Commodore Kilburnie

COMMODORE KILBURNIE

· A Novel ·

WILLIAM P. MACK

Naval Institute Press
Annapolis, Maryland

Naval Institute Press
291 Wood Road
Annapolis, MD 21402

Library of Congress Cataloging-in-Publication Data

Mack, William P., 1915-
Commodore Kilburnie : a novel / William P. Mack.
p. cm.
ISBN 1-55750-480-6 (alk. paper)
1. Napoleonic Wars, 1800–1815—Fiction. 2. Copenhagen, Battle of, 1801—Fiction. 3. Trafalgar, Battle of, 1805—Fiction. 4. Scots—Foreign countries—Fiction. I. Title.
PS3563.A3132 C66 2002
813'.54—dc21

2002002672

Printed in the United States of America on acid-free paper ∞
09 08 07 06 05 04 03 02 9 8 7 6 5 4 3 2
First printing

CONTENTS

ACKNOWLEDGMENTS

I AM INDEBTED TO the United States Naval Institute for continuing to bring to its membership works of fiction, adventure, and humor; to my editor, Therese Boyd, who was able to make necessary corrections without losing any saltwater; and to Elsie Mack for her editorial assistance and tenacious search for typographical errors.

Commodore Kilburnie

CHAPTER 1

New Beginnings

CAPTAIN FERGUS KILBURNIE, Royal Navy, pushed back in his chair and stretched carefully. He had been napping on his front porch, catching the full sun of a cool Scottish fall. He noticed that the creel of salmon he had caught that morning, which had been at his feet when he fell asleep, was gone. The cook must have picked them up to prepare for lunch.

A handsome Scottish naval officer, Fergus was accustomed to much more activity than he was presently enjoying. But he had suffered serious injury months before as captain of the *Imperious.* When his ship was wrecked in a violent storm in Donegal Bay, Ireland, Fergus was nearly given up for dead. Although now nearly recovered, and ready to return to Navy service, he still followed his doctor's prescription of exercise and an evening tot of rum for the lingering stiffness.

Finally Fergus awakened fully and stretched his six-foot frame again. He heard footsteps and saw Shannon coming up the stone terrace. She was still the beautiful young woman he had met so many years ago in Ireland, then lost, found, and wed. Her long, red hair glowed in the sunshine, and her full figure strained against her expensive London frock.

When she realized he was awake, Shannon grinned warmly, her beautiful eyes sparkling. "Well, my sailor, I see you are ready for lunch. While you have been sleeping, the cook has poached your salmon. I just came out to call you and the girls."

"Where are they?"

"Down in the stream. You know, they're quite disappointed you didn't take them fishing this morning. Mary says they are too old to keep using pins and string. And you know Margaret echoes whatever Mary says."

"Yes, I was fishing by their age. And soon they'll be in school and we'll have no time for fun."

"And you'll have a command again. Have you heard from the Admiralty since you wrote to tell them you were physically fit for duty and wanted a command as soon as possible?"

Fergus stirred lazily and stretched again. "Not yet. But I'm ready for deeper water than the salmon stream."

"You'll hear soon enough. Let's go get the girls and have lunch, my dear."

The noontime meal was interrupted by a shout from the kitchen. The cook, always with an eye on the approach road, called out, "Ma'am! Three men are heading this way. They're riding horses and leading several others. I've never seen them before."

Shannon leaped up excitedly. "It must be Liam Shaughnessy with my horses from Ireland!" Dessert was forgotten as Shannon dashed outdoors, Fergus and the girls following.

Even before the riders reached the little family, Shannon cried out, "Liam!"

The handsome young Irish lad smiled, his dark eyes shining. He quickly dismounted, took off his cap, and nodded at Shannon's greeting. "How do you like the horses, ma'am?"

"They look wonderful, Liam. They made the trip just fine. And how are you?"

"Thank you, ma'am. The horses were better sailors than we were, but we've all recovered."

Shannon looked behind Liam at the other two riders, now gathering the horses and tying their lead ropes to nearby trees. "Who are your helpers?"

Liam laughed. "I guess you don't recognize them. You know them both."

The two took off their caps as they walked toward Shannon, and she could see that they weren't men, as the cook had said, but a very young man and a woman.

Shannon gasped. "Is that Ellen? Wasn't she in training to be a housemaid? She's as pretty as ever, though last time I saw her she was just a stick of a girl."

"Aye, she was," Liam said, "and only twelve when you left. She came out to the barn whenever she could, and your father kept chasing her back. Now that he's gone, God rest his soul, she's out there with me all the time. First she said it was just to see the horses . . ." He smiled shyly and bowed his head.

"Will you be sending her back?"

Liam answered quickly, "Oh, no, we both want to stay here, get married, and work for you, if that's all right."

Shannon laughed. "Yes, that's fine. Don't worry, I'll make sure everything is arranged."

Fergus cleared his throat. "That's fine with me, too. We'll be leaving for

London soon, so you can stay in the big house. I'm going to have to get a crew from town to build a horse barn and paddock for the new horses anyway; I'll just have them build a small cottage, too." He motioned toward the younger riders. "Now, tell me, who is that boy?"

"That's Patrick Egan. He was even younger than I was when you left, and just a sprout around the place. He's a good carriage driver and would be happy to work for you, too. You can see he's only about the size of a jockey now, but strong enough to handle four horses and a large carriage, and he's growing fast."

Fergus looked at Patrick and liked him instantly. "How about London?" he said to the boy with a smile.

Patrick grinned back. "Aye, sir, I'd like that."

Shannon laughed. "Well, that takes care of all of us. Now stake the horses out well so they can get some good Scottish grass. When you've finished, come into the house and ask the cook to give you some poached salmon and a place to sleep upstairs tonight."

Liam's eyes widened. "You mean the farm hands get to eat poached salmon?"

"Yes. We have it almost every day."

Patrick beamed. "I might change my mind and ask to stay here."

"Don't worry. I'll see that you eat well in London, too," Shannon replied.

At supper that night, Shannon asked Liam for a report on her family's business in Ireland. She had inherited estates from both her father, Lord Inver, and her first husband, Lord Malin, but hadn't been back to Ireland for a while.

Liam shrugged. "Since your father died, his estate has been under the care of an old Irish farmer who does his best, but he is far too old to keep up with the young workers. He needs lots of help."

Fergus thought a moment. He said to Shannon, "You know, I met a young Scot in the village yesterday. He was graduated recently from Edinburgh University in agriculture. He was telling me that he has six older brothers so there is no place for him on the family farm. I will try to arrange to bring him out tomorrow so you can meet him. Maybe we can send him over to Ireland to take over the estate."

Liam, still busy eating a large piece of salmon, nodded eagerly without opening his mouth. When he could talk, he said, "That sounds good. There aren't any overseers in Ireland near us. Can you tell me why so many Scots leave their country to go to Ireland to run estates?"

Fergus sighed at the question. "Scots are cash short and have plenty of skilled manpower. They go to Ireland to earn money to pay the taxes and other expenses so they won't have to sell their estates at home."

Shannon nodded in agreement. "Now tell me how the Malin estate is doing, Liam."

"Well, your late husband kept it in excellent shape. It still supports a large string of racehorses he put together. Sometime soon you'll need an overseer to run it."

"Thank you, Liam, I'll think about that," Shannon said and passed him the plate of salmon.

Ellen, who had been carefully putting away a second helping of salmon, spoke up. "Ma'am, I don't feel comfortable calling you 'Shannon.' Shouldn't I call you 'Lady Shannon'? Your late husband was Lord Malin, and before that your father was Lord Inver."

Shannon nodded. "You are right. They were both English and liked those titles. But my mother was Irish and was never called 'Lady' Justine. Titles aren't of much importance to the Irish, or the Scots, for that matter."

Ellen chewed thoughtfully. "But what happens when you go to London?"

Shannon laughed. "Even more so. English women who are entitled to be called 'Lady' because of their husband's status call each other 'Lady So-and-so,' but when I am present they carefully avoid addressing me as 'Lady Shannon,' although technically I am as English as they are. But my mother was Irish and that seems to set the English ladies off."

Ellen frowned. "Well, I don't like that." She put down her fork and pushed the plate away. "But I like the Scots." Her face broke into a big smile. "I hope to stay here for the rest of my life."

Liam laughed. "After you marry me you'll have to stay because I'm never leaving."

Ellen looked back at Shannon. "I don't see how you can leave either, particularly to go to London."

Shannon patted her hand. "Don't worry, my dear. I rather like London. I've learned to get along with the English."

"Don't you have a house there?"

"Yes. Lord Malin had business interests in both Belfast and London. He bought what is now Malin House from a bankrupt English nobleman." She sighed heavily. "But it's too big. It takes six maids to keep it up. I have taken a large flat and I'll sell Malin House when I can."

Ellen shuddered. "I wouldn't want to help with all that housework. I want to stay here, with the horses." She looked at Liam.

Shannon laughed. "Don't worry. You won't be going with us. I know you'll enjoy being here, with the horses."

Liam nodded vigorously. "Oh, yes. She will. We love Scotland. We're going to grow old here."

CHAPTER 2

Moving to London

A WEEK LATER, Fergus was sitting on the terrace, drinking coffee and watching the work crew install a fenced paddock and the foundations for a large horse barn. Liam sat beside him, studying a design plan of the new barn.

"This barn is far bigger than we'll need for the horses we have," Liam said.

Fergus smiled. "Don't worry. I'm sure Shannon will fill it up."

Shannon came out of the house behind them and looked out over the fields. "Why don't you boys go out for a ride like I'm going to do?"

Fergus put down his coffee cup and looked at her. "I'll be taking Liam out later to see the whole place."

Liam said, "I hear it's half again as big as the Inver estate!"

"It is." Shannon said. "I'm going to take the stallion out for half an hour." She bent over Fergus's shoulder and took a handful of lumps out of the sugar bowl next to the coffeepot.

Half a dozen horses milled about in a temporary paddock made of lines of rope strung around a succession of small saplings and trees. Liam and Fergus watched Shannon walk gracefully down the gentle slope, stepping carefully to avoid small depressions in the sod.

Liam whistled. "What a graceful woman, even from the rear. That riding habit doesn't hide much."

Fergus's eyebrows firmed. He was about to make a reproving remark but changed his mind and said only, "Liam, watch your whistles in Scotland."

"But in Ireland . . ."

"This isn't Ireland, Liam, and the Scottish men are different. If you do that for the wrong woman, some Scot might deck you."

Liam reddened. "Thanks for the warning. Most of them are bigger than I am."

Fergus said, "At the rate you are eating salmon you will soon be as big as any of them."

Shannon opened the paddock gate and called the stallion. The beautiful horse trotted over willingly when he saw the lump of sugar in her open palm. When he reached out to take it, Shannon quickly whisked off his paddock halter and slipped on his regular bridle. The stallion pulled his head back, but he was trapped and Shannon quickly tied him to the fence.

Another lump of sugar kept him docile while she threw on her saddle and cinched it. She led the horse out of the paddock and threw the reins over his neck. With the moves of an experienced horsewoman, Shannon adjusted the reins and put a foot in the near stirrup. She threw her leg over his rump and pulled herself into the saddle with one graceful movement. Her riding skirt flew in all directions. When she tapped the stallion lightly, they started off over the hill behind the house in a flurry of hooves and flying sod particles.

Fergus sighed at the sight of her. He could remember when he first saw Shannon Inver, a slim, headstrong, thirteen year old. Fergus had been hired to care for her father's horses and to teach her to ride. Two years later, she was a beautiful fifteen year old, flirting with him at every opportunity and driving him crazy. Although Fergus was in love with her, he knew the trouble a relationship with his employer's daughter could cause and so he tried to hide it. But Shannon could not be avoided forever. When her father discovered them in an old churchyard, under a blanket, it was the end. Fergus was fired and sent back to Scotland. He thought he would never see her again. At this memory, Fergus sighed again. All these years and he knew he was still very deeply in love with her.

Liam brought him back to the present when he started to whistle again at the sight of Shannon's red hair flying, but he stopped himself and only said, "That is some beautiful woman, and a great one with a horse."

Fergus pointed to the design plan and changed the subject. "Let's get back to this. Unless you can come up soon with where you want the entrance to the haymow, the builder won't be able to go ahead with the framing."

They talked about alterations for half an hour. Suddenly there was a burst of noise, flying hooves, and loud whinnies as Shannon came riding over the hill, headed for the temporary paddock. She pulled the stallion up gradually, and he slowed and came to a halt before the paddock, breathing easily. She threw the reins over his head, brought her right leg over his rump, and jumped lightly to the ground. She landed firmly, her riding skirt again flying in all directions. Her breasts bounced firmly as she hit the turf.

Liam could not contain a groan.

Fergus sighed impatiently. "Liam, why don't you go down there and help Shannon with the horse? You could burn up a little of that nervous energy."

Liam laughed. "Are you kidding? You trained her. You should know that she expects to take care of her own mount. If I go down there and offer to take over, she'll backhand me with her crop. She'd do the same thing to you if you tried it."

Fergus laughed. "Oh, yes, I remember now."

Shannon took off the bridle, slipped on the paddock halter, and tied him to the paddock top rope. She took off the saddle and picked up an old piece of towel from the paddock ropes and rubbed the stallion down. Then she released him into the paddock after giving him the remaining lumps of sugar in her pocket.

Liam nodded knowingly as he watched her. "She does it all just like you trained her to do—and trained me, too."

Shannon walked up to the terrace and sat down with the two men. "That's a top horse. We should be raising racehorses that he could sire."

Liam shrugged. "We don't have Irish grass here. The experts say that's what gives horses speed."

Fergus bridled. "There's nothing wrong with Scottish grass. If there is, I'll import Irish hay by the boatload and do everything else we need to do. Let's do it all."

Shannon laughed, got up, and started for the house. Over her shoulder she said, "Well, that's settled. Now get on with your ride. Be back in time for lunch, or I'll give your poached salmon to someone else."

Liam jumped up. "Let's go. I'll saddle the horses. Poached salmon is next to nectar."

Fergus went off to get his riding gear and Liam went down to the paddock to saddle the horses. He bent down and plucked a tuft of grass to chew. He shook his head and thought, here I am, a poor Irish lad. But wasn't Fergus poor, too, at this age? Now look at him. Rich as hell. Liam drew down his black brows. "Damn!" he muttered aloud. "I'll make it some day, too."

Shannon came out of the house, freshly changed, followed by Fergus. They strolled down to the paddock. When she saw the troubled look on Liam's face, she asked, "What's wrong?"

Liam lowered his head and dug his toe into the ground. "I was just thinking about your idea. I don't see how we could raise good racehorses here. We need the Irish grass, fresh, and lots of other things."

Shannon laughed. "You just don't think big enough. We can work it out between here and Ireland. Remember, my father used to raise good racehorses on the Inver estate."

"Yes. Real winners. I trained most of them and rode a lot of them in races—I won, too."

Shannon went on. "The Malin estate legally belongs to my daughters, so I can't use that. But . . ."

Liam saw a gleam of light. "But the other," he interrupted. "The other was your father's, and you can do anything you want with it."

Shannon stopped him. "Exactly. But think even bigger. I'll ask Fergus's father to start a horse-breeding farm on the lower part of this estate. He's an excellent farm manager. And there's plenty of room. We could have breeding barns and a mile-long track for exercising and training." She turned to Fergus. "Angus would like that, wouldn't he?"

Fergus shrugged. "Sure, but you can't damage the trees and the streams. The runoff from the barns will kill the salmon or keep them from coming upstream."

"You know we can control any runoff," Shannon said. "We can build cisterns and containment walls."

Liam shook his head. "It isn't that easy if you're worried about the salmon." Then he grinned. "I've become very fond of the 'little blighters,' as the English would say."

"Well, we'll leave that to Angus." Shannon looked at Liam. "Now what about the training of the horses?"

Liam became very serious. "That's *my* business."

Shannon nodded her head as she smiled. "All right, then, I'll make you a partner in my horse-racing business."

Fergus hardly heard them as he was thinking ahead. He said, "So far so good. I said I'd ship over all the Irish grass we needed, but I think we can do better. Why don't we breed and raise the horses on the good strong Scottish grass right here for the first year? Then we'll ship them to Ireland to finish them off on the Inver estate while they get bigger and faster."

"Would your brother, Ennis, agree to go over there and take over?"

"I don't see why not. Now my young Scottish lad can stay here."

"If this works, will you take the horses to London for racing?" Liam asked.

Shannon laughed. "Think big again. Why just London? After we train them we'll ship them to other tracks around the world!"

Liam slapped his thigh and rolled on the grass in delight. "Mother of Mary, I can't wait!" he shouted.

Shannon laughed at his youthful exuberance and said with mock sternness, "Get up. You're scuffing up your riding boots and your clothes are covered with dirt. Now that you are a young businessman you must look neat at all times."

Liam wiped his eyes and got up. "I can't believe my good luck." he said.

"Thank you both so much for giving me this chance."

Fergus said, "Well, after we ride, you can go tell Ellen all about it. You've been neglecting her."

Shannon and Fergus sat late that night at the dinner table with Liam, Ennis, and Angus discussing details.

"I'm glad you thought to bring in Ennis," Angus said. "He needs a bigger challenge in his life."

Ennis laughed. "I've been spending twelve hours a day following slow-moving animals around these fields. I need a change."

Angus scratched his chin. "I'll have to hire two or three young boys to take over from you."

"You'll need at least three to do what I've been doing," Ennis agreed.

"Father, do what you want about everything," Fergus said. "We expect to be leaving soon, but I'll leave a large draft of money at the bank for you."

"Good," Angus said. "I'll need to start a lot of things as soon as possible. The best breeding season for horses is coming soon. I'd like to get roofs up for the mares and put them to work."

"If you need more money, Shannon can send it up on the daily packet." Fergus paused. "There's just one other thing."

"Yes?"

"Please make sure the barns and paddocks don't drain into the salmon runs."

Angus laughed. "For a seagoing man you don't think very clearly about running water. All of them will be below the salmon runs."

"No, Father, that may be true, but the salmon will have to swim upstream and downstream through it."

"Right you are, lad, but I'm taking that into account. Cisterns will hold the runoff during those seasons. When the salmon runs are finished, I'll empty the cisterns."

Fergus smiled. "I knew you'd be on top of it."

The next morning, at breakfast on the terrace, Fergus heard a horse clopping down the approach road from Kilburnie. The postman was making his daily delivery, and Fergus went out to meet him.

"Morning, sir," the mailman said as he pulled up in front of Fergus. "This must be an important envelope—it has seals all over it."

Fergus took the large brown envelope and signed for it before running inside to find Shannon. "It's here!" he shouted. "It's here!"

Shannon ran down the stairs. "Open it," she said eagerly.

Fergus opened it carefully and drew out several pages of fine handwriting. "It's from Uncle Jeris," he said, "and it's signed over his title, Secretary to the First Lord for Personnel."

"Read it," she said impatiently.

Dear Fergus:

I have in hand your recent letter reporting your physical condition and requesting a return to sea.

It was most opportune. Admiral Nelson has been in correspondence with me, too. He is enroute to England overland in Europe and expects to return to London in November. He wants to have a direct hand in assignments to command the ships for any force to be assigned to him. Two new frigates are to be completed in our Royal Navy dockyards in late November. They will be two of the fastest ships our Royal dockyards have ever turned out. Their speed and maneuverability will surpass that of any of the French ships. Only some of the American schooners with fore and aft rigs can outspeed them, but you are unlikely to come across any of them. Admiral Nelson is looking forward to his next assignment and wants to use these new ships as fast scouts. Your name and that of Captain Essex are in his mind as leading candidates, and I do not think the Admiralty will dare impress on him some of the dull, sycophantic aristocratic candidates who daily flood my office. It is therefore important that you be in London by the first of November.

I trust you will leave some salmon in your streams for me. I hope to make a trip up there after your affairs are settled and the Admiral is safely out of town and at sea.

Congratulations on your recent marriage. Shannon is a lovely girl. I will have her townhouse ready for you and your new family when you arrive. The fact that you and Shannon are now married should have some bearing with certain parties in the Admiralty but of course will mean nothing either way to Admiral Nelson.

I look forward to seeing you soon.

Best regards,
Jeris

Fergus had begun to pace up and down as he read the last lines, and he slapped his leg as he read the signature. "There! We have it now. All we have to do is to get there. We can leave within a week. I have already looked into travel arrangements."

Shannon sighed. "I'm very happy for you, but there's something you should know. I didn't want to say until I was sure, but I believe I'm pregnant."

"What? You didn't say a word."

"I wasn't sure myself. I'm about two months along."

Tears welled in Fergus's eyes as he thought of their firstborn. It was only after the *Imperious* shipwreck, when Shannon was nursing him back to health, that she told him that she had given birth to his son while still married to Lord Malin. But baby Fergus had died of typhoid. Now that they were finally married, this would be their first child together. He blurted out, "Oh, you shouldn't travel."

"Don't be silly. I can do anything when I'm pregnant. Let's just not go all the way to London in a stage or a carriage."

"All right then, we have a few choices. We can travel by carriage to Edinburgh and then by sea to London. Or we can go to Glasgow by carriage, and by sea to Southampton, which would mean another, shorter trip by carriage to London. The Irish Sea will be much milder than the North Sea and English Channel."

Shannon nodded. "I'm for the Irish Sea. We'll take the girls with us. They'll be starting school a little late, but I think they'll be fine."

"Good. Now let's go down to the new paddock and talk to Liam. We need to tell him about the changes and see that he and my father get started."

They strolled over hand in hand, Fergus watching carefully for hummocks and holes in the lush turf. Shannon giggled and slapped his arm. "Stop that. I'm as agile as ever and will be for several months."

At the new paddock Liam and Patrick were directing the workforce. Fergus interrupted them. "Liam, I just got a letter telling me to leave for London next week. I plan to take my carriage and horses to Glasgow and load them on a ship. My father will lend us his carriage and driver to take the overflow to Glasgow. We will land in Southampton and hire a second carriage there. I will need someone to drive the second carriage to London. Patrick, would you like to go as my driver? Once she's in London, my wife has her own carriage and driver."

Patrick grinned. "Certainly, sir, although I'll miss the salmon."

"Then it's decided," Fergus said. "You and Ellen will stay on here, Liam."

"Of course. We are to be married next week. Then I think your parents might feel better about the sleeping arrangements."

Fergus laughed. "We Scottish Presbyterians aren't that bad, but it's a good idea anyhow."

For several days Shannon bustled about packing for the trip. When she announced she was ready, Fergus said, "That pile of baggage is much less than I expected."

"Don't worry," Shannon smiled slyly. "I expect to buy out all the millinery stores when we get to London. I see you are traveling in your usual naval fashion. A seabag and a spare uniform. Not even a sword."

Fergus laughed. "All of my uniforms went down with the *Imperious,* as did my grandfather's sword. I'll have to get a complete kit for myself in London. In the meantime, I hope to borrow Jeris's sword."

A week later the Kilburnie clan gathered to see Fergus and Shannon off. Ennis supervised the stowage of the baggage in the second coach, and yards of cordage were used to secure the cases and bags the family had rounded up. Ennis's wife, Eileen, played with Shannon's two girls, giving each big hugs and telling them how much she would miss them.

Only when the packing met with Angus's approval did the little family clamber into the seats of the larger carriage, which Fergus's grandfather, Strath Kilburnie, had made years ago. Liam climbed up to the box and looked expectantly at Fergus.

Fergus grinned, "Up anchor, Liam, and hoist all sail."

Liam laughed and urged the horses forward. Behind them Patrick followed, and the carriages drove slowly up the road to Kilburnie village that in turn led to Glasgow.

While there were tears in many eyes, Fergus's dry eyes fixed on the road to Glasgow and London. He was anxious to resume his career. He remembered how he had followed the same road as a young man just off to join the Navy. His career years had been very rewarding. He concentrated on feeling for the bumps in the road, keeping a careful eye on Shannon, who seemed to be taking them easily.

She caught him. "Fergus, stop worrying about me. These are all small bumps and your grandfather built your carriage well. The way it swings and sways make it seem almost like we're at sea."

Shannon was torn between her desire to stay at the estate and the benefits of London. Her two girls had been born in the large hospital there, attended by a famous obstetrician. Here in the small town of Kilburnie she would have had to rely on the country doctor. She waved back once and then, like Fergus, turned toward Glasgow. "Fergus," she said, "are you sure you made all the travel arrangements?"

Fergus nodded reassuringly. "The ship we'll be on is the largest of its type making regular trips between Glasgow and Southampton." He grinned at Mary and Margaret. "You'll like it, too, girls."

Mary spoke up. "Father, will we have our own room on the ship?"

"Certainly. But we'll still eat in the dining room together."

The ship was all they could have wanted. The trip south was comfortable in the Irish Sea, but a little rough when they rounded St. David's Head and headed up the English Channel.

The business of loading and unloading ships at the docks at Southampton intrigued the girls while Fergus headed off with Patrick to arrange for a second carriage and driver to carry their baggage.

The huge cranes creaked and groaned as they turned carrying large loads at the end of a whipping snake-like cable. When they turned, clanging bells warned anyone who might be standing in the way of the huge vehicles. When they moved a load over a large hatch, a man standing near its edge who could see the bottom of the hatch raised his hand and displayed various numbers of fingers to signal to the crane operator what he should do with the load. Soon it disappeared into the open maw of the hatch as the man watched it carefully. After a few minutes the empty hook snaked upwards en route to another load. The little girls were held captive by this fascinating operation, expecting that some time the man directing the operation would make a mistake and the load would come crashing down. To their disappointment it never happened.

After an hour or so Fergus came back with a carriage and driver and the baggage was loaded onto it.

The seventy-mile trip through the Hampton countryside was a pleasure. No one had seen before houses of the type that dotted the towns and country farms, and the countryside seemed to be almost like a garden.

"Not like Scotland, but just as pretty," Fergus said.

Halfway in the trip they stopped at a quiet inn. "Beautiful," Shannon said, and she took the girls on a sightseeing trip while Fergus tested the beds with a short nap. When she got back she woke Fergus up. "You missed a lovely afternoon with your daughters."

Fergus stretched. "I regret it, but I'll make it up to them. I'll take them shopping while you rest."

Shannon yawned. "Good deal. Thank you."

The trip ended when the carriage pulled up to the front door of Shannon's flat the next day.

Uncle Jeris and Aunt Martha came down the stairs to greet them. On first glance, Jeris's empty sleeve and eyepatch gave him the appearance of a pirate, but there the resemblance stopped. He truly looked like the kindly old gentleman he was.

Martha was about fifty pounds heavier than she wanted to be because she liked her own excellent cooking. She had never had children, but she looked at Fergus as the son she had never had. Her gray hair was pulled back severely from her soft, kindly face. She reached out to hug first Fergus, then Shannon, and then said, "There's a fire laid against the fall chill. Dinner will be ready shortly."

The girls asked, "Can we help?"

"Of course. You can set the table. I think your parents would like to join your Uncle Jeris for a little refreshment in the parlor."

Dinner was pleasant, with Martha's cooking as good as it smelled, but Fergus could tell Jeris was bursting to talk with him privately, and, after dessert, Jeris rose rapidly and said to Fergus, "Now we'll have some port in my study. I'm sure the ladies will excuse us just for a short time."

In the study Jeris handed Fergus the port decanter and sat down. "I can't pour well any longer. My right hand is tired from writing all day. Your affairs are going along splendidly. I have an appointment in a week in my office in the Admiralty for you and young Essex to meet with Admiral Nelson. I am sure how it will go."

Fergus nodded. "I'll be ready."

"There's one thing first. You are to have dinner with Lord Satterfield tomorrow. You've been to White's Club before."

"Yes, but I'll need to order some uniforms. Mine were all lost."

"You won't need them tomorrow night. Civilian clothes will do this time. You can go to Gieves to order a complete outfit before you see Admiral Nelson. Tailoring all of it will take two weeks or more, but they can rush one complete outfit for you in time."

"Thank you, Uncle. I can never thank you enough."

Jeris smiled. "Yes, you can. Just keep my cottage on your place in shape for us to use and notify your gillie about our plans. I'd like to fish before the winter comes and after Admiral Nelson is out of town."

"Your place is being kept up along with mine by a couple who came over from Ireland to look after Shannon's horses. They'll have everything ready for you except the fish. You'll have to do that yourself. And one of these days you'll find a surprise."

"Yes?"

"We'll be raising Scot-Irish racehorses as well as salmon."

"What for?"

"We hope to ship them all over the world to run them against the best competition."

"What do you mean they're Scot-Irish?"

"We'll breed the best stallions and dams we can buy in addition to the ones we already have. We're going to do it in barns and paddocks already being built on my estate. They'll grow there for a year on Scottish grass, and then they'll be shipped to Shannon's estate in Ireland. Then they will get another year of conditioning and training."

"Sounds like Lord Satterfield will be intrigued. He loves horse racing. May I tell him?"

"Of course, but I'll probably inform him first."

CHAPTER 3

Dinner at White's

THE NEXT MORNING Fergus left the townhouse early in Shannon's carriage with her driver, Shepherd, on the box and Patrick beside him.

"For indoctrination and sea trials," Fergus had explained to Patrick, "you ought to have a few days in heavy London traffic with Shepherd before you try it yourself. He can make it a lot easier for you and he is very experienced."

Patrick had shuddered. "I've already seen some of it on my way here. Not like Donegal, or even Glasgow. These drivers are like sharks. Shepherd is a real gentleman, and I don't see how he puts up with the scoundrels out there."

The carriage stopped in front of Gieves Naval Tailors. Fergus left the carriage and paused before going inside. The uniforms displayed in the windows looked just as they had for decades; naval uniforms had not changed in a long time.

As Fergus pushed the door open, it creaked loudly. A gray-haired older gentleman with a tape measure draped around his neck appeared suddenly. "May I help you, sir?" he asked.

Fergus looked at him closely and said, "I'm Captain Kilburnie. I need your help."

"A uniform?"

Fergus laughed and shook his head. "No. A whole outfit, including a sword."

"Ah, your ship was sunk?"

"Yes, but I'd rather not talk about it."

The clerk chuckled. "None of them does, but I'll keep quiet and get on with my job." Suddenly he exclaimed, "Wait a minute! You're the famous Captain Kilburnie. I've heard about you. You should be very proud of your exploits."

Fergus spent an interesting morning being measured in all directions while telling sea stories. As soon as the word got around as to who he was, every tailor in the place swarmed around him. By noon he escaped poorer by several hundred pounds and with a promise that his uniforms would be magnificent, "not like the ones in the window."

While Fergus was busy, Shepherd took Patrick for a trip around London. The two on the box were quite different in appearance. Shepherd was a middle-aged Englishman with a dignified mustache and slight sideburns. His slightly bulging stomach contrasted with Patrick's trim figure and Celtic looks—his snub nose, slightly crooked teeth, pale complexion, and shock of red hair. Shepherd and Patrick were quite different in many respects. Nevertheless, they soon became fast friends.

Shepherd drove around the main area of London, pointing out the street names and areas to Patrick. Patrick was soon lost, but maintained his approximate bearings in spite of the lack of any plan on the growth of the London streets.

In heavy traffic carriage movement often stopped. On one occasion two young ladies standing on the curb stepped off into the street. One of them glanced into the interior of the carriage. "Ah," she said, "I see you don't have any customers in there." Then she put a hand on her hip, used the other hand to hoist her breasts almost to the top of her gown, grinned wickedly, and said, "Sir, would you like to give us a ride about town? We'll give you a ride, too, and I'd favor that young man. Cleo, here, can take you on, Dad."

Shepherd grinned, tweaked his moustache, and said, "What do you say, Patrick?"

Patrick looked at Shepherd, closed his open mouth, and said indignantly, "Never! They would infect the upholstery. I wouldn't let them in my barn."

Shepherd laughed so hard tears formed in his eyes, "Lad, you just passed the first test. We never let anyone inside the carriage."

The traffic eased, and Shepherd shook the reins. As they moved off, he looked back at the women, tipped his hat, and said, "Maybe some other time, ladies."

The two stepped back on the curb and tried to clean their shoes of the filth in the street. One said, "Dammit, that was for nothing, although I'd have favored the young'un. I need a little young stuff now and then."

The other shrugged. "I favored the old geezer. He'd have been easier on me, and I think he's more experienced."

"Forget it, dearie, it's in the past."

They came back at noon to pick up Fergus. Patrick was slightly shaken by the traffic but still confident, "If I can get down off the box to argue with some of these blokes, I'll do all right. They aren't all that tough. Take away their whips and I'll take them on even up."

Shepherd laughed. "Don't try it. If you get down or put down your whip, they'll run over you. Learn to shout loudly and make obscene gestures. I'll give you lessons. You have to learn to speak London English instead of Gaelic or even the Irish version of English. Otherwise your efforts to argue or shout them down are wasted." He laughed again. "You've already learned to stay away from the ladies of the street."

Fergus chuckled. "This is worse than being at sea in Naples Harbor. The Italian captains are masters at gestures and swearing in every language. Shepherd, you have to take me to White's Club tonight. I should arrive at the door just a few minutes before seven."

"Yes, sir, I know White's well. You should know we will have to leave home just after six."

Shannon and her maid had Fergus's evening dress ready for him, and the two women and the two drivers managed to get him to the club on time.

It had been a long time since Fergus's first visit to White's. He had been only a young lieutenant then, but still managed to impress Lord Satterfield at dinner with his appetite for good food, knowledge of horses, love of Satterfield's favorite claret, and lack of political opinions. That meal had been important to Fergus's future, but this one was even more important. Fergus hoped that his patron would know something of his record as a naval officer. And soon he might even be able to tell him that he was about to race his wife's racehorses.

Promptly at seven, Fergus walked up the steps of White's Club. Not impressive at the front, it was still one of London's most exclusive clubs, having in its membership only men who were large property owners, held political office, or were members of the aristocracy. He was surprised when the porter at the door recognized him instantly. "Ah, Captain Kilburnie, you have been promoted since I saw you last, and you have become moderately famous." He bowed slightly.

Fergus nodded in return. "Thank you. I am here again at Lord Satterfield's invitation."

"Of course." The porter stepped aside. "The hall porter will escort you to him."

As Fergus stepped inside, another porter appeared almost magically and said, "Good evening, Captain. Allow me to take your hat. Ah, as usual you are punctual." The porter motioned to still another porter. "Please take

Captain Kilburnie to Lord Satterfield. He is expected."

They passed through the usual small groups of men, talking in low tones, reading papers, or playing cards. The smell of expensive cigars and whiskey was pervasive.

As he had been before, Lord Satterfield was sitting alone in a quiet corner, reading a newspaper. The servant stopped, cleared his throat, and said, "M'Lord, Captain Kilburnie."

Satterfield dropped his paper, and said to the porter, "Ah, my good man, thank you."

Lord Sinclair Satterfield was every bit the English aristocrat. He was slightly stooped with age, but his tall, slim figure was topped with a still thick shock of gray hair. Although his hearing and sight were failing, he refused to use glasses. His voice, once booming, was still strong. When Lord Satterfield told a story at dinner, diners at tables for several yards around stopped to listen to him. What he said was always humorous, important, or at least confidential, depending on his subject. Now he had taken to using a quieter conversational tone, and Fergus hoped he would use it that evening.

Lord Satterfield got up slowly, turned to Fergus, and held out his hand. "My boy, I am glad to see you again. Let's go to my table. We will have to go slowly. I am not as agile as I once was when you were here last time. My gout, you know. May it spare you for years to come."

Fergus offered his arm to Lord Satterfield, who staggered slightly even with his cane. They moved between the upholstered chairs, occupied by elderly persons wreathed in strong Cuban cigar smoke.

At one point Satterfield wrinkled his nose. "Smelly damned weeds," he muttered. Then he stopped and pointed to a servant carrying a basket of candles and standing under a sconce. "Watch him," Satterfield said.

The man reached up to the sconce and took down a sputtering, half-used candle. He put it out and threw it into the basket before replacing it with a new one.

Satterfield grinned. "White never lets a candle burn more than halfway or smoke or sputter. That man spends his entire day patrolling the hundreds of candles in sconces and in holders on the tables."

Fergus shrugged. "Seems to me a waste of valuable candles."

"No, the old gentlemen need plenty of light to read their newspapers and menus."

Satterfield started to walk on again but stopped and stomped on the carpet. "See this carpeting? It is laid over an oak floor three inches thick. It mustn't dare creak to wake up these old gents. You will notice the many flecks of cigar ash and traces of food stains. Although the carpet is thick and very expensive, it is changed every six months."

Fergus whistled quietly. "I'm glad I don't have to pay dues in this club."

Satterfield laughed. "You will want to join it some day. I'll put you up for it." He started to walk forward again, keeping a close eye on the chairs ahead.

When they came to an elderly gentleman sprawled in a chair, sound asleep, with his feet extended into the aisle, Satterfield paused, shook his head, and poked him with his cane. The old man came to quickly, opened his eyes, and glared at Satterfield.

"Oh, it's you, Sinclair. Why don't you look where you're going. You trampled on my gout."

"Well, keep those damned things out of the aisle, Clarence. I almost fell over them."

"Would have served you right. Next time try hopping over them."

"Hopping! I haven't been able to do that for twenty years. You might try cutting down on the rum and whiskey. My doctor says my gout will tolerate claret. Try it."

"Off with you, Satterfield. Let me sleep."

Fergus hurried him by the reclining old gentleman and toward his table. Lord Satterfield led the rest of the way into the dining room, occasionally looking back at his friend who was nodding again.

The waiter gestured to a quiet table in a corner, and Satterfield nodded in assent. He lowered himself carefully into a chair. "We will have my usual claret," he said to the hovering waiter.

The waiter brought out a bottle and passed it without even bothering to display it to Lord Satterfield.

Satterfield chuckled. "I gave instructions years ago never to serve me anything else and to test it in the wine cellar. I don't need to waste time sniffing it. They never fail. I hope you like it."

Fergus remembered. "Whitechapel '77, I believe, and the best claret I've ever tasted."

Satterfield laughed. "You learn fast and you never forget. By the way, I knew I made a good choice when I, er, backed you for command. You made a remarkable record."

Fergus hesitated. "Well, sir, thank you, but I did lose my last ship."

Lord Satterfield shook his head. "No! No! You took great risks and carried out your orders, thereby saving a large and valuable convoy, many times the value of your ship. I hear you carried out your duties against great odds. The

Admiralty likes that sort of thing, and they said so. They like captains who can perform in the face of strong enemy opposition and heavy storms. There aren't too many of you in the Navy."

"Thank you, sir. I hope I am still in that category."

"You certainly are. Most important, Admiral Nelson thinks the same way. I have been in constant correspondence with him on his trip home. As you know, he's due to arrive in England any day now. He will want to see you soon after he arrives. Of course he will have to settle his domestic affairs first. As you know, he is having trouble keeping his present wife and his mistress apart."

Fergus blushed, thinking of his own wonderful relationship with Shannon, and changed the subject. "And how is my good friend, Captain Essex?"

Lord Satterfield beamed at the mention of his son and poured more wine, not waiting for the steward. "Let's drink to the young lad. I'd say you two will make a superb pair of thoroughbreds capable of carrying any cargo and winning against any enemy." He finished his glass, and looked at the waiter over his shoulder. "We'll dine now, if you please, and you know what I've ordered." Satterfield turned to Fergus, "I hope you like this menu. It doesn't vary much, but it's the best in town."

The headwaiter wheeled up a cart filled with a huge roast of steaming beef. He cut two generous slices for each diner and filled the rest of the plates with large helpings of Yorkshire pudding. He placed one plate in front of each diner and filled the rest of the table with large tureens of vegetables and containers of hot rolls.

Satterfield surveyed it carefully and began to rub his hands. "Fine!" he said to the beaming waiter. "Your usual superb job. Now we'll have at it."

Fergus was overwhelmed. "A magnificent feast, sir."

Satterfield chuckled. "Then let's attack it."

They ate in silence, interrupted only by Satterfield's call for more claret.

Finally, when both plates were empty, Fergus said, "You started to tell me about Captain Essex."

Satterfield beamed expansively. "Of course Jason has done splendidly. He is, perhaps, more highly spirited than you are, but you complement each other well. One of you always takes the initiative and the other holds back for a little. You will make a great team. And Admiral Nelson agrees."

"And Essex's present assignment . . . ?"

"He has been, as you may know, in command of a cutter for some time, in charge of landing raiding parties and agents along the French coast. It has been damned dangerous, and he has done it quietly and well. Now he is to be rewarded, as you are. He will give up his present command next week and come to London to meet with you and Admiral Nelson."

Fergus drew in his breath. Perhaps Lord Satterfield was trying to tell him something. "Are you telling me we are to command other ships in company? Jeris didn't say anything about this."

Satterfield laughed. "He has certain responsibilities that prevent him from telling you, even such information as this. I am not inhibited by such restrictions. I do what I please as long as I do not damage my country. This information is to be held between us. Do not even share it with your uncle. He knows it anyway and will tell you after Admiral Nelson confirms the good news."

Satterfield turned to the waiter and waved at the table. "Jasper, my Chilton cheese and port, please."

When the cheese, port, and bowls of nuts were in place, Lord Satterfield said, "Now tell me about your last encounter with the two French frigates and how you saved the convoy. I read all the splendid official reports, but I'd like to hear your version."

Satterfield listened to half an hour of Fergus's recital of his exploits. Then he raised his hand. "I could listen to this all night, but at my age I only have so much time. Tell me something of your family life and your beautiful wife."

Fergus smiled at the thought of Shannon. "She is still just as beautiful. We married after Lord Malin was killed in a riding accident. She has two little girls, you know. And of course I've spent the past months recuperating from the shipwreck." He paused, not wanting Lord Satterfield to think he'd been idle too long. "We have plans, though. We're going to breed, train, and race horses."

Lord Satterfield's face lit up.

Fergus continued. "My father is building barns and paddocks on my estate now. He will breed the horses there and feed and train them for a year. When they are ready they will be shipped to Shannon's estate in Donegal, where they will feed on Irish grass and be trained some more. We hope to race them in London and throughout the world."

"My God! You have both been busy. I want to get some bets down when you are ready to race. Please keep me informed and," Lord Satterfield smiled warmly, "tell Shannon to call on me frequently. I would like to be able to help her. After all, I've been in horse-racing for a lifetime."

An hour later Fergus judged that Lord Satterfield was growing drowsy, and he thanked him profusely for the evening and asked for permission to withdraw.

Lord Satterfield nodded and said, "Forgive me if I do not rise to see you off. This has been a splendid meeting for me, too, and I hope to repeat it with both you and my son after you have seen Admiral Nelson."

Shepherd and Patrick were at the door with Fergus's carriage. Patrick climbed down, opened the door, and unfolded the steps. Then he stepped back and said, "What do I do now, Fergus? Help you down?"

Fergus said, "First, don't use my first name out here in public. Save it for home. And never help me in or out. Help the older ladies but not the younger ones. They might belt you with a handbag if you touched them."

"Ah, I see. *Belt* means the same in Ireland. I'd rather step back and get a good look at their ankles."

At Shannon's townhouse, Fergus got out, thanked the two drivers, and bounded up the steps of the townhouse. Shannon met him and, after a warm kiss, said, "Your Uncle Jeris is waiting to see you in the parlor. He seems very anxious. I'll leave you two alone."

Fergus found Jeris standing in front of a coal fire and nursing a glass of port. "Ah, Uncle, I see you are waiting up for me."

Jeris sighed. "Of course, dear lad. I want to know how it went with you and Lord Satterfield."

Fergus shook his head, "The whole affair is ridiculous. You know what happened, and I know what is about to happen, but we can't talk about it."

Jeris sighed, "Yes, my boy. I'm sure you know my official constraints. All in all, I'm very happy, and I'll be able to celebrate with you as soon as you've seen Admiral Nelson. By the way, settle one point for me. A man from Gieves Naval Tailors called on me today and wanted to know why you had ordered a special version of a regular naval cutlass instead of a dress sword."

Fergus laughed. "You know I lost my grandfather's regulation sword when I lost my ship. Will you loan me your sword so that I can take it to sea for ceremonial purposes?"

"Of course. It's yours. But why the cutlass also?"

"The regulation sword will be all right for ceremonies, but it's no good for fighting. Jason Essex taught me that. He had the ship's armorer grind down the regular broad-blade cutlass until it was narrow and sharp all of its length. That way he could cut sideways with its length and still thrust with its point like a foil. He did a lot of destruction with it. I mean to carry one in battle. I'll feel a lot better than I would trying to defend myself with a ridiculous ceremonial sword."

"Anything you want, lad. You'll find one complete uniform ready for your Friday meeting with Admiral Nelson. Send Shepherd to pick it up. You won't need to try it on any further. Gieves Tailors never miss. When you are overseas, write to them and they'll send you anything you need. Of course you will have to keep your middle, er, waist, the same size."

"And when is our meeting again?"

"It will be at 10 A.M. in my office. Now if you'll excuse me, I'll say good night and wish you luck."

CHAPTER 4

The *Daring* and the *Dashing*

THE NEXT WEEK passed quickly. Shannon was busy putting the girls in school and seeing her obstetrician. He pronounced her healthy, and she was happy except that her clothes soon would no longer fit.

Fergus made preparations for sea, expecting that orders would come to him soon from the Admiralty after his meeting with Admiral Nelson.

On Friday Fergus arrived well before the scheduled meeting time and found Uncle Jeris very nervously pacing his office. A few minutes before 10 A.M. Jason Essex burst into the office, and the two captains and old shipmates embraced each other. Fergus stepped back and looked at Essex's handsome face and athletic form. They were about the same height but otherwise not the same. Where Fergus was definitely of Gaelic origin with a little Scandinavian thrown in from some invading ancestor, Essex was completely Norman, probably of French descent, although the Satterfield name had been in England for centuries. Essex had thick, dark brown hair, kept short, and his eyes were a matching brown. He had a nervous energy that always seemed to be just below the surface. He was much quicker in his reactions than Fergus, but somehow he made mistakes that the more cautious Fergus avoided.

Fergus said, "You're still in good shape. Did you keep that way by climbing to the foretop every morning?"

Essex laughed. "Lord, no. My cutter's mainmast wouldn't challenge anybody."

Jeris was bewildered. "What are you two talking about?"

Fergus said, "When we were shipmates, this fellow used to climb up to the top of the mainmast every day on the morning watch."

"All right. Tell him all about it," Essex said.

Fergus slapped his knee. "Oh, yes. The first time was a real dasher. You came on deck when I had the morning watch, walked over to the mainmast ratlines, looked up at the top of the mast, and shook your head. The senior top man of the watch walked over and said, 'What's the matter, Lieutenant Essex? I don't see anything,' and you said, 'I think I see an Irish pennant up there.'

"Shaughnessy, the senior top man, looked up again and said, 'It looks all right to me.'"

"Oh, yes, I remember," Essex laughed. "I took off my jacket and hat and handed them to you. Then I said to Shaughnessy, 'Shall we take a closer look?' 'Oh, yes,' he said."

"Just so," Fergus said. "Then you put your hand on the ratlines and said 'Start us.' Shaughnessy put his hand on his side of the ratlines. 'Go!' I shouted, and you both took off. You were even at the main top, and you gained going around the outside of it. You both went hand over hand past the ratlines there, and I was afraid one of you would fall."

"Not a chance!"

Fergus went on. "At the top you were a fathom ahead and when you got to the deck you were two fathoms ahead. You dropped down to the deck breathing easily and Shaughnessy was puffing. The crew of the watch had been cheering Shaughnessy, but when you hit the deck they cheered you, too."

"Ah, yes, Shaughnessy was a fine young man, but I was in better shape," Essex bragged.

"Then the captain burst out of his cabin door and strode forward, trying to keep his shirttails and trouser tops together. 'What the devil is all this racket about? You woke me up!' I tried to calm him down because he was a very popular and able captain. 'Sir, Lieutenant Essex and Shaughnessy were aloft trying to take care of, er, a problem in the rigging.'

"'Haw!' said the captain. 'I don't buy that. Next time let me know when you have one of these affairs, I'd like to get a bet down.' He pushed his shirttails the rest of the way inside his trousers, turned, and went back to his cabin, trying to suppress a laugh."

Essex sobered. "It was a great morning. I'll always remember it. Now let's get down to business before the admiral arrives. I trust you know why we are here."

Fergus was still laughing. "Now, Essex, calm yourself. I don't know anything officially other than we are to be here, and as usual you were almost late."

"Aw, fiddlesticks! I made it." He looked at the brass clock on Jeris's desk, just striking six bells for 10 A.M. "It's the admiral who is late. Maybe his new mistress detained him a bit in bed?"

Jeris colored and clasped his hands nervously. "Please, Captain. Be careful with such comments. He might come in suddenly and hear you."

It nearly happened. An aide knocked on the door, opened it quickly, stood aside, and said ceremoniously, "Sirs, Admiral Horatio Nelson."

An unprepossessing man in a vice admiral's uniform, of short stature and slim body, walked in, paused, and looked around. There was nothing startling or striking in his appearance. He had short brown hair, and his eyes seemed to be smaller than average and clouded slightly by some lingering infection. Other than that, he had regular features. His forehead was marked by a long scar, still healing. At first he held his right arm, missing the forearm, behind him, but as he strode forward he brought it around to balance himself, and no one seemed to notice.

Fergus thought Nelson seemed to change as he walked and talked, and soon he was only aware of his striking personality. All his physical problems faded away.

Nelson waved the aide aside. "Never mind the ceremonies, Lieutenant Sinclair. I know these gentlemen well. Now please go out and take care of my barge, er, carriage, and have it ready when I call for it in about an hour."

The aide left, somewhat subdued.

Essex giggled quietly and said behind his hand to Fergus, "I never wanted to be an aide. I'd have been fired before the first day was over. This one might not make it much longer."

Nelson walked to the middle of the room with a firm stride and shook hands with Jeris. "Please excuse his pomposity, Fairlie, he has just been appointed my flag lieutenant, and I will have to break him in. I don't like all that officiousness, particularly ashore."

Essex raised his hand again. "Well, I might have agreed to serve as his aide."

Fergus said, "For God's sake be quiet. You'll get us both fired."

Jeris nodded politely. "I can understand, sir. I am sure you know Captains Kilburnie and Essex."

"Like brothers, sir." Nelson strode over to each and shook hands warmly. Then he turned back to Jeris. "Could we be seated and have a glass of your good port to celebrate the occasion? I find the dust in your London streets opprobrious. I'd like to get back to the clean sea air."

Jeris rang for refreshments, and the four sat down at a conference table. As they sat, Fergus was quick to note that the damaged eye was a little better than he had remembered, and that the large scar on his forehead that Fergus had seen at the Battle of the Nile was still obvious. He was accustomed to Nelson's short stature and the absence of his forearm, but he noticed that Essex seemed to be perplexed. Essex leaned over to Fergus and said behind his hand, "I only met him once years ago, and we were seated at a dinner table. I thought he was taller."

Nelson looked at the two young officers and laughed. "No secrets, gentlemen. The only secret now is which of the two ships each is to command."

"Yes, sir," Jeris said, "but at present they do not even know that they are to command any."

"Well, Fairlie, you have maintained security well. Now please tell them something of the nature of the ships they are to command and when."

Jeris seemed to be relieved of the strain of maintaining secrecy. He cleared his throat. "As I understand it, sir, Kilburnie is senior by two months and is therefore to get the larger ship."

"Fairlie, you jest. They are exact sister ships. One is a foot longer than the other because the figurehead sticks out a foot further."

Jeris cleared his throat. "Well, sir, it seemed the thing to do. I must say that in the dark I couldn't tell one from the other if I were in bed with them."

Nelson looked at him with a twinkle in his eye. "Now, sir, you could."

Jeris colored and coughed. Fergus rolled his eyes in consternation.

Nelson retrieved the situation. "Tut, tut, Fairlie. I could have told the difference. One figurehead is male and the other female. Otherwise the ships are the same tonnage, the same design and dimensions, and will carry the same number of men and guns. Their speed remains to be tested, but I am informed they will be the fastest large square-rigged ships afloat. I expect them to sail against and fight our enemies frequently, but I also expect to send them off both together and individually on dangerous and important tasks. They will form the nucleus of a scouting force. If they are as successful as I expect, I will add more fast frigates some day and immediately, as messengers, two or three small fast sloops. I will add one more fast frigate when it is completed. Together the force will seek out the enemy, tell me where they are, and bring me to them."

Jeris beamed. "A new concept, sir?"

"Not quite. Kilburnie served in a ship in a fast frigate force, which was the eyes and, I must say, the ears for Admiral Jervis at the Battle of Cape St. Vincent's."

"Ears, sir?"

"Yes. Their ship located the Spanish fleet by the sound of signal guns in the fog. I understand that Lieutenant Kilburnie first noticed the significance of the single shots as being a Spanish custom in the fog and the information was passed up the line."

Jeris looked curiously at Fergus. "Fergus, you never mentioned this."

Fergus shrugged modestly and started to speak, but Admiral Nelson interrupted. "Fairlie, get him in front of a good fire with some good port some night. He'll tell you many a tale of his exploits. So can Captain Essex. If you include Lord Satterfield in the audience, they'll burn your ears. Essex has been carrying out exploits along the French and Spanish coasts that even the Admiralty doesn't know about yet. Only Lord Satterfield and I know."

"But sir!" Jeris said. "Can we talk about such things?"

"Oh, yes, their own sense of intelligence is far superior to that of the ponderous group the Admiralty calls the Intelligence Service. Sometime you and I will have to conduct our own personal conversation over port on this subject. Now, Fairlie, my good man, I must get off. I must get back to a personal and, er, family matter. I assume this decision is to be final and these two young bucks can now see their new commands and get acquainted with them."

"Yes, Admiral, with your consent, the decision is made, and I will inform the Lords of the Admiralty."

"And the king?"

"He will know almost immediately, as will the hordes of sycophantic would-be captains who have been hounding my outer office."

Nelson laughed. "Tell them to leave you alone. This decision is as firm as Gibraltar."

"Ah, thank you, Admiral. This will make my task easier."

Nelson rose slowly and clapped each captain on his back in a firm embrace. To each he said, "You are now in Nelson's Navy. We will do wonders together. One final word. Never fail to take the most daring course of action you can discern, just as I would. I will back you to the hilt no matter what happens as a result of your actions."

Essex said quickly, "Of course, sir, you can always count on both of us."

Fergus was more deliberate, as he always was, and said, "Sir, we dedicate our lives to you."

Nelson grinned. "And to the country and our Navy."

Both captains' eyes grew moist at those words, and Fairlie suppressed a sob.

"Of course, sir," they said, almost in unison.

Nelson smiled, touched his brow in a form of salute, turned away, and walked out. Outside the door they could hear him raising his voice. "Lieutenant Sinclair, where the hell is my barge, er, carriage?"

"Just outside, sir."

Fergus grinned. "Lieutenant Sinclair is learning very fast, but he'll have to move even faster to stay ahead of his new boss."

Essex laughed. "I think he'll make it."

Once the excitement of Admiral Nelson's departure abated, Jeris said, "I suppose you two young 'bridegrooms' want to see your new 'brides.'"

Essex laughed. "I'm a bachelor, so this ship will be my new wife. Fergus here is already married. I suppose this will be like meeting his new mistress."

Fergus was impatient. "Never mind the words. I want to see my new ship. Incidentally, what are the names of the two beauties?"

"Yours is named the *Daring,* and Essex will command the *Dashing.* Both very appropriate names, don't you think?"

"When will they be ready to go to sea? I am very anxious to get there."

"Not more than a fortnight to prepare them and another similar period to work up."

"I see." Fergus nodded.

Essex frowned. "I wish it could be sooner."

"The Admiralty has put a lot of money in these ships and wants to begin to get a payback soon. You should be ready to fight by the middle of February. Admiral Nelson expects to be at sea in the north in two months," Jeris said. He turned to Fergus. "Remember, it is Royal Navy custom that once you commission your ship, you may not come ashore in England for any reason unless the Admiralty orders you to do so."

"But I also remember that my wife can live aboard with me when I'm in port, and I think Shannon is willing."

"That's still so." Jeris winked at Essex. "And you, my boy may embark a dozen 'wives,' but only one at a time. Please be discreet."

Essex laughed, "Don't worry. You'll never hear anything about what I do. I'm getting too old for anything fancy enough to get to your ears."

Soon Jeris's carriage drew up to the gate of the Royal Navy dockyard. Jeris leaned out and said to the gate guard, "I have here the newly ordered commanding officers of His Majesty's ships *Daring* and *Dashing.* May I escort them aboard?"

"Of course. Identify yourself at the yard master's office in charge of construction of ships. Since the ships are almost identical, you can save yourself a lot of traipsing around in dust and dirt by just going about one ship."

Essex said, "That's all right with me. Let's see the *Daring.* I'd rather only see mine when she's dressed in her final finery anyway."

Jeris nodded. "Then that's the way it will be. When we leave them today in the tidying phase you two will not be allowed aboard until the day they are commissioned."

Fergus was growing impatient. "Yes, Uncle, I understand. Let's get on with it."

The carriage drove up to the side of the *Daring.* The pier side and the ship's decks were a shambles of ship's equipment, construction equipment, and scurrying workmen. The outline of the ship was apparent, and the guns peeked out of the gun ports as the workmen hoisted and fitted the heavy gunport covers. As they climbed up the makeshift brow and stood on the deck, Fergus stopped and looked around the masts that had been stepped. An antlike array of workers was clambering aloft, installing the standing rigging that was designed to support and brace the huge masts.

Other men were festooning the masts with hoisted yards supported by filaments of rope used to control the slim sticks of wood that would someday display the sails attached to them. As soon as the pieces of rope being installed were made up to suit their purposes they were no longer "rope" but "lines." "Halliards" hoisted the sails and "sheets" controlled the angles the yards made with the keel. Other lines had names indicating their purpose, such as "log" line.

Below, carpenters were sawing and banging with great abandon. Despite what seemed like confusion to outsiders, the two experienced captains knew by looking at the ship's pieces that it would all be finished and in good order in less than a month.

A quick trip to what would be the living quarters was satisfactory. Fergus was sure that Shannon would be reasonably comfortable in his cabin for the short visits she would make aboard.

Finally Fergus said, "I've seen enough. Now let's get a look at the ship's lines from the pier."

Essex nodded. "That's where we'll be able to tell whether the ship will be fast or not."

On the pier the three started at the stern and walked slowly forward. At the bow Essex snickered. "Pretty sexy figurehead you have on your ship. You ought to put some clothes on her upper works. I understand that what makes your ship a foot longer than mine."

Fergus sighed. "I think that's so. Your Greek warrior figurehead is very muscular but still flat-chested compared to mine. My sailors will think that's fine. They don't care how much it sticks out. They just like the beauty of it."

Essex shrugged. "I doubt that, but so be it. That won't make your ship fight any better."

The two captains stopped and looked at each other. Essex, as usual the first to speak, whistled. "They're going to be fast all right."

Fergus nodded soberly. "They stole the hull lines from the French."

Jeris said, "Of course. They've been doing that for years. French ships have always been the fastest in the water because of their hull design. Now we think our hulls are the equal of theirs and changes in ballasting and mast placement may add another knot."

Fergus shrugged. "That's all we can ask."

"No, it isn't. Every time we capture a French ship we test it to see if it is fast. If it is, we copy her lines exactly and incorporate them in our next ships."

Fergus shook his head, "Why can't our designers figure this out in the first place? There's nothing magic about it."

Jeris nodded. "I've wondered about that myself. I even asked the designers of the Royal Navy dockyard why our ships are always so slow. They shrugged their shoulders and then nodded wisely, saying, 'That is the way it has always been and the way we've done it. Ours are supposed to be broad, strong, and heavily constructed. The French like theirs to sail fast.'"

Essex, listening carefully, said, "If I'm lucky some day, I'll get somewhere in the Admiralty. I hope I can change things if and when I'm alive."

Fergus poked him in the ribs. "I wouldn't count on it. You live too close to danger to get much higher in rank. You are lucky to have lived thus far."

Essex nodded. "You are probably right, but in the meantime we have to do the best with what we have. My father says he will see that we are given a couple of fast sloops to use as scouts and messengers. The use of American fore and aft schooner rigs will let them outrun any ship in the ocean by five knots."

"Somehow getting free from the stultifying conservatism of our country and her designers seems to free the minds of the Americans," Fergus observed. "They've already come up with several inventions and been willing to try several we have rejected. They use many schooner-rigged ships that can out-speed our square-rigged ships by four knots. Now they can be expected to try new methods of shipbuilding. I don't think they can ever build a very large schooner-rigged ship. Its very narrowness would prevent it from carrying many large guns. But, mark my words, they will try to construct a hull that will be as strong as iron, and at least they'll have a lot of iron in it."

"How so?"

"By using large oak beams in the hull joined by iron bolts. They have thousands of large oak trees, whereas we have used almost all of ours."

"And what else?"

"Perhaps cross scantlings that give the hull greater strength? The possibilities are frightening."

Essex nodded. "And you and I will be fighting these monsters some day. They might control the seas then."

Fergus said, "That's the future. Now let's use these beautiful ships in the present. Well, we've done all we can here, Essex, and we have to meet soon to figure out what we are to do to carry out Admiral Nelson's plans. How about next Wednesday?"

"Good, but my father would like to sit in. We owe him that much, at least. He'll invite us to White's Club if we ask him to join us."

"You are right. I'll ask Lord Satterfield as soon as I can and send word to you. Now let's go home."

At Shannon's townhouse, Fergus burst in the front door and called upstairs for Shannon. She came downstairs as fast as she could and he carefully took her in his arms.

Fergus grinned. "I'm glad to see you are being very careful with my son."

"Why do you think it's a boy?"

"Just wishful thinking. Actually I'll be happy either way."

"You already look very happy. What happened?"

"Admiral Nelson is as inspiring as I remembered him. Our meeting was very pleasant."

"Stop stalling and tell me . . ."

Fergus smiled. "Oh, of course. He did confirm that Essex and I are to command the two fast frigates we've heard were being built in the Royal Navy dockyards. Mine is to be the *Daring,* and Essex's is named the *Dashing.*" His face broke into a grin. "Mine is a foot longer than his."

"I thought they were sister ships."

"They are. Mine has a very buxom female figurehead. His has a flat-chested male warrior."

"And she sticks out a foot farther than he does?"

"Oh, very definitely. And she is as bare as the day she was born, er, sculpted."

Shannon sighed. "You would get into something like that."

"I had nothing to do with it, and if you don't like it, just think of Uncle Jeris as the salacious old man who made the decision."

"Stop it. He's a nice old man. Now tell me about your ship's cabin."

"Right now it is full of wood shavings and lumber. You get to sleep on the bare lumber and maybe a few shavings I'll put on top of it."

"Stop all this kidding," Shannon said. "Losing you to that naked woman at sea for months at a time is bad enough. By the way, what is the figurehead's name?"

"I don't know. I think I'll have her christened 'Shannon' after you," Fergus teased.

Shannon groaned. "That's enough or you'll get no supper. Now sit down in my parlor and wait for me. I'll be with you as soon as I've talked to the cook. And I suggest you find some other name unless you want shavings for supper."

As she was leaving he said, "Oh, I remember now. They told me at the dockyard that the figurehead had already been named Eurydice. You're safe."

"So are you. Sit down."

The next evening, while being driven home in his carriage, Fergus began to think about the horse-training system he and Shannon had set in motion. Letters from his father, Ennis, and Liam all reported that the operation was proceeding. The final part, a plan for establishing a complex for entering the London race-course operations and for shipping horses onward, had not been taken care of. As he swung out of the carriage, after arriving home, Fergus looked up at Shepherd on the box. "Shepherd, after you put the carriage and horses up, come into the parlor and have tea with Shannon and me."

Ten minutes later, Shepherd arrived, hat in hand, somewhat uncertain. As she always did so well, Shannon put him at ease. "Shepherd, put your hat over there and come sit with us. How do you like your tea?"

"Plain, ma'am."

Shannon poured his tea and began. "You must have heard that Fergus and I have begun to raise racehorses in Scotland and have shipped some to my estate in Ireland for finishing,"

"Yes, ma'am, I've heard that from Patrick, but I don't know any details. I've always liked horses. I spent years training my father's and riding them when I was small enough to be a jockey."

Fergus perked up. "Your father was a horse trainer?'

"Oh, yes, he raced several horses. But he died several years ago," Shepherd bowed his head. "Since then my mother and I tried to make a go of the farm and racing, but we couldn't make it financially. I had to go to work to keep the farm going."

Fergus looked at Shannon and pursed his lips. "We were going to ask you to take Shannon on a tour of the territory surrounding London looking for a location to put together a station for the final finishing and racing of her horses. You may have the answer. Take Shannon out to your farm first thing tomorrow."

Shepherd rose, smiling. "I'll have the carriage ready right after breakfast."

"Good. You take Shannon out. Patrick can take me to the shipyard. I'll see you tomorrow night."

Shannon nodded. "I think we'll make a lot of progress tomorrow."

At supper the next night, Shannon and Fergus sat late over coffee. Fergus said, "First, this whole project has to be yours and in your name. As a naval officer, I can't do anything publicly except cheer for your horses. I'll like that, but I'll have to learn that they belong to you."

"I understand," Shannon said.

Fergus sat back and poured more coffee. "Now tell me what went on today."

"Well, we didn't know what a gem we had in Shepherd. His father trained and raced horses. Shepherd has raced as a jockey and worked with his father for years, just as he said last night. I looked him up in all the racing records."

"I take it that they weren't too successful."

"No, but it was not their fault. They lacked the capital to buy good horses and carry out the rest of the requirements of a successful operation."

"And the so-called farm?"

"It's really an old estate. The house is an old stone mansion, in good condition except for the roof. Ten bedrooms, an enormous kitchen, and a large dining room, too. The barn is also stone, and needs a new roof. Ten stalls."

Fergus said, "We need room for a staff of thirty jockeys, exercise boys, and trainers."

"Yes, and we will have to build a small bunkhouse back of the main house. Also a barn with twenty more stalls and a large storage area."

"I take it you want it," Fergus said.

"Very much. I'd like to offer Shepherd a ten-year lease and an agreement to make the necessary repairs and build the extensions. The lease can provide that we leave them in place if we do decide not to renew the lease."

"Will he accept this?"

"He was ecstatic when I proposed it. He volunteered to stay on as manager, and his mother wants to run the house and its kitchen. Two of his brothers will stay on with him."

Fergus sat back and smiled. "Well, it's all settled then. Patrick can become your driver, and Shepherd can find a replacement for himself as my driver."

Shannon went on. "I propose to offer him a contract for a year as manager at a handsome salary. If he succeeds I will increase it."

"I'm glad to hear it's all arranged before I have to leave. After all, we should be racing in a year. I can hardly wait to tell Lord Satterfield the details. He will be ready to help you when I am gone. He has been racing horses for many years."

"I think we can do it all ourselves," Shannon said stubbornly.

"Don't try it. Lord Satterfield has helped us already, and he is a very influential person in politics and racing."

"I'll remember that."

"You know the king controls most of the racing tracks and all of the horses in England."

"Yes, I know, and getting around him will be difficult."

Fergus nodded. "Lord Satterfield is a favorite of the king. Keep that in mind."

Now Shannon grinned. "And he seems to like me also."

CHAPTER 5

Under Way

WHEN FERGUS INFORMED Lord Satterfield of the outcome of the meeting with Admiral Nelson, Satterfield immediately invited Jeris and the two captains to dinner at White's.

Satterfield was a superb host as usual and remained quiet as the claret loosened the tongues of the two young captains. They described the characteristics and qualities of the two ships and propounded ways to get the maximum speed and maneuverability against one, two, and three enemy ships.

"Speed, always speed," Essex said excitedly. "That's what Admiral Nelson wants."

"And maneuverability," Fergus chimed in.

Jeris said, "Your speed will always enable you to back away from any engagement."

Both frowned and said almost with one voice, "We are part of Nelson's Navy, and we don't back off. Never! The enemy does that."

Lord Satterfield slapped his thigh and roared. "You have been had, Jeris! You miss the next round of claret."

Jeris colored. "Sorry, sir, I am sure they are right. I was just theorizing."

Satterfield's roaring laugh subsided, to the relief of several nearby dozing gentlemen in overstuffed chairs. "All right, old friend. I know you were, but you still lose the next round of claret."

Fergus leaned over to Satterfield. "Sir, I want to inform you that Shannon will be racing some winners next year. I'll give you some tips when they are firm."

Satterfield beamed. "I knew there was some racing blood in her family. I will be her chief representative to the king."

The meeting broke up at midnight, and the captains walked out arm in arm, still deep in conversation.

Satterfield, following after them with Jeris, helping him to negotiate the sprawling legs in the club, poked him playfully in the ribs. "Look at those two young cubs. There will be some sorry Frenchmen soon. You'd better hurry out to your carriage. They may not even notice that you have been following behind, and they may drive off without you."

Jeris laughed. "You're right. I thank you for a superb evening."

Satterfield nodded. "I am the one who should be thanking all of you together. They made an old man feel vigorous and important again."

The next two weeks were busy for Fergus. He contrived to spend as much time as possible with Shannon and on weekends visited her daughters at school. He had his uniforms fitted and refitted and checked the work on his cutlass until the Gieves' clerks sighed and told him openly that they wished he would hurry to sea and ease their work.

Fergus became increasingly restless and eager to see his ship. On two occasions he snuck a peek at his ship. With his face muffled against the increasing fall coldness and sitting well back in Jeris's carriage as it drove slowly through the Royal Navy dockyard, Fergus could catch a glimpse of the growing *Daring.* Finally satisfied with the progress of his ship he returned home to report to Shannon that all was well.

"Have they carried aboard to your cabin any feather mattresses for me yet?"

"No. So far all they have done is convert more of the lumber stored in my cabin to shavings. That may be the best that you can do."

One evening Shannon almost broke into tears as he kept on about shavings, and he hastily retreated. "Don't worry. At the least we can sleep together in one large cot."

"Can we both sleep in one cot?"

Fergus looked at her growing girth and laughed. "I don't think we should try that, at least for a while. I'll make sure they send aboard two."

The day set for commissioning was a beautiful cool Monday. The crew was about three-fourths recruited, as word got around London and the other ships of the Royal Navy that "Lucky Kilburnie" was going to sea again and they could expect to bring back the usual amount of prize money.

Fergus tried to deny the rumor when Essex heard it, but Essex only laughed. "You are lucky. Don't deny it. I just hope your luck holds."

Shannon's carriage drew up to the bottom of the brow promptly at 10 A.M. Fergus had already stopped by the dockmaster's nearby office to draw a commission pennant, now clasped firmly in Shannon's hand.

They climbed down the carriage steps, Shannon taking great care, and walked to the bottom of the brow and up the long distance to the deck above.

Since the ship was not yet commissioned, the colors were not yet flying. Nor was the quarterdeck ready. At the top of the brow Fergus was greeted by his lieutenants, who saluted, and he returned their salutes. Fergus was very fortunate to have such a group sailing with him. His senior lieutenant, Poston, had served with Fergus on the *Athena* and later became a lieutenant. Lieutenant Puller had been a midshipman on the *Aberdeen* and under Fergus's tutelage had succeeded in making lieutenant. Also in the officer group was Doctor Pollitt, who had served as surgeon when Fergus was on the *Athena.* And in the ranks of the enlisted men were several familiar faces from his old ships. Lieutenant Poston gestured to the men in front of them. "It won't be hard to fill their ranks, sir. We'll go to sea filled up and ready to fight."

"Thank you, Poston. Now please go ahead with the ceremony." He took the commissioning pennant from Shannon's hands and handed it to Poston.

The dock manager stepped forward. "Captain, it will be a pleasure to turn this fine ship over to you. The *Dashing,* astern of you, will be commissioned at the same time and will follow your motions in raising her flags and pennants. Now, if you are ready, I turn this ship over to you. Please proceed with the rest of the ceremony."

By now Lieutenant Poston had stationed his quartermaster mates at the appropriate points on the ship to hoist the commissioning pennant and the Jack, and the Royal Standard. "Ready, sir," he reported.

Fergus glanced at the *Dashing* and received a wave of readiness from Captain Essex. He waved back and turned to Lieutenant Poston. "Sir, commission the ship."

The flags and pennants broke free from the strings that restrained the small bundles hoisted at the proper halliards. The brilliant bunting spread out, caught the breeze, and flew freely in the cool breeze. The crews of both ships broke into cheers.

Shannon wiped her eyes. "Magnificent!"

Fergus took off his hat and raised it. "Three cheers for the *Daring!*" he shouted.

The roaring cheers from the two crews could be heard all over the dockyard, and work stopped for a few minutes.

"Two more ships for the king," one man said.

Another nodded. "And the Spanish and French will be in for more trouble."

Fergus looked toward the *Dashing,* now flying bright flags and pennants. Essex waved back, and Shannon, standing by his side, wiped more tears from her eyes. Fergus said, "He and I will do our best for the king."

Shannon was more practical. "And for Admiral Nelson."

Fergus, now recovered emotionally, laughed. "Oh, yes, that too. He calls us a band of brothers."

The bustle throughout the shipyard did not stop for long. An hour after the ceremony, the task of ammunitioning and provisioning the ships started. Huge drays drew up alongside and dock cranes began to lift barrels and crates aboard. The heavy barrels were rolled about the deck and lowered into the proper holds.

When the provisioning was completed, ammunitioning started. The powder kegs were treated carefully and even gingerly. The captains were on deck from the moment this phase started. Then the heavy balls were hoisted aboard in cargo nets and rolled to their storages. When this had all been completed, Poston reported, "Sir, the magazines are full and secured. All safety precautions have been complied with."

The second day Fergus allowed Shannon to come aboard, followed by a small amount of baggage. Other women began to come aboard, and Fergus turned his eyes away as the "port wives" disappeared below. "Get them all off two days before we sail," he said to Poston.

Poston grinned. "Aye, aye, sir."

Shannon took to shipboard life quickly. Fergus had recruited a handsome young Welshman named Evan Radcliffe as his steward and sent him ashore to fill the larder for the cruise. Radcliffe came back with a good selection of canned goods and as much fresh vegetables and fruit as he thought would last without spoiling. A crate of chickens was added to the forward compartment, known as the "manger" for the growing supply of small animals to be slaughtered at the proper time. Most captains used the majority of the farm animals for their own meals, but Fergus had vetoed any animals for himself, disappointing young Radcliffe. "You'll regret this, sir," he said in his Welsh accent, but the captain had held firm.

"I'll give the crew all the space up there I can," Fergus said, "and I can do without it."

The month allotted for outfitting passed quickly, and Shannon left the ship with quiet tears in evidence, but quickly blotted them out with a kerchief.

"I'll be back home in about a fortnight after our workup cruise," Fergus said, "and I'll miss you and the girls all the time."

"Oh yes, you will, and soon there will be four of us for you to miss."

On the last day of the period of outfitting, Fergus and Essex opened their sealed orders sent to them in heavily embossed envelopes and read them to each other.

"Simple," Fergus said, "We get under way as soon as possible, go to sea in the English Channel, train our crews to the maximum extent, and then come back here to this pier and prepare for active duty."

Essex nodded. "I presume we'll use our signal book to the maximum to teach us to maneuver together."

"Yes, I'll be in tactical command today, and you'll be in command every even calendar day."

"Suits me," Essex said. "Now let's stop stalling and get under way. The wind and tide are fair."

Fergus shook his head and laughed. "You really are dashing, just like the name of your ship. I'll see you here in two weeks."

Essex saluted formally, took his leave of the officer of the watch, and trotted aft to his ship.

Fergus grinned and turned to Poston. "All hands to station for getting under way."

Poston looked bewildered. "You mean now, sir?"

Fergus nodded. "Damned right. We can't let the *Dashing* beat us."

The men scurried to their stations aloft followed by the loud voice of the sailing master, Lombardi, cursing alternately in Italian and English. Workmen strolling down the pier side stopped and listened to Lombardi's tirade as he tried to speed up the men in the foretop.

Fergus said to Poston, "He's not a very patient man."

"He's reasonably so," Poston shrugged, "but many of our crew are green. He'll have them dancing a jig up there when we return to port."

Fergus grinned. "Like old times."

"Yes, sir, but I don't remember this demand in those days for all this speed."

"Well, we'll all hear more of that from now on at sea. We're part of Nelson's Navy now, or soon will be, and he likes lots of speed."

"And we don't?"

Fergus laughed. "We always liked it, but we never had ships under us before that could provide the speed."

In a few minutes Poston yelled at some workmen idling on the pier to cast off their lines. The light, offshore winds moved them slowly off the pier, and Lombardi ordered the main courses hoisted. Now the ship moved slowly ahead. As soon as the ship had steerage way, the sailing master set a course for the main channel. Fergus looked up and noticed that the *Dashing* was following at a cable's length. "Well done, Sailing Master, we're out first, just as we always should be."

For the first week, as agreed, the ships sailed in sight of each other, conducting internal drills and eventually test-firing their new guns. The last quarter of the crews and two lieutenants and three midshipmen had come aboard both ships in the last week, and all the sail-handling teams and gun crews had to be instructed by the hard-working boatswain, gunner, and the two new lieutenants. Poston declared the newcomers "surprisingly good material. They all wanted to come aboard this ship."

"Tell me something about them," Fergus asked. "I know all about you and Puller."

"Well, the older lieutenant, Ballinger, has ten years at sea and has been wounded twice. He just got out of the hospital and limps slightly, but the surgeon says he'll be recovered completely soon."

"He's a very distinguished looking officer. And Lieutenant Meadows?"

"Young and inexperienced, but smart and eager."

"Can he navigate?"

"I think so. At least he says so, but I'll have to test him. He's been at sea for five years and earned his commission in battle. He hopes to take his final examinations for lieutenant soon."

"Good. I like that kind. How about the midshipmen?"

"Two young lads 'bought in' by rich fathers, and one a favorite of an admiral. We'll have to look at them closely."

"Poston, you don't know much about our sailing master."

Poston laughed. "I hear he has a very good voice. He shakes the men up in the tops if they loaf."

"Yes, I understand he could sing opera."

"He did," Poston said, "but he says he hated dressing up in those silly costumes. Also the Italian theaters smelled just like pig stys, garlic, unwashed bodies, and what-not. He says he likes the fresh air out here much better."

"Well, our crew's quarters won't smell so good after a month at sea." Fergus wrinkled his nose at the thought.

"I don't think Boatswain Terwilliger will let that happen. He's a stickler for cleanliness. They'll be scrubbing everything in sight. He's the first Londoner I've known who was not only personally clean, but also wants the ship to be just as clean. He really drives the crew on this. There's not a rat left on the ship and even the bilges smell good."

Fergus laughed. "He's very strong physically, too. Does he beat his men with the rope end he carries?"

"I've never seen him have to use it. In the first place, his orders always make sense to his men, and even if they doubt them, they would only have to look at his large muscles. They scare me, too."

"I think his forearm is as large as his starter," Fergus said.

"That heavy-handed Norwegian, Gunner Jansen, is getting his share of the crew's time. I'm surprised that the two don't come to blows," Poston said.

"Frankly, I'd bet on the boatswain, although the gunner is faster on his feet. You may have to step in. I think both officers are doing well now."

"I just don't want to get caught between them."

"Tomorrow I want to rig a floating target out of the barrels we have emptied," Fergus directed. "Try at least three and a mast on top. I see the *Dashing* on the horizon has already started gun-crew firing procedures and, like us, yesterday they completed test firing of their guns."

The next morning, after Fergus had instructed his officers in procedures, he pulled out his watch and ordered, "Man battle stations!"

When Poston reported the ship ready and at battle stations, Fergus looked at his watch and frowned. "Not good enough! Five minutes. The Spanish and even the French would have holed us by now."

Lieutenant Puller, the most experienced lieutenant, was ordered to fire his battery in succession as the sailing master brought the floating-barrel target abeam. The serving of the guns was deliberately slow to check the safety regulations for loading and firing. Nevertheless, several balls fell near the target and brought cheers from the gun involved.

Lieutenant Ballinger, given the other battery, produced almost as many near-misses. After three more passes, the barrel target received several hits and began to disintegrate.

"Enough!" Fergus ordered. "We'll do this several more times. Save the empty barrels."

At the end of the week, by mutual consent, the two captains decided that their ships were reasonably well trained in individual tasks and decided to sail in close company, maneuvering using signal flags during the day for the first week and for the second week using hooded lanterns for maneuvering at night.

Fergus and Essex were unusually skilled in handling frigates individually and in close formation. The rest of the officers learned quickly from their captains' examples and their own mistakes.

On the last day the two ships stood north in the English Channel, headed for the dockyard. It was Essex's turn to lead the formation, and Fergus strode up and down the quarterdeck watching the seagulls flying astern.

Suddenly the lookout aloft shouted, "*Dashing* is signaling man overboard!"

Then one yelled, "I can see a man in the water."

Fergus picked up a long glass, focused it, and yelled, "I have the conn. I have the man in sight. Prepare to pick him up when I back my sails."

The boatswain's mate on watch ran up the deck, sounding his pipe down each hatch and roaring, "All hands to quarters! Man overboard!"

The crew boiled up out of the hatches, adjusting their clothing as they ran to their stations.

In a few minutes, with the man just ahead and slightly to starboard, Fergus ordered, "Starboard your helm!"

The ship swung rapidly to starboard, the sails luffed, and the ship coasted to a stop.

As the ship slowly passed the man, lines were thrown to him, and he was pulled aboard by several men clinging to the sea ladder and laid out on the quarterdeck. Pollitt examined him quickly and pronounced him cold and temporarily out of breath, but in good shape.

"Looks all right to me, but the channel water is very cold at this time of year."

Fergus, bending over him, noticed a carpenter's auger tethered to his waist with a small piece of line. "What the hell is this?" he asked the recovering sailor.

The sailor sat up slowly and grinned. "It's an auger. I borrowed it from the carpenter."

Fergus pulled at his chin. "And what the devil were you doing with it?"

"Boring a hole in the bottom of the figurehead."

"And then?"

"The crew was going to hand me down a two-foot piece of mop handle to stick in the hole."

Fergus slapped his knee. "That wily so-and-so. He was going to claim that his ship was longer than mine."

Poston looked bewildered. "I don't get it."

"Don't you see what he's trying to do? The figurehead's two-foot penis would be a foot farther out in front than our figurehead's breasts."

The men surrounding the recumbent figure roared.

Fergus refrained from smiling. "Well, if you all think it is so funny, I'll detail you to row this man and his tool back to his ship." He turned to the officer of the deck. "Send a signal to the *Dashing:* "Am returning your culprit and his tool, less his mopstick, by boat."

The sailor stirred and stood up. "But, sir, I'm afraid Captain Essex will punish me. He doesn't know a thing about this."

Fergus laughed. "Don't worry about that. I know him well. He'll probably make you a petty officer when he finds out about your, er, *Dashing* initiative. Give him my regards, and tell him I ask him to give you an extra ration of rum."

Surgeon Pollitt laughed. "But I just gave him a ration of rum to take care of the cold."

Fergus grinned. "The next one will be a reward, and he deserves it." He turned to the quartermaster. "Change my last signal. Make the word 'culprit' read 'hero.'"

CHAPTER 6

The First Battle of Copenhagen

THE NEXT DAY the two ships sailed up the Thames River and moored at the Royal Navy dockyard. Jeris had been informed of the ships' progress, so he was already sitting in his carriage awaiting an opportunity to board the *Daring* when they arrived.

As soon as the brow was in place, Jeris left his carriage and walked up the brow. Since he was not in uniform, he did not salute the colors, but he held out his hand to Fergus. "Good to see you back, my lad. I have secret orders and information for you and Captain Essex. Please send a message to him to come aboard as soon as he moors."

"Fine. In the meantime I have some good port and a good sea yarn for you. Let's go to my cabin."

Once they were seated Jeris took the port Radcliffe poured for him. "All right, go ahead. I need a little laughing. The Admiralty is a pretty heavy place to be."

Fergus told him of the incident of the overboard "carpenter" from the *Dashing* and the young sailor's efforts to lengthen his ship by two feet.

Jeris slapped his thigh and almost spilled his drink attempting to manage both tasks with one hand. When he calmed down, he said, "That yarn will be all over the wardrooms in the fleet in a week and of course in the Admiralty by tomorrow. I'll wager the king will be telling it at port sessions after state dinners at the palace in a few days. I'm afraid that the young sailor from the *Dashing* will make you both famous with his exploits."

Fergus sighed. "I wish it would go away. I'm thinking of cutting the, er, protuberances of my figurehead by a foot to stop the competition."

"No, you don't want to do that. Sailors always love competition of any kind."

Just then Captain Essex burst in the cabin door. His arrival on the quarterdeck was so quick that Fergus had not been able to meet him there.

Essex said, "Good morning, Mister Fairlie. I presume Fergus has told you about my carpenter."

"I hope you have rewarded the lad." Jeris laughed again.

Essex smiled. "Yes, but first I thought about keelhauling him. Do you have orders for us?"

Jeris nodded. "Don't be in such a hurry. Have a glass of this good port first."

"Well, all right." Essex sat on the edge of his chair and watched Jeris pull the envelopes out of his jacket pocket without spilling his port.

Jeris gave identical envelopes to the two captains. "They're the same. Fergus, please read yours."

Fergus tore open the envelope and read the orders from Admiral Nelson.

> I am about to become second in command of a fleet under Admiral Sir Hyde Parker. We are forming up in order to leave for an adventure against the Danes at Copenhagen. The reason for our action is far too complicated to recount here. We will leave about the 12th of March and plan to arrive off Copenhagen about the first of April.
>
> The *Daring* and *Dashing* and two fast sloops will remain under my command and yours, Captain Kilburnie, although also a part of Admiral Parker's fleet. You will leave England the 10th of March, sail north while avoiding all ships if possible, proceed to the Kattegat through the Skaggerack, and take station twenty miles south of Copenhagen. It will be necessary to pass Copenhagen at night and, if possible, not to be identified by a potential enemy before the first of April. After taking station, patrol vigorously, looking for ships of any of our potential enemies. I do not need to name them, but they will include the Danes, Russians, Prussians, Swedes, and French. Shadow them, sending word to me using your fast sloops. When you hear that there has been action at Copenhagen, leave your patrol station and report to me off Copenhagen for further orders.
>
> Faithfully
>
> Nelson of Bronte

Essex shook his head. "What the hell does 'Nelson of Bronte' mean?"

Jeris cleared his throat. "That's the signature of a newly made peer as duke of Bronte."

"I'd rather be a vice admiral," Essex said.

"You will be one or the other some day. Now both of you must excuse me. I have a long ride back to the Admiralty."

The two captains escorted him to the quarterdeck and watched him depart. Then Essex turned to Fergus. "So I guess we'll be leaving very soon."

"Just staying long enough to load victuals."

"And Shannon?"

"She'll have a quick visit."

Essex laughed. "Also my current wife, of course."

"The poor girl will hardly have time to get your bed warmed," Fergus said.

Shannon's carriage drew up to the *Daring*'s brow that evening, and her driver, carrying a single bag, escorted her up the brow. Fergus folded her in his arms as soon as she stepped aboard. After a few seconds, Shannon said, "We'd better save this for your cabin. Your sailors will begin to snicker."

Fergus laughed. "No, they won't. Their minds are elsewhere. As soon as you are inside my cabin the port wives will dash aboard and disappear below."

"Are any of your sailors *really* married?"

"Only one elderly petty officer really is. The other women are all 'regular wives.' They just come aboard whenever the ship is in."

Shannon cocked her ear and listened carefully. "There! I hear loud giggling."

"You'll hear more than that. They sneak aboard with a lot of rum under their dresses. I don't bother them unless it gets out of hand and interrupts my sleep."

"I'll see that there's enough action here to keep you awake tonight." Shannon smiled and lifted her skirt to pull a bottle out of her waistband. "I'm learning fast. Here's the start of our own party."

"You're learning," Fergus agreed.

Shannon reached down and pulled loose the blue ribbons tied around her pantaloon bottoms.

Fergus said, "That's very pretty, but what is it for?"

Shannon raised her eyebrows archly. "If the bottle had slipped down inside my pantaloons the ribbons would have caught it before it hit the deck and broke into a million pieces of whiskey-soaked glass."

Fergus roared. When he stopped, he said, "A brilliant idea. I can't imagine what the crew would have said if the bottle had ended up in a pile of glass and Irish whiskey."

Shannon smiled. "Speaking of Irish whiskey, that's for me. You can drink that old stuff I've seen Evan put in your cabinet—rum, brandy, Scotch, wines, all that crude stuff. Although I'll say some of the wines look passable. I compliment him on his choice there."

Fergus took two heavy glasses out of the cabinet and poured Irish whiskey in one and Scotch in the other. He handed Shannon the Irish whiskey. "Here's to our party."

Shannon raised her glass. "My, the party up forward is getting noisy." She stopped, listened, and said, "Maybe we should join them."

Fergus laughed and shook his head. "No, the officers drink with the crew only on Christmas Day. If the noise gets out of hand the boatswain will step in and take charge. He likes his sleep." He looked at Shannon's waist as she was settling her skirt and whistled. "From the increase in your girth, I'd say our party is well along."

Along about midnight the noise forward and below got out of hand. Shannon finally protested. "Dear, how will we be able to sleep, assuming we are able to get into these cots?"

"Don't worry about it," Fergus answered. "The boatswain will get it in hand when he gets sleepy."

Just after a sudden burst of laughter below came a firm knock on Fergus's door. Fergus recognized it as the boatswain's knock, and sure enough Terwilliger was standing there when the captain opened the door.

Fergus's eyebrows shot up. "Well, Boatswain, what's that all about? It sounds like the ship is in danger."

Terwilliger shifted his large feet tentatively and shrugged his massive shoulders, "Well, sir, I apologize. I'll get it under control. The ship is safe."

"What is going on?"

Terwilliger rolled his eyes. "Well, sir, you remember when the ship was being built, you decided to make the midshipmen's mess below into a storeroom."

"Yes, I remember. It was too dark and too small so I ordered a corner of it to be made into a midshipmen's mess with light partitions that could be taken down when the ship was prepared for battle."

"Well, the three midshipmen were very happy with your decision." Terwilliger rolled his eyes. "In fact, I would say they were in heaven."

"How so?"

"Well, sir, you know their wives are aboard."

"Yes."

"Well, sir, the midshipmen decided to have 'horse races' in their wardroom."

"Horses? I don't understand."

Terwilliger took a deep breath and said in a low voice, "The midshipmen each took a name from Lady Shannon's stable."

Shannon giggled.

Fergus turned to her, "Please, this is serious."

Terwilliger, now at full speed with his explanation, went on. "The girls were mounted on the shoulders of the three midshipmen acting as horses, so to speak, and were racing around the table." He stopped his explanation and colored and stammered.

Fergus sensed that Shannon was up to something behind him and moved to block Terwilliger's view. "Well, go ahead. What were the stakes?"

"Each losing jockey had to take off an article of clothing."

"And?"

"One was down to one stocking and her chemise." He paused again. "So on the last race the leading horse stopped to get a better view of the losing jockey and the others piled into him. The whole group crashed into the bulkhead."

Fergus grinned. "The bulkheads are very flimsy. I can imagine the mess."

"I'm not sure you can, sir. All the bulkheads fell into the wardroom."

"What a mess!"

"Worse than you can imagine."

"What else?"

"They fell on the three wardroom officers who had their eyes on the race through cracks in the bulkhead and were making bets."

"Was anybody hurt?"

"Oh, no, sir. They have all gotten together and are now racing a new series of steeplechase events using the wardroom furniture as obstacles."

"Well, Boatswain, I think we've about reached the end. I want the officers and midshipmen to have some well-deserved rest, too. Perhaps you can call an end to the festivities at the end of the next race."

Terwilliger sighed with relief. "Ah, yes, sir, with your wise sailing directions, I think I can take charge."

Fergus watched him leave, closed the door, and turned to Shannon. "What were you doing that disturbed the poor boatswain so much?"

Shannon pulled a blanket up around her chin, batted her eyes, and said, "I was just getting into bed. Perhaps my nightgown slipped. I thought you two would take all night."

Fergus walked over to Shannon, leaned over, and pulled the top of the blanket down. A flurry of pink lace fell out. Fergus laughed. "No wonder. You must have shaken the poor old man."

Shannon laughed. "Stop being silly. Come to bed."

"Soon," Fergus said. "Let's have a glass of champagne first while the noise below dies down."

Four days later Fergus sent Shannon ashore amidst a few tears and asked Essex to join him.

Essex came aboard an hour later, yawning and adjusting his uniform. "Fergus, next time give me a little more warning. My 'wife' was a little miffed when I sent her ashore. I figured you'd already made plans to depart."

"Yes, it's true."

Fergus spread a large chart covering the area of the North Sea as far east as the Baltic Sea. He pointed to the mouth of the Thames. "We'll leave at dawn tomorrow and take up an easterly course for at least fifty miles to get well clear of the shipping lanes for foreign ships bound for the Baltic Sea. After that, we'll head for the mouth of the Skaggerack. We'll avoid other ships if we can, and if we can't we'll scatter. Ships that can't get away will hoist a neutral flag. The passage through the Skaggerack and the Kattegat will be difficult, but not as hard as passing through the southern mouth of the Kattegat and the entrance to the Baltic Sea."

Essex looked carefully at the chart, measuring the width of parts of the passages with his fingers. Then he shook his head slowly. "Difficult, but possible."

Then he grinned. "I'm going back to my ship and catch up on my sleep. This life in port is too strenuous. I may have to get married."

By now the crews of the two ships were well broken in, and the departure from port was flawless, except for one "wife" who had only been found by the boatswain at the last moment and had to be escorted ashore just as the lines were being taken in.

The four ships sailed undisturbed out the mouth of the Thames and ran east as planned. Then they turned northeast in a sea barren of ships.

As they steadied on course, Lombardi ordered the sails set for the long run across the North Sea. Poston came up to Fergus, who was standing by the quartermaster, watching the ships form up behind the flagship. Poston said, "Captain, just what the hell are we about to do that no one should see us do? You have the lookouts and the officers of the watch in a dither, and they don't know why."

"You have a point," Fergus said. "You should know more, particularly if something should happen to me. I have in my shirt a set of secret orders given to me by Admiral Nelson. Captain Essex has a duplicate set. If anything happens to me, you will take over command of this ship and Captain Essex will take command of the flotilla."

"But I still won't know what to do," Poston protested. "I can't see myself scrambling around in your shirt trying to read a set of blood-soaked orders while the rigging is falling around us and somebody is blasting at us with 32-pounders."

"Yes, Poston, you are right. The best I can tell you is that we are ordered to transit the Skaggerack and the Kattegat and pass Copenhagen at night en route to the southern opening of the Kattegat. We will arrive there in the dark and establish a patrol. Of course, we are supposed to do all this without being seen or identified."

"Then what? We argue with fishermen over what they are catching?"

Fergus laughed. "You always did get to the point. I know you have been hearing of the encounters between British ships and Dutch and Danish ships the past months. This has blown up into an international argument. The Russians have taken advantage of the fracas, too, organizing what they call 'armed neutrality' between their country and Denmark, Sweden, and Prussia. Denmark has assumed leadership of the organization and placed an embargo on British ships in her ports. Denmark also occupied Lubeck. The British government saw these moves as the beginning of bigger troubles, eventually leading to war, and decided to take the initiative against Denmark before it gets out of hand."

Poston nodded. "I'm for that, but that coalition sounds pretty stupid. You forget that in the pubs I frequent they don't know or care much about this political stuff unless there is actual fighting."

"It might become fighting soon. Admiral Nelson thinks he can strike a blow at the Danish navy that will deprive the Danish government leadership of the neutrality organization. Once this is done, he thinks the organization will fall apart and the danger to us will disappear."

"How can he do that without bringing the other members into the war?"

"That's the key. He's always been as good a diplomat as a fighter. We'll see."

"But he won't be in command."

"Admiral Hyde Parker is leading the fleet to attack the Danish forces off Copenhagen. As you might expect, Admiral Nelson will lead the actual attack."

"And what do we do?"

"We will be patrolling the southern mouth of the Kattegat to detect any movement of the other navies in the Baltic. Once the action off Copenhagen is over, we will join Admiral Nelson for further orders."

"Now I feel better," Poston said. "I think I can take over if I have to without tearing up your shirt."

Sharp lookouts and quick maneuvering by the officers of the watch brought them to the mouth of the Skaggerack undisturbed. The 100-mile transit up the Skaggerack was more difficult, and false colors had to be hoisted twice. The 150-mile leg through the Kattegat was easier, and Fergus hugged Sweden's shore to avoid either merchant ships or Swedish naval vessels.

A good wind took them through the narrow passage off Copenhagen in a few hours of one night. Without further incident they entered the narrow mouth of the Kattegat without having been identified, although one warship tried to catch them without success.

Fergus set up his patrols on 29 March. Nothing passed except the usual fishing vessels and an occasional small merchantman. Fergus did his best to keep his lookouts and watch officers alert. The political situation was far too complicated to hope they could understand what they were doing, and the average officer or sailor was not even aware of the potential enemies or how they might change from day to day. Fergus himself could only guess. Poston alone walked about seemingly confident that he knew what was happening in the distant capitals and the closer Copenhagen.

The hours dragged on, and then, without warning, a lookout called out, "Sail ho! Single warship to the north!"

Fergus at first was confused, expecting warships to appear from the south. The ship came on and soon turned to port, evidently trying to pierce the patrol line. All of Fergus's ships were at battle stations and maneuvered to counter every move of the strange ship. It was flying a Danish flag and Fergus estimated it as a large frigate, about forty-eight guns or more.

Fergus gave the order, "Fire a shot across her bow!"

The shot landed well ahead, and the Danish ship was not in the mood to fight. She soon rounded up into the wind. Fergus brought the *Daring* under her counter and also rounded up into the wind. As the *Daring* slowed and passed the other ship close aboard, Fergus grabbed the speaking trumpet and shouted in English, "Captain, please come aboard."

There was some disgruntled conversation on the quarterdeck, but the sight of the *Dashing* circling with guns ready made up the captain's mind.

Soon the Danish ship launched a boat, and it was rowed over to the *Daring,* the captain fidgeting in the stern sheets.

Poston had side boys ready, and normal honors were rendered. The captain appeared through the gangway, stepped on deck, and saluted the British colors and then Fergus.

His English was good as he looked around and said, "Captain Johanneson of the Royal Danish ship *Komso.* May I ask why you are detaining me?"

Fergus set his jaw. "I am Captain Kilburnie of the HMS *Daring.* I am under orders of Admiral Nelson of the Royal Navy to detain all ships in this area. Please come to my cabin, and we will discuss this further." When Fergus used the name "Nelson" the Danish captain seemed to wilt, and he gave no further resistance.

When they were seated below, Fergus said, "I presume the action off Copenhagen is over, and I estimate from the condition of your rigging that you were in the action. How did you avoid capture?"

The Danish captain seemed to know that it was all over for him, and he spoke freely as he watched Radcliffe pour port for the two captains. "I was anchored off the entrance to the harbor with two other frigates."

"And the rest of the Danish fleet?"

The Danish captain took a sip of the port handed to him. "They were anchored in a line in front of the fortifications next to the king's channel."

"I passed Copenhagen at night, so I don't know how your defenses were set up. Can you describe them to me?"

"I suppose there's no harm in telling you this now. After all, the war is over."

"Thank you. Please do. I know what the chart says about Copenhagen. I understand the city runs north and south. The coast is defended by large fortifications along the coast and ends in an even larger series of forts at the entrance to the harbor named Trekoner. Off the coast are two channels running north and south separated by a shallow bar. The outer channel is the deeper one."

Captain Johanneson nodded. "You have it right. The coast is further defended by a chain of interlocking armed hulks and active naval vessels. The hulks are manned by army infantrymen and artillerymen. Frankly, the fortification was thought to be formidable, even impregnable."

"And I suppose Admiral Nelson proved you wrong?"

"He did, and I can't believe it."

"Now tell me what he did."

Captain Johanneson stood and paced up and down for a few minutes, his brow knitted in thought. Then he sighed deeply and sat down. "On the first of April Admiral Parker's fleet appeared in the north and transited to the south through the outer channel."

"No firing then?"

"No one fired. They were outside of range. They anchored to the south in a compact group at the juncture of the two channels."

"That is unusual. Admiral Nelson seldom wastes any time."

"I think they had to make some plans, and they quickly discovered that we had removed all navigational markers from all the channels."

"That could have slowed them. Admiral Nelson almost ran into a disaster at the Battle of the Nile when he tried to enter too fast."

"Not much time was wasted, though. Small boats began to move up the channel, sounding the limits of deep water and thrusting large poles into the edges. They also placed temporary buoys made of barrels. Other small boats scurried between the larger ships, obviously carrying planners to decide about their moves."

"Nothing was done before dark?"

"Nothing that I could see, but I wager that there was a lot of conferring going on in the flagships."

"Of course."

"At first light I climbed up to the main cross tree. We were anchored in the entrance to the harbor with two other frigates where I had a good view of the English fleet. We were the only ships able to get under way, and I felt very vulnerable."

"I don't blame you. I wouldn't have liked that position either. Now what happened?"

"As the light increased, through my telescope, er, as you call it, a long glass . . ."

"Yes, we do. Please go ahead."

"Well, I watched the English fleet carefully. At first the small boats continued to move about. I thought they were delivering plans the admirals had put together during the long night."

"We do that. Please go ahead."

"At about 7 A.M. the English ships all got under way and formed two columns. One was obviously made up of larger ships that forged ahead, led by Admiral Parker's flagship. This one proceeded up the outer channel and anchored opposite the harbor entrance out of gun range."

"Hmm!" Fergus said. "Not the most courageous move I can think of."

"About twelve of the smaller ships formed a column behind the *Elephant,* Nelson's flagship. A frigate and three other smaller ships proceeded independently ahead of him and approached the entrance to the harbor."

"My God, that's not like Nelson! He was sending them to the lion's den."

"He was. We beat them badly, and they had to retire."

"I'm sure Nelson was headed for the inner channel and prompt action."

"He was, but he had difficulty getting it started. The first two and the biggest of his ships ran aground in spite of their temporary navigation aids.

Eventually the *Elephant* bypassed them and got into the inner channel and headed north, firing as it went. The rest of the smaller ships followed him and took on the Danish ships as they progressed north."

"That doesn't sound like much of a fight yet."

"Not at first, but by noon all of the English ships were heavily engaged. The ships aground were still there, but Nelson didn't pay any attention to that and kept moving his force north. The fire became so heavy that the smoke interfered with my observation of the action. I could see that the Danish gunners were having trouble firing on the moving targets. They weren't used to it. The hulk guns were manned by unskilled army infantrymen and the Danish navy ship's men were without practice. The balls fell like rain around the English ships and made the observers on Admiral Parker's flagship think that the English were taking a beating. Further, the English balls were either hitting aboard the ships in the barricade or were passing overhead and landing ashore where the observers could not see them."

"And the English observers?"

"It was difficult for them to make judgments. I think Admiral Parker was very conservative. He sent a boat in with some officers in it, apparently to find out what was actually happening, but they never seemed to get to Nelson's flagship."

"How did you think the action was going now? Who was winning?"

Johanneson shrugged. "Roughly equal, but the English were dogged and determined. The Danish, on the other hand, were not very well organized. Some flags began to flutter down, and they surrendered one by one. None of the English struck at all. As usual they were very brave and tenacious in spite of the damage I could see to some of them."

"What happened then?"

"The English flagship in the outer reach, Admiral Parker's, I think, hoisted a numeral hoist signal. All the ships repeated it but Nelson's flagship never did seem to know what it meant and never acknowledged it."

"And how did the action finally end?"

"It just petered out, as you English would say, and the English assumed that they had won. I did, too, and when dusk came I cut my cables and started out of the harbor entrance. I ran right through the English fleet in the outer channel. They were surprised, I think, since I wasn't firing. Maybe they thought I had surrendered along with the other ships. When they made up their minds they fired heavily at me, but since I was in the middle of them they had to be careful not to hit each other. I headed south as soon as I got clear, and here I am."

"Thank you," Fergus said. "That fine rendition answers some of my questions. I'll find out the rest when I join Admiral Nelson."

Johanneson said, "I'm sure you'll learn all of interest to you."

"Up until this meeting I didn't know whether we were in a state of war or not," Fergus said. "You confirmed that we are, and I therefore accept your surrender. Now you must return with me and be turned over to Admiral Nelson. I am sure you will be treated well. He always admires daring, and he demands that prisoners be treated properly."

Johanneson sighed. "I see your position, and I am afraid I have no course of action but to surrender."

The British force sailed north, followed by the Danish frigate, and the three large ships anchored near Nelson's flagship, the *Elephant.*

Admiral Nelson was ashore, but Fergus and Essex boarded the flagship to wait for him to return.

As they boarded the *Elephant* they were greeted by Nelson's aide, Lieutenant Sinclair. "Good evening, Commodore and Captain. Please come aboard. The admiral is ashore but he will be back soon and he wanted to see you both the minute you arrived. Please come down to his cabin and have some port. I know that is what he would want."

"Very well," Fergus said.

In the cabin they sat down and Sinclair ordered port.

Fergus asked, "Well, how are you getting along as an aide?"

"Fine, I guess," Sinclair shrugged. "I like him and he hasn't fired me yet. I'm learning to keep ahead of him and always can anticipate his wishes."

"That's the way to do it. But you don't seem happy."

Sinclair shifted in his chair. "I guess so. Before today I was satisfied."

"And today. What happened?"

"Well I was bustling about in all those signal bags, thumbing the books, and keeping track of all those signals through a long glass."

"What set you off?"

"Well, I heard all that clanging and banging. All that firing of guns, and I realized I wasn't part of it. I was born to be a gun-battery commander and here I was a signal jockey and, most of the time, a tea caddy."

Fergus laughed. "You've got a problem."

"What do I do about it, sir?" Sinclair asked.

"Just keep on doing your present job as well as you can and wait for an opportunity."

"An opportunity?"

"Yes. there will come a time when a ship is in dire need of a battery commander when the present one is killed. If my ship needs one, you're the first lieutenant I'll ask for. Then volunteer and keep after the admiral until he gives in. He'll let you go."

"And what about a relief?"

"Don't worry about that. There will be a dozen lieutenants asking to be Nelson's aide."

Lieutenant Sinclair sighed. "Thank you, sir. Now what can I do for you?"

"Tell me all about the battle. The captain of the Danish prize I brought in told me about it from his point of view. He said a strange numeral hoist was flying for a long time."

Sinclair laughed. "Oh, you mean number 39."

"I guess so, what about it?"

"Well, the battle was going badly, or so it must have seemed to Admiral Parker. I think he couldn't see well. He should have been in a lot closer."

"Yes. A lot of critics will say so in the future."

"A lot of Danish balls were falling all around us, but few hit. Our balls fell well, but no one out in the outer channel could see them. Apparently Admiral Parker thought we were losing, and he put up hoist number 39, meaning 'withdraw.'"

"What happened then?"

"A lot of balls were falling all around us, but Admiral Nelson just laughed and at one point said, 'This is the best place to be.' I thought he was wonderful, and I wanted to be just like him some day."

"And then?"

"I told the admiral the signal was flying to withdraw. He laughed and said, 'I can't see it,' and he put his long glass to his blind eye. I stopped bothering him and watched the action. I didn't want to take the hoist down because all the other ships would think it had been executed and would stop the action and withdraw."

"And no one stopped?"

"No. They just followed Admiral Nelson's motions instead of the hoist. We just kept firing and all the other ships did, too. We got better and they got worse. Finally the Danes ceased firing, one by one, and some of them struck their colors. Eventually all of them did and the battle was over. Then I took down old number 39."

"And what did Admiral Nelson do then?"

"He got in his barge and went over to the harbor to end the hostilities. He'll be back soon to change his uniform to make formal calls on all the big-shots, the sort of thing he does so very well."

"What about the light vessels he sent to the north, to the mouth of the harbor?"

Sinclair shook his head dolefully. "It was a mistake. Captain Rioux, heading them, was killed in heavy fire as he tried to lead them back out."

"I didn't know him very well."

"Admiral Nelson didn't know him either. This was the first time they had fought together."

Fergus shuddered. "We might very well have been here and sent in place of Rioux's flotilla."

"I don't think so. You were both lucky and speedy."

"Speedy?"

"Yes. Admiral Nelson wanted your speed to get you to the south in order to blockade the entrance to protect his rear."

"Thank God! I hope you are right. Though I do feel for Captain Rioux's wife."

Sinclair shook his head. "He's not married. He leaves only an invalid mother."

"Can I help with her?"

"That won't be necessary. Admiral Nelson will take care of her."

A messenger knocked on the door. "Sir, the admiral's barge is returning."

Fergus and Essex walked up to the quarterdeck to watch Admiral Nelson's return. As he came aboard he saw the two officers standing there. "Ah, gentlemen, this is fortunate. I've been needing you. Come below."

After they were seated in his cabin, Nelson said, "Tell me all you've been up to, and I'll sit here and write my battle report while you talk."

While Fergus narrated their experience, Admiral Nelson wrote his report. Every so often he interrupted Fergus to ask questions.

Fergus saved the best for last. "Sir, on patrol I took into custody, and also as a prize, a Danish frigate. I've brought her in. She's anchored nearby. What shall I do with her?"

Admiral Nelson gave Fergus his full attention. "Do? What you always do with a prize. Take her with you to England. She is your prize and belongs to you and your flag officer, me. All the other prizes captured belong to Admiral Parker."

"I see, sir."

Nelson laughed again. "I, er, need all the prize money I can get, and I'll get very little out of this action. Honor doesn't pay much."

Essex grinned. "I understand, sir. The ladies are very expensive."

Fergus interrupted as quickly as he could and signaled to Essex to keep quiet, but he was not fast enough.

Nelson frowned at Essex. "I guess you, as a young bachelor, wouldn't understand matters of domestic finance, but I'm sure Fergus does. Now, as to our other prize, I'll land all her officers and crew and you put aboard a prize crew. Turn her over to a prize court in London. Your four ships won't end up with much prize money, but I will. After all, you didn't have to fight very hard to take her. But then neither did I, and a flag officer never does."

"Sir, what other orders do you have for us?"

"My flag lieutenant will deliver to you a sheaf of papers in about half an hour that will include my report of the recent action that I am writing now. I want it in the hands of the Admiralty as soon as possible, certainly before Admiral Parker's report can arrive. It will differ in some details from mine. If you are about to be captured, burn it, eat it, or otherwise destroy it."

"I understand," Fergus said.

"Speaking of prizes, Admiral Parker has sent word that it will be difficult to return our prizes to England. He thinks they might not survive the weather or might be recaptured. Therefore he wants me to burn or destroy all of our prizes."

"What! That doesn't make sense. I could easily get them all home. I hope it doesn't apply to the one I captured."

"No, it doesn't. That one belongs to me. Take it with you." Then Nelson said, "Here are more orders for you. I gave you orders to put a prize crew aboard the other Danish frigate anchored nearby. It is in the same category as the one you captured. It belongs to me. As I said, you are to take her with you."

"But won't that be a violation of Admiral Parker's orders?"

Nelson sighed. "Don't worry about it. I'll take the responsibility. After all, I've been violating his orders all afternoon long."

Fergus grinned. "Sir, I'm learning from you."

"Now remember, after you have completed this mission, I will have others for you. I expect to be placed in command of the blockade force about to be activated off the coast of France, and I will need you both. Now go back to your ships and await my flag lieutenant. Good work, and smooth sailing. I must change uniforms and get ashore for a negotiating session."

"I know you are good at that. Your success will reduce the amount of fighting we will have to do," Fergus said.

Nelson nodded. "You are kind. That is exactly what I try to do. Again, smooth sailing and be fast about it."

An hour later, after Fergus and Essex had returned to their ships, Admiral Nelson's barge drew alongside the *Daring* and Sinclair climbed aboard. "Here are your documents, sir. You are supposed to get under way immediately. Good luck."

As Sinclair climbed down the ladder, Fergus shouted, "Prepare to get under way immediately! Quartermaster, make the signal to all of our ships including both prizes."

The quartermaster said, "Prizes, sir? We only have one."

Fergus pointed to the second Danish frigate nearby. "We have two, and on the watch before you, I sent a prize crew over to her. They'll be waiting for your signal."

They were, and in a few minutes the flotilla plus the two prizes got under way and sailed north, well clear of Admiral Parker's fleet.

As they stood up the coast, the quartermaster said, "Sir, there's a flag signal to you from Admiral Parker's flagship. It is hard to see, but I think it is telling you to send your prizes back."

Fergus laughed and looked back at Admiral Parker's flagship. "Seems pretty dark to me, and I can't really make it out. We'll just sail on as we are."

The quartermaster wrinkled his brow. "But won't Admiral Parker get mad at you?"

Fergus laughed. "Someday, son, you'll hear about how Admiral Nelson put his blind eye to his long glass."

"Never heard of it, sir."

"Well, you will. It will be famous some day, and you will have been here."

"And Admiral Parker, when he gets back, what will you both say?"

"Probably nothing. Probably by that time Admiral Parker may not be an admiral."

"I don't understand."

"You don't need to." Fergus patted his jacket. "The reason is in this envelope."

CHAPTER 7

Secret Plans

THE TRIP BACK to the Thames was expected to be uneventful. Fergus knew that the navies of other potential enemies, except for the French, were in port while their governments negotiated. But three days out of port he became anxious about the slowness of the prizes that was holding him back from delivering the dispatches and he left Essex in command and went on by himself.

When the *Daring* was secured to a pier in the Royal dockyard, Jeris came aboard. Once in possession of the ceremonial glass of port, he said, "Well, what happened? Where are your other ships?"

Fergus laughed. "I've learned my lesson. When I carry important dispatches for the Admiralty and the king, I get them in the proper hands right away. I left the other ships coming on at their best speed, but they were held back by two prizes. The Danish don't make them very fast, but they are certainly strong and pretty."

Jeris chuckled. "Admiral Nelson can use all the prize money he can get. The word around here is that his mistress is spending it faster than he can bring it back."

Fergus grinned. "I hope Shannon is not doing the same thing."

"No. She's spending a lot of money on horse-racing, but it's her own money."

Fergus pulled out from his jacket the large brown envelope given to him by Nelson's flag lieutenant and said, "Here they are. But please finish your port first, even if they are very important and should go back to the Admiralty and the palace right away."

Jeris sighed. "My boy, you don't know just how important they are. I think the future of Admirals Nelson and Parker will be decided soon after I get these in the proper hands." He gulped down his port, got a good grip on the heavy envelope, and hoisted himself from his chair. "I'll send Shannon down to you tonight, and I'll be back to see you two nights from now. The information I'll have for you will be important to your career. I'm sure you will be a lot richer and so will Admiral Nelson. As far as the envelope, the politicians around here always seem to believe the first version of anything they hear. In this case, you've made it happen."

Fergus nodded. "We'll be sure that the facts, properly known, will be in Admiral Nelson's favor. He took some very big chances, and, as usual, came out ahead. I'm afraid Admiral Parker stood by out of range and did nothing. No matter what he reports, the facts are against him."

"Fine. Please plan to stay for dinner tonight."

"I shall, but I won't stay late. I want Shannon to have as much time with you as possible. By the way, her doctor says she should deliver within a month."

"Will I be in port then?"

"I doubt it. What you will be doing, when, and how long will depend on decisions to be reached in the next two days. This will be a decision far above my office."

Shannon came aboard, walking slowly up the brow, and stood for a moment in Fergus's arms. "These boarding arrangements on your ships aren't made for fat ladies. I don't like these separations either, but I'm glad this one was relatively brief."

"I feel the same way, but you know retirement isn't far off."

As they went to the cabin arm in arm, Shannon relaxed. "Oh, Fergus, you are so young and you have so much to do for your country and you'll have to do it. I will be patient, and I'll wait for you."

Two days and nights together restored their enthusiasm, and on the evening of the second day Jeris drove up in his carriage. Fergus was waiting for him, and dinner was ready. The steward Radcliffe's best efforts, with a little help from Shannon, produced a simple but excellent dinner.

Jeris accepted a glass of port after dinner, complimented Evan, and asked him to leave the cabin. He asked Shannon to stay. "She's capable of keeping secrets and she should hear about your future," he said.

Fergus nodded, remembering their conversation about his career of two days ago. "Yes, she shares the best and the worst with me," he said.

Jeris asked for a second glass of port. "This is going to be a big evening," he said.

Fergus got up and filled all the glasses. He laughed. "I suppose Admiral Nelson's version of the Battle of Copenhagen was somewhat different from what you received from Admiral Parker yesterday."

Jeris nodded. "Certainly, but differences of opinion were confirmed from other sources. Frankly, they all told us what we expected. Admiral Parker was an old, conservative leader, and Nelson, with his young, vigorous style, saved the day, so to speak."

"I didn't see the actual fighting, but the Danish captain I took as prize and Admiral Nelson's aide certainly confirmed what you said. Now, what has the Admiralty done?"

"It's all over now. Westminster received the news in the dispatches you brought with great enthusiasm. The incident you related to me about the long glass hasn't surfaced yet, but it will. Lord St. Vincent, the head of the Admiralty, wrote a letter to Nelson that I was privileged to see. It said, 'It is impossible for me to describe the satisfaction expressed by His Majesty, his confidential servants, and the whole body of the people over the conduct of your Lordship.' He went on to describe Nelson's ability as a negotiator."

"He certainly turned a losing situation into a victory, didn't he?" Fergus said. "That was what he always does."

"Well, the truth won't hurt him at the Admiralty. All the world will accept it, too. The Admiralty has expressed its opinion and gratitude by sending him orders to relieve Admiral Parker about the fifth of May."

"And Admiral Parker?"

"He will shift his flag to a frigate when relieved and return to England. I am afraid his career is over, although the Admiralty will find some chore for him to perform. He deserves to be let down easily."

Fergus shook his head. "When we left Copenhagen, I took a second prize with me. I'm sure it was in violation of Admiral Parker's orders to destroy all prizes and he was trying to stop me."

"He signaled to you?"

"Yes, but it was getting dark, and I couldn't see the signal very well."

"You left anyway?"

"Yes, but I pulled a 'Nelson.' I told my quartermaster I couldn't see it." Fergus winked.

Shannon giggled. "You bad boy."

"But you could?" Jeris asked.

"Maybe. But I didn't look very well. Now it won't make any difference, which I thought would be the case."

Jeris shook his head. "Forget about it. Admiral Nelson knows, doesn't he?"

"Of course. He's the one who told me to do it."

"Then for sure forget about it. The Admiralty and particularly the king will care more that you brought back two valuable prizes."

"Worse than that. Admiral Parker gave orders to destroy a dozen prizes that I could easily have brought back. It will deprive the palace of millions of pounds."

"I hope the king never finds out." Jeris shook his head dolefully.

"And Admiral Nelson and Admiral Parker? What about them?"

"As you might expect, there is no animosity between them, or at least not publicly expressed. Nelson has by now taken over the fleet and made several moves against the Swedes and Russians. There has been no fighting though. As the Admiralty hoped, Admiral Nelson's very boldness has cowed the Swedes and Russians and maybe other allies."

"Just what I expected," Fergus said. "Now what will happen to me? My ships and I are still under his command."

"You are under his command, and the Admiralty realizes that. I must tell you in all confidence, and you and Shannon must not reveal this information, that Admiral Nelson is not well physically, and his, er, family problems are weighing heavily on him. The Admiralty expects that his duties in and around the Baltic will end in July, and that soon after that he will come home."

Fergus shook his head, still not satisfied. "And then what for me?"

"Nelson will be put in command of the forces blockading the French ports along the Atlantic coast. You will be part of this particular command, and from that you can deduce what you will be doing."

Fergus frowned. "Days and weeks of fighting the weather in the English Channel and chasing elusive French ships, scuttling from one port to another."

Shannon had been quiet, but now she spoke up. "It could be worse. You will be quite close to the Thames. Being in distant waters would be worse. We do have a baby to think about."

Fergus smiled. "Thanks for those good thoughts." He turned to Jeris, "Uncle, now that you have settled the distant future, what do my ships do now?"

"I think the Admiralty has something important for you in a week or two. I hope it will hold off until Shannon's blessed event occurs."

Shannon sighed and surreptitiously felt her swelling belly. "Tonight I think it will be soon. Tomorrow I'll call my doctor. Maybe he can speed this up. I'd like Fergus to see this child before he leaves."

One week later Shannon called for Surgeon Pollitt. He examined her carefully, and on his orders she left immediately for the lying-in hospital. Her carriage driver had been standing by in a stable next to the Royal dockyard for just this occasion.

The next morning Jeris came speeding up to the ship's side, his horses in a lather. He leaped out of the carriage, ran up the brow, and met Fergus, who had been summoned to meet him by the watch. "It's a boy!" he shouted. "Six pounds!"

"And Shannon. How is she?"

"Fine, and she sends her love. I have obtained special permission for you to visit Shannon in the hospital. Get in my carriage."

Fergus spent the better part of his day at the hospital holding his new son, Strath. Finally Jeris pried him loose. "You must get back to your ship. I expect that your group will have sailing orders tomorrow."

The next morning, just after breakfast, Jeris showed up, trying to be businesslike but still very excited. As soon as he came aboard, he said, "This time I don't have sailing orders for you."

"What happened?"

"I don't know. I have orders directly from Lord St. Vincent, the head of the Admiralty, to bring you and Captain Essex immediately to his office."

"And the captains of the two fast sloops attached to my flotilla?"

"Apparently they will remain under your command, as Admiral Nelson arranged, but their commanding officers are not required to attend. Now let's depart. We'll pick up Captain Essex on the way."

Jeris's carriage driver kept his horses going as fast as possible, and just before noon the carriage drew up in front of the Admiralty building. Jeris leaped out and shouted over his shoulder, "Follow me!"

Within minutes they were in front of a large but plain mahogany door displaying a highly polished brass plate with the words "Lord St. Vincent." There was no need to add a second line.

Essex raised his eyebrows as he read the plate.

Jeris laughed. "I know what you are thinking about, but it's not necessary to tell you who he is. Everyone knows he's the head of the Admiralty. As you two may have heard, he's a rough, gruff disciplinarian at sea and not much different ashore."

Jeris knocked on the door. A deep voice within said, "Come!" Jeris turned the shiny brass knob and pushed the equally shiny door open.

Essex laughed and said to Fergus quietly, "If I were leaving here, I'd pull out my kerchief and wipe off that perfectly polished brass knob."

The door swung wide open, and Jeris went in, signaling the other two captains to follow. He looked at Lord St. Vincent. "M'Lord, may I present Captains Kilburnie and Essex of *Daring* and *Dashing* respectively."

Lord St. Vincent rose and came out from behind the enormous mahogany desk. He shook their hands cordially. "Ah, young men, I'm glad to meet you. You have both been just what Admiral Nelson said you'd be. Now that he has been detained in the Baltic area for a few weeks, I have decided to borrow you for a special mission. Please sit down." He motioned to a group of large, heavily padded, mahogany chairs around an equally large mahogany table.

Lord St. Vincent still had some of the suntan he had accumulated from years at sea. There was a permanent squint about his eyes, also from years on the quarterdeck, looking through strong sun. His middle was beginning to show the change from sea to shore. Now he was eating high-caloric food instead of the spare rations he had consumed at sea. His weakness was that rich food; even now his stomach was calling for it.

As they sat down, Essex said behind his hand to Fergus, "Doesn't look gruff and tough to me."

Fergus whispered back, "Don't rush to judgment. We're not at sea yet."

Lord St. Vincent did in fact look tough, but his lips were thin and compressed and his eyes protruded. When he talked his words seemed to come out of his mouth like projectiles. But there was something likable about him, and both captains knew they would find it.

Jeris said, "Lord Entwistle, head of operations, and Lord Greenway, head of intelligence, are on call and will be here in a few minutes."

"Good. Please get them, and while they're on their way we will chat a bit."

Lord St. Vincent took a seat at the head of the table and gestured to the chairs next to him. "Please sit down." Then he pointed to a series of paintings along the walls. "Some of this will be known to you since you were present at the battles. That one is of the Battle of the Nile. You will recognize Aboukir, the heavy fortification at the head of the bay. The next two paintings gave me my title. They are about the Battle of St. Vincent. I am indebted to both of your ships for your assistance in all of those endeavors."

Fergus nodded. "Thank you, sir, but you are too kind. Our parts were very small."

"Not so. A machine depends on all of its parts, no matter what their size."

Suddenly the door swung open and Lords Entwistle and Greenway came in. "Good morning, M'Lord," they both said.

Lord Entwistle was a bustling, earnest man of about forty. He wore heavy sideburns that covered part of his ruddy face. His accent betrayed his private schooling, and his voice was loud and high-pitched. Lord Greenway, on the other hand, looked like a merchant wearing a uniform. His voice, unlike Entwistle's, was low and he was inclined to stutter. He wore heavy glasses that didn't fit well, and when he was talking he had to pause frequently to push them up on his nose.

Fergus and Essex started to get up, but the First Lord waved them back. "Good morning, M'Lords," St. Vincent said. "These are the two captains we were talking about. Kilburnie of the *Daring* and Essex of the *Dashing.* Now please sit down and spread your charts. I hate the damned things, but we've got to look at something while we talk."

Both lords unrolled charts and picked up weights to hold down the corners. The two officers appeared to be fussing with each other, each apparently trying to get his chart closer to Lord St. Vincent.

The First Lord sighed. "All right, gentlemen, let's get this thing settled right now. Operations always takes precedence over intelligence and commands any operation. Are we clear on this point?"

Lord Entwistle beamed and cleared his throat. Lord Greenway opened his mouth and frowned but kept quiet, pushing his glasses up firmly. Essex looked at Fergus and both smiled and nodded.

Lord St. Vincent nodded, too. "So it will be at sea. Also, Captain Kilburnie, you are senior and will be in command, no matter what. Captain Essex is our expert in intelligence affairs. He has landed half a dozen agents successfully, and knows the territory in which you will operate very well. Nevertheless, you, Kilburnie, will command the whole operation and will bear full responsibility."

Essex started to speak, but decided to remain quiet.

Fergus, always slower and more deliberate, said, "M'Lord, I think I can speak for both of us. We have served together since we were lieutenants. There will be no friction of any kind, and Lord Greenway, I assure you that whatever Captain Essex will present, all aspects of intelligence will be listened to carefully." He turned to Essex. "Captain Essex, do I speak for both of us?"

Essex nodded. "Completely."

Lord St. Vincent, obviously already slightly bored, got up and began to stride up and down. "All right, Lord Entwistle, outline the operation."

Lord Entwistle took up a pointer and put the point on a small inlet along the French coast. "First, this is where you go, about ten miles north of Dieppe. Unsettled woods to the beach line and next to deep water. If the wind is not blowing on shore and the general weather is not too bad, you should not have any trouble sending a boat ashore to the beach containing a half-dozen marines and three agents. Your mission is to put the agents safely ashore. If anything happens that you cannot cope with, your alternate landing point will be here, forty miles to the south. Now Lord Greenway will take over the briefing."

Lord Greenway got up, almost fell over his chair, grabbed the pointer, and looked a little miffed at taking second place at an obvious intelligence operation. He cleared his throat and said, "I will not give you the names of the three agents or their exact mission. Captain Essex will know. He has already made two landings in this area, but he cannot reveal the names of these agents. They will each carry a heavy bag, as you can guess, filled with gold and some paper currency. Captain Essex will put them in a secure place when they are aboard." Lord Greenway finished speaking and sat down heavily, obviously still disgruntled, glaring fiercely behind his glasses at the others.

The First Sea Lord stopped pacing. "Any questions, gentlemen? My luncheon awaits me."

Fergus said quickly, his mind also on Lord St. Vincent's stomach, "Sir, one question. What will we do after we complete the landing?"

Lord St. Vincent nodded vigorously, patting his stomach. "Remain off the coast of France on patrol. Shortly after that, I expect Admiral Nelson to have more exact orders for you. Good day, gentlemen, and good lunch."

Fergus and Essex scrambled to their feet, pushed a covey of chairs aside, and made for the door, ignoring Lords Entwistle and Greenway, now busy rolling up their charts.

"Thank you, m'lord," they both said as he disappeared down the corridor toward his dining room.

Jeris sent them back in his carriage after a meager lunch and with a parting admonition, "Good luck."

Fergus said, "Wait a moment. When do we leave?"

Jeris looked puzzled. "Why, whenever Captain Essex says the agents are on board and are ready."

Essex laughed. "This seems to be intelligence dictating the operation, but don't worry. I'll let you know when they are ready."

CHAPTER 8

Espionage

TWO DAYS LATER a carriage drew up to the bottom of the brow of the *Dashing.* Three men got out, stretched their legs after the long ride from London, unloaded obviously heavy canvas bags, and toted them up the brow.

Captain Essex met them at the gangway. The officer of the watch ordered three men to take over the bags, but the captain held up his hand. "Thanks, but no. They will want to take them down to the brig themselves, and I will personally lock the door to it, give them the key, and post a marine guard in front of it."

Essex, followed by the other men, went below.

The officer of the watch looked bewildered, but did nothing except recall the three seamen. "Damned funny," he said. "Those three look like they came out of the slums of Paris."

The senior lieutenant, watching it all, said, "That's what they're supposed to look like, or so Captain Essex told me yesterday."

Half an hour later Essex came back on deck and said to the officer of the watch, "I'm going to the *Daring* to call on Captain Kilburnie. Make all preparations for getting under way. I expect to leave port just after I return."

Essex walked forward along the pier side and boarded the *Daring.* Fergus had been watching the arrival evolution, and he suspected the three men were the agents. He greeted Essex on deck.

"Good morning, Kilburnie," Essex said. "I hear your son is doing well. Have you named him?"

"Shannon named him Strath, after my grandfather. Looks just like him."

"How would you know?" Essex teased. "He was forty-five before you recognized him."

"Of course. All Kilburnies look alike."

"I'll take your word for that. Now let's get to your cabin and consult that large chart I know you have spread out on your table."

Fergus rolled his eyes. "Of course. Let's go."

It was there as expected, the corners held down by two cups and two apples. Essex promptly pointed to the plotted-in point of the landing plan. "Hmmm, a breach of security," he said, and he reached over and quickly erased the plotted point. "Anyone could come in here."

Fergus smiled guiltily but remained quiet.

"What Lord Greenway failed to take into account," Essex began, "is that I have landed the head of this agent group twice before at the same point. That point may be 'old hat' now and a little suspect, but we have to go ahead. The agents may have talked to the locals before and they may be expecting us. Further, one of the agents is a replacement for a man lost on the last trip. However, the moon, tide, and expected weather will be all right and we should go ahead."

"Shouldn't you have said something to Lord Greenway about all this?"

Essex shrugged. "Lord Greenway is notoriously bullheaded. He wouldn't have listened. Lord St. Vincent was obviously hankering for his lunch and wouldn't have listened to me anyway. We will just have to play it carefully. I plan to go in the boat myself."

"I hate to play the heavy leader right at the beginning," Fergus said with hesitation, "but I don't like to see you endangered like that. You might spend years in a ratty and drafty French prison. They are supposed to be horrible."

"And so you have decided that I shouldn't go?"

"Yes," Fergus said firmly.

Essex grinned in relief. "Thanks for getting me off the hook. I didn't like the idea, but I felt I had to live up to my reputation as a daring and dashing agent. Maybe I'm getting old, and I need to be an old married man like you. Holding your son got me thinking. With a little practice, I think I could take to this married man stuff."

Fergus got back to business. "I suggest you follow your boats as close in as you think it's safe, although I see the water is deep up to a hundred fathoms out from the beach. I'll take a position well clear of you so my guns will bear on the beach and still have maneuvering room. I assume you will be ready to recall your boat quickly."

"Naturally. Let's go. My crew is ready, and I don't want to wait any longer."

"So is mine. I noticed yours bustling about your topside when you left."

"Oh, yes. They always know what I want."

Four days later they were off the designated landing position. Fergus examined it carefully by long glass and couldn't detect any sign of movement or settlement in the heavy growth behind the expected landing area.

That night, the moon was just bright enough to allow the boat coxswain to see his way. Fergus tested his own eyesight and could see enough to advise the coxswain.

The night was ideal, the tide near slack and the wind light. This should be just right, Fergus muttered to himself, but somehow he didn't like it. He searched the underbrush again. It was nearly impenetrable.

Fergus watched Essex take his ship close to the shore and lower a boat. The boat crew reached up and grabbed the bags and the three men followed and sat in the stern sheets. The coxswain ordered the oars out, and the boat was rowed quietly toward the shore. The stillness was complete, but again Fergus felt a gnawing sense of unease. He sighed. This might be too easy after all.

The boat crew stopped rowing, waiting for the boat's bow to grate on the beach.

Fergus sighed again, hoping that it would be all right. They were just a few seconds away from a landing.

Just as the boat crew stopped rowing and the bow grated on the beach, all hell broke loose with firing directly in the faces of the boat crew. The men in the boat began shouting and cursing and the marines returned the fire. From the shore came an answering volley of curses in French.

Fergus expected that most of the crew would be hit, but few of them seemed to be down. The force ashore was for some reason firing at the *Dashing*.

"My God!" Fergus yelled. "We've been betrayed!"

Poston, watching carefully, said, "You're right! I count ten flashes from field pieces and about twenty rifle flashes. Thank God the boat isn't any closer than it is! There's an army over there, but they were a little too eager, and they seem to be ignoring the boat."

The *Daring*'s guns were loaded and aimed at the landing area. Fergus shouted, "Commence firing!"

The guns boomed out and fired salvo after salvo. Fergus swore and stamped his feet. In spite of the heavy fire from the *Daring* and *Dashing* pouring ashore, the well-concealed heavy guns ashore kept firing, and several shots landed on the quarterdeck of the *Dashing*. The small-arms fire was aimed principally at the boat, although a few tried to reach the quarterdeck of the *Dashing*. All of the small-arms fire fell short of the *Daring*.

Fergus continued to swear, but there was little else he could do.

Soon the heavy guns firing from ashore slowed and appeared to become disorganized. Fergus stole a look toward the *Dashing*. He could see by the light of the firing several forms lying on the deck. Men were running around the quarterdeck, and he knew there had to be several casualties.

By the time the fire from ashore ceased, it was too late. Fergus could still see men running about the stern sheets of the *Dashing* helping the casualties. Her boat was now pulling frantically away from the shore to escape the dwindling small-arms fire. The muskets shifted their fire to the boat and the balls peppered the water around the boat, but soon it pulled around under the protection of the *Dashing*'s counter where the deck force threw a tow line to them. The *Dashing* hoisted sails and soon drew out of range of the shore.

Fergus took a deep breath. They were safe, but they had suffered casualties, and he would have to wait for daylight to assess the situation.

Suddenly there was silence. Poston, searching the shore, said, "They pulled their batteries out with horses and the small-arms carriers ran into the bushes."

Fergus shouted, "Lombardi, change course to sea as soon as the *Dashing* is outboard of us." He paced the quarterdeck, waiting for daylight, muttering imprecations against the intelligence branch of the Admiralty. Poston, listening carefully, heard him mention the words, "Greenway, Gervais, traitor," and a series of oaths, but he couldn't connect them, and he was afraid to ask.

Finally Fergus used one word he could understand. "Bastards," he growled.

At dawn, Fergus directed Lombardi to pull under the counter of the *Dashing* so he could inspect her damage. He could not see Captain Essex on deck, and he said, "Lombardi, ask the officer of the deck to order the *Dashing* to come into the wind. When she does, do the same, and lower a boat for me to board her. I'll take Surgeon Pollitt with me. I've got to see the situation in person."

In a few minutes the *Daring* had coasted to a stop alongside the *Dashing.* Fergus quickly climbed down the sea ladder to a waiting boat, which was rowed to the *Dashing.* He prepared to board her and ordered the coxswain to wait for him. He climbed the sea ladder quickly, followed by Pollitt, and saluted the colors and the officer of the deck, who was the youngest of the lieutenants Fergus had met on his last visit. "Are you in command?" Fergus asked.

"Yes, Sir. Captain Essex is badly wounded and is in his cabin being tended to by the surgeon. Lieutenants Easterling and Cobb are also wounded seriously. The surgeon can tell you more about them. If you will follow me, sir, I will lead you to the captain."

"Don't bother. I know the way. You should remain on deck in command. Pollitt, check on the wounded lieutenants and then meet me in the captain's cabin." Fergus, his brow furrowed as he digested the news, strode rapidly aft to the captain's cabin and entered quickly without knocking.

Essex, his head and left shoulder swathed in heavy bandages, was lying in his cot with the surgeon bent over him examining his head.

"My God, Essex, why didn't you let me know before this that you were wounded?"

Essex smiled wanly through the maze of bandages. "Sorry, old man, I didn't think it was this bad, and I thought I'd have us back on the line by noon. Now my carpenter and boatswain have made a thorough inspection and tell me that repairs will take a day or two. The murderous bastards dealt us a proper bad hand on the quarterdeck and the rigging above it. Those of us on the quarterdeck caught bloody hell."

"Do you have any idea what happened?"

"Oh, yes, I know it all now." He gestured to a tall, husky man with a small mustache standing nearby. "This is Monsieur Gervais. He is the head of what was the three-agent team. I am sorry to say it has now been reduced to two."

"One was killed?"

"Not yet. He'll have to be tried first."

"I am mystified."

Essex laughed faintly. "I don't doubt it. The intelligence business is always mystifying. You wanted to know what happened. Monsieur Gervais was as suspicious as I was of the third agent that was added to the team by Admiral Greenway's group. After firing had started and when the boat was pulling away from the shore for its very existence, the third agent muttered some suspicious remarks. Gervais says he heard him say, 'My God! They weren't supposed to shoot at the boat!'

"Even though they didn't shoot at the boat much, from what he said he was sure he was a double agent, and on the way back Gervais threw him in the bottom of the boat and choked the truth out of him. It seems the group ashore was supposed to let the boat land, capture the crew of the boat and the agents, and then try to sink the ship. Well, you know the revolutionaries. Poor discipline. They all want to command. Someone couldn't resist shooting at the ship, and before long all of his companions were shooting. Apparently they didn't like our heavy return fire and soon cleared out, probably leaving some of their heavy guns in the bushes. I think we destroyed a few and killed a few of the French crews."

Essex's voice was getting weak, and the surgeon raised his hand, "That's enough for now, Captain Kilburnie. Captain Essex is seriously wounded, but there is no doubt he will recover."

"Could he stay aboard? My surgeon will be back here soon to confer with you."

The surgeon laughed. "By no means should he stay aboard. You should get him to a proper hospital as soon as possible. I have packed the wounds in his shoulder and arm, but quite a bit of repair needs to be made as soon as possible to the tendons, nerves, and blood vessels involved in the wounds. Also the two lieutenants are wounded beyond my capacity to care for them here and they have similar problems."

Fergus turned to the officer of the watch, who was standing outside the doorway. "Lieutenant, please make a signal to the fast sloop *Hatchet* and order her to come alongside. Then prepare to receive her. I will be with Captain Essex. When the sloop is alongside, ask the captain to join us."

Surgeon Pollitt came running up. "Sir, the lieutenants should get to the hospital as soon as possible."

"Thank you. Please step into the cabin and confer with the ship's surgeon. I am sure you will agree with him that all of them should be sent to the hospital as soon as possible. I can get them there."

Fergus stepped back into the cabin, asked the surgeon to step out, and sat down next to Essex. "I know you want to stay aboard and keep your command, but it's not possible. You must have expert medical help soon. I am going to send you to London as soon as the *Hatchet* is alongside. I will also send your two lieutenants with you. I estimate she will be in London in two days. Her captain will be here soon and I will instruct him to give you and your officers all comfort and assistance.

"The ex-agent is in chains, and I will instruct the captain to take him. I will depend on you to report the incident to the Admiralty. Otherwise I will make a letter report in due time to the Admiralty."

Essex nodded. "I trust you will try again to land the agents at the alternate site. Gervais is anxious to vindicate himself and I'd like to do the same. The alternate landing area looked safe, and we never have used it."

"Certainly. Now here is another matter. Do you think your young lieutenant Craig is capable of assuming command of your ship?"

"Frankly, not at this time. He is a good battery officer and an average watch officer, but not much more. He is still young, and he is intelligent. He will make the grade some day. Obviously he needs time."

"Then I will send Lieutenant Puller over to assume command. Admiral Nelson knows him well, and I assume he will approve, possibly allowing him to retain the command of the ship until you are well."

"I agree. I will do my best to get well and carry out your plans."

Just then there was a knock on the door. Fergus rose and opened it. "Ah," he said. "Captain Harley of the *Hatchet.* Please come in."

Harley removed his hat, and frowned when he saw Essex's condition. "Damn!" he said. "I didn't know. There was a hell of a ruckus around your stern last night, but I thought the frogs quit quickly."

Fergus nodded. "They did, but their treachery did the damage. Now I must ask you to take Captain Essex and two of his officers to London for hospitalization. They are all badly wounded, but not in the critical stage. I also want to send in chains the culprit who caused all of this."

Captain Harley frowned. "I'll keep him well trussed up. I'll also do my best to keep Captain Essex and his officers comfortable."

"How long will the trip take?"

"I guess it at no more than two days. The winds off shore are favorable and I should average ten knots. Schooner-rigged ships are always faster and more able to sail into the wind. I'll have no trouble."

"Thank you, Captain Harley. You have my gratitude. Please rejoin my command after you have completed your task. We'll miss you."

Harley bowed. "Then, sir, I'll return to my ship and see that arrangements are made."

After Harley had withdrawn, Fergus sat down again next to Essex. "I do not know how to advise you to report the double agent's actions. Normally I suppose you would report to Lord Greenway."

Essex laughed even though the effort hurt him. "Hell, no. I'll go right to Lord St. Vincent. Lord Greenway will be bound for his country estate in hours. I've waited a long time for this welcome event."

"I don't see how Lord Greenway could have been duped by this bastard."

"I don't know, but we'll find out soon enough. I have always felt he was a little off the mark. I guess I was too loyal to the Admiralty to do anything about it."

Fergus laughed. "Enough advice from me. You don't need any on this subject." He bent over Essex and patted his good arm affectionately. "Old chum, this pains me to see you suffering. Now get well and come back out here. There is still much left for us to do."

"I won't be long."

Fergus walked out on deck and called over the young officer who had the watch. "Lieutenant, your captain has agreed with me that you need help after he leaves. I'm sending my senior officer, Lieutenant Puller, over to take command of this ship. You will remain aboard as second-in-command, and I hope you won't take this too seriously."

The young officer looked relieved. "Yes, sir. I'll have the ship ready for him. The carpenter and sailmaker are hard at work making repairs, and we should be ready for full operations by noon tomorrow."

Fergus nodded. "Well done, young man. I know you will be qualified soon."

When Fergus returned to the *Daring* he called Puller to one side. "Puller, gather your gear in a hurry and take my boat over to the *Dashing.* You are to take command. Captain Essex and his two senior lieutenants were badly wounded by a salvo last night. I'm sending them to the hospital in London on the *Hatchet.*"

Puller was puzzled, but at the same time pleased. "Aye, aye, sir. What will we do next?"

"As soon as we are ready we will try again to land the two agents."

"Two? I thought there were three."

"There were. Now one is bound for London in chains."

"I will do my best to carry out whatever is left of the plan."

"You could do the job as well as I could, but still I will change the plan as soon as you take over command. Send over to me Agent Gervais, his assistant, and the three bags. Guard them carefully until you turn the bags over to me."

"I assume, sir, you will do the landing."

"Yes. The two ships will reverse their roles, and I will make the landing. Be sure you guard my rear end better than I did during the last event."

Puller laughed. "You can count on me, sir."

Later the next day Fergus led his flotilla south, going far enough to sea so no one could guess that their destination was to the south.

On the way south Fergus gave Agent Gervais an excellent dinner and pumped him of all the information he could extract. By the time dinner was over, Fergus was convinced he was honest and would do his best.

About midnight Fergus brought his ship close in to the shore at the alternate site, and came into the wind to kill their way. He ordered the boat lowered and loaded it with the agents, their bags, and five marines.

The boat pulled away from the side quickly with muffled oars toward the shore. Fergus anxiously scanned the green bushes, and the gun captains kept their crews alert. The scene appeared to be even more peaceful than it had the night before, and the bushes were even more dense.

There was absolute quiet, the boat grating on the beach the only noise. Gervais and his companion jumped over on the beach, unloaded the bags, and dragged them into the heavy underbrush.

Fergus heaved a sigh of relief. The boat pushed off of the beach and began its trip back. For a moment he thought he heard voices in the underbrush. He listened carefully. Nothing except some muttering in English. Fergus relaxed. They had made it, and Essex was avenged.

The next morning the small flotilla headed south to go on patrol. Fergus, drinking a cup of tea, put it down, raised his long glass, and looked aft at the *Dashing*. He could see, through the rigging, Lieutenant Puller, with his hands behind him in his best imitation of a captain, pacing up and down.

Fergus grinned, and said to Poston next to him, "He looks like he's been a captain all his life. Look at the way he paces."

Poston nodded. "I guess the first twenty-four hours is the easiest. Then the responsibilities and the constant stream of officers and men asking questions begins to catch up with you. He'll be frowning by tomorrow."

Fergus shrugged. "I don't think so. You and I might be, but that young man will never grow up. He'll die a young man, and I like him for it. That's why I chose him, and I hope we'll fight together soon."

"Do you think the Admiralty will send out a replacement for Captain Essex or wait for him to get well?"

"Maybe the latter. I have a plan and I think Admiral Nelson will help me carry it out."

CHAPTER 9

Capture of the *Mystère*

FOR TWO DAYS Fergus sailed his flotilla southwest to a position off L'Orient. Intelligence had informed him that one or more French frigates would arrive from the Caribbean carrying a valuable cargo. Since a frigate could not carry much cargo, intelligence estimated that it would be either gold or silver.

As they sailed south, Fergus paced the quarterdeck talking with Poston.

Poston asked, "Where do you suppose intelligence got that information?"

"I don't think that's the level those agents we landed could have gotten next to."

"Maybe," Poston said. "That guy Gervais was pretty smart. He seems capable of dressing up and passing into fairly high circles."

"That's possible. If so, we may hear more from him. You have to remember that the whole French government is now in a state of change. Supposedly members of the government talk to all sorts of people when they shouldn't."

Fergus stopped pacing and talking and turned to the business of running his ships. He spaced his three ships in a scouting line across the course line from the Caribbean to L'Orient.

On the fifth day the *Hatchet* returned from London, and Fergus stationed her on the northern end of the line. Still, nothing happened. Before she left, Fergus called her on his quarter and asked through a speech trumpet if Essex was recovering. The captain nodded a vigorous yes, and Fergus relaxed.

For over a week the ships ran north and south changing course every four hours. On the next day a ship was sighted north of the northern end of the scouting line. Fergus immediately turned his ships toward it, but the tactic was futile, although Lombardi put up all the sails the masts would hold.

The *Hatchet,* on the northern end, and the fastest ship of the group, closed her enough to be able to identify her as a French frigate. "She's the *Mystère,*" he reported, but the *Hatchet* was too small to attack her alone and so just trailed her. To get the last fraction of a knot out of them Fergus brought his ship as close as he could with all of the sails Lombardi could use and then ordered Lombardi to trim them. Unfortunately the *Mystère* had the speed of a French ship and she drew away very slowly.

Fergus was able to follow her at just out of gun range. In spite of all the canvas Lombardi had piled on, the Frenchman drew away slowly and headed right for the harbor entrance.

"Dammit!" Fergus said, "She's going to make it."

Poston nodded. "She will, but Lombardi has done all he can to catch her."

Fergus followed her right to the entrance to the harbor and finally gave up just short of the gun range of the shore batteries. Fergus, using his long glass, watched the quarterdeck of the French ship closely as she coasted to a stop and moored at a pier.

"What's going on?" Poston asked.

"The bastard I take to be her captain is strutting up and down and waving his arms. It looks like he's dressed up like a fighting cock. I'm sure he's telling his officers he defeated a whole British squadron."

"Sure, and he'll tell the admiral in port tomorrow the same thing."

Fergus banged his fist on the taffrail. "Well, he won't get away with it."

"But what can we do?"

"We'll give him a day to let his crew get ashore and get well drunk. It's in the dark phase of the moon now, and I plan to take a boat inside the harbor tonight and reconnoiter. If I think it's possible, the next night I'll take in four boatloads of marines and sailors and cut her out."

"Sounds risky if you try for her. We could see where she moored. A lot of other ships are moored at the other piers that might be easier to get at and cut out."

"Yes, but sometimes the unexpected is the best way. They'll never think we would do such a stupid thing."

That afternoon, out of sight of land, Fergus called for the captains to come aboard. When they were seated in his cabin, he began to set out his plan. "Tonight the *Daring* will close the harbor entrance just after midnight. I will take a boat with muffled oars in the harbor to see just where the *Mystère* lies and how we can plan to cut her out."

Poston interrupted. "But why do you want the *Mystère*? She didn't look like much of a ship. There might be some other, better ships that are easier to get at."

"We already talked about that. I want that French bastard. He irritated me. Besides, he might not have unloaded his valuable cargo yet. He's a Frenchman, and he'll want to celebrate whatever the holiday is before he goes to work. So far intelligence has done very well."

Poston asked, "What holiday?"

Fergus shrugged. "Who knows? They have three a week or maybe more."

The marine captain had been a student of French culture, and he spoke French. He said, "You can count on at least three holidays a week at this time of the year. If no holiday is at hand, they will designate some saint and drink to him all night."

About midnight, Fergus, in the stern sheets of a boat being pulled rapidly toward the harbor entrance, raised his long glass and searched the entrance of the harbor, carefully looking over the fortifications at the mouth of the harbor. Obviously it was well defended with several embrasures visible in the faint moonlight. He could not see anyone or any moving lights. The boat crew pulled them silently inside the entrance with no indication of alertness ashore.

Inside the harbor several ships were visible in the light from the shore. No men or lights or sentries were visible. Most ships were moored in nests of two or three at narrow finger piers. To the north was a larger finger pier, and the *Mystère* was moored by herself at the south side of the pier. Other ships were moored in front of her, but none astern.

Fergus searched the topsides of *Mystère* and then the weather decks of the other nearby ships. "Damn!" he said. "I can't see a single sentry."

The coxswain said, "Sir, we could board her right now. It would be easy."

Fergus laughed. "I like your spirit. You'll be the coxswain of the lead boat tomorrow. Now come about and take me back to the ship."

"Thank you, sir. I'll be ready."

The next afternoon Fergus held another conference. The officers were ready.

Puller was eager. "Sir, do we take her?"

Fergus laughed. "Oh, most certainly we do."

"Then I can go in with my boats?" Puller asked.

Fergus frowned. "I know how much you all want to go, but I want to make sure a competent senior officer is left in each ship."

Captain Harley of the *Hatchet* was equally eager. "And the sloops? I could load fifty men and marines and land them right alongside the *Mystère*."

Fergus sighed. "I'm sure you could, and I've thought about it, but there will be other problems."

Harley fidgeted. "Can you tell me about them? Maybe I can solve them."

"I am sure you could. In some ways your plan would be far simpler, but I don't want to take unnecessary chances with your ship. You would be in some danger, particularly when you are alongside the ship. It is possible that they would never see you, but you are a lot to see and if they do, you will also be a large target. I believe we can do the job with pulling boats with less risk."

Harley subsided, obviously disappointed. "As you say, sir, but if you change your mind, we'll be ready."

"I'll remember you. You two will guard our rear to sea. If any French ships show up, do your best to lead them off until we can get together and escape."

Poston growled, "I take it I don't get to go with the boats either."

Fergus nodded. "No. I will be going in command of the boats so you will have to remain in command of the *Daring* and the whole flotilla. I think this is a good opportunity for you exercise command, even if it is only against a bunch of drunk and sleepy Frenchmen."

Poston sighed. "I guess I'd do the same if I were you. Now tell us the rest of the plan."

"All right. We'll go near the harbor entrance at midnight and lie to just outside of the sight of the fortifications. Each frigate will lower two boats. Five sailors and five marines in each in addition to the crews will be loaded. Muffle all oars. Observe strict silence. Form in column aft of my boat.

"*Daring* boats will come alongside the starboard side of the *Mystère* and we will board by sea ladder or grapnels if necessary. The *Dashing* boats will come alongside the pier opposite the ship and board her from the pier side. Be quiet. Last night there wasn't a sentry in sight, and I don't think they will change anything tonight. The lazy frogs hadn't even lowered their yards or sails after they moored. Just dashed ashore for the nearest bar, I suppose, just after their captain and their officers had left, but there may be a few left aboard.

"The *Dashing* boats will carry axes to cut the mooring lines as they board. The marines will go below and take over the ship and secure it. Those aboard will probably be asleep below. Frenchmen don't seem to like fresh air.

"*Dashing* sailors will go aloft and unfurl the main courses. They probably will be loosely furled. That's all we'll need to sail the ship out stern first. I'll take the wheel."

Poston snickered. "But, Captain, can you steer?"

Fergus guffawed. "What? You taught me when we were quartermasters together."

The others laughed, finally getting the joke.

Poston said. "Sorry. You were pretty good as a helmsman as I remember it."

As the laughter died away, Fergus resumed, "As the boats are unloaded, have your coxswains take their boats astern and prepare to take the ship in tow. Take your own tow lines. Spread the towing points so that each boat will have maneuvering room. The *Daring* crew will take along two hooded lanterns. Leave them with me on the quarterdeck. The marines can pick them up as they go below. I am hoping that the *Mystère* can be steered going astern, but if she's cranky the towing boats will help steer. I'll use the lanterns to signal to the coxswains. One lantern, change course two points to the north, two lanterns, change course two points to the south.

Poston asked, "Are there any questions of the commodore at this point?"

No one spoke up.

Fergus said, "I think this is all we need to provide for. In an operation like this we'll just have to be ready to improvise. Remember that we British have always been able to outsmart the Frenchies, and now they are worse than ever. They have killed off most of the smart ones.

"Poston, if anything happens to me, you will take over the flotilla and the ship, of course. Lieutenant Ballinger will be in my second boat and will be second-in-command of the boats. Any questions?"

The officers looked at each other, and a few wrinkled their brows, but no one asked a question.

Fergus stood up "Then let's have at it. We'll get under way for the harbor entrance as soon as possible."

At midnight all four ships came up to the harbor entrance. The two sloops turned away and took up prearranged patrol stations within sight of the entrance.

The *Daring* and *Dashing* lowered their two boats and quickly loaded marines and sailors. There was absolute quiet as they entered the boat. All hands had secured their equipment so it wouldn't rattle.

As all four boats started off in column, Fergus stood up and listened carefully. Nothing could be heard from any of the boats. The oars were well muffled, and the coxswains gave orders in whispers. He could not see any lights so he sat down, opened his long glass, and began to search for the harbor entrance headlands.

Suddenly there was a splash near the bow in the first boat. One of the oarsman had "caught a crab" with his oar. He recovered quickly, but the stroke oar said in a hoarse whisper, "Braxton, do that again, and I'll brain you right away with my own oar."

"Damn," Fergus muttered.

The coxswain started to remonstrate both men, but Fergus raised his hand and whispered to the coxswain, "Don't bother. I don't think it will happen again."

The *Daring*'s marine officer, Captain Larsen, was sitting next to Fergus. He whispered, "Commodore, I don't think you have to worry about noise. When we get into the harbor, the whole place ashore except for the French ships will be one big noise. Mister Gervais told me this day would be one of the many new revolutionary holidays, and they'll all be drunk. As I told you before, if this isn't a holiday, they'll still find an excuse to get drunk."

Fergus nodded. "Thank you, Captain, maybe we're in luck tonight."

Soon Fergus sighted both headlands and changed the boat's course carefully and enough to bring the boats in the middle of the channel.

When they could see the French ships in the harbor, Fergus, as on the night before, could not see any lights or movements on the topsides of the ships. The four boats separated near the end of the pier, where the *Mystère* was moored. The coxswains gave commands by hand signals and brought the pairs of boats alongside the ship and the pier opposite the ship almost simultaneously.

One *Daring* boat found a sea ladder over the side of the ship and the second boat came alongside the first. The marines clambered up the sea ladder, followed by the sailors. No one was on deck, and the marines headed for the hatches leading below, taking the lanterns with them.

In spite of the *Dashing*'s men's efforts to cross the pier quietly, Fergus could hear them faintly. But still no one on board was roused. The first sound was the ringing of the axe blades as the mooring lines were cut, and quiet was no longer important.

Captain Larsen and his marines went down all the hatches at the same time. A few French sailors were still aboard. At first there were shouts by the marines and a string of English curses. No Frenchman in the room could get to a firearm and the marines didn't fire but used their muskets as clubs. Then there was a dying string of French curses, and the noise ceased. The marines routed them all out of their bunks and put them under guard. The captain sent a man above to tell Captain Kilburnie the good news, but then a French sailor surprised him coming from a small room below. The man was naked and shoved the marine aside and ran up to the quarterdeck and across to the side. One of the marines, standing near the commodore, raised his gun. "Shall I shoot him, sir?"

Fergus laughed. "No. Let the poor bastard go. A shot might warn men on the adjacent ships too soon. He'll do it soon enough."

The French sailor jumped over the side and began swimming for the adjacent pier. Fergus watched him and shook his head. "He thinks he can rouse somebody. We certainly couldn't even with all the noise we made."

The marine shrugged. "Those Frenchies certainly can sleep."

On the quarterdeck at the wheel, Fergus watched the *Daring*'s sailors climb aloft and cast the three main course sails free. They were poorly furled, obviously by sailors in a hurry to join the festivities ashore. They fluttered down in cascades of white canvas, catching the lights of the nearby town and some wind. The sailors came down and trimmed the sails so they could draw better. Soon they bellied out and the ship began to move astern.

Suddenly a shout came from one of the ships at the nearby pier, and men came topside and began to run around, shouting loudly in French. Apparently the naked swimmer had found someone.

Larsen, who had come up from below, asked, "Commodore, should my men put a few balls over there?"

"Good idea. It will give them something to do dodging your fire." Fergus looked over the side, noting that the debris in the water was passing the side with increasing speed. "We're moving astern now."

There was a gentle offshore breeze, and the *Mystère* began to move slowly astern with increasing speed. Fergus said to Larsen. "Keep those hooded lanterns nearby. I may need them for signaling."

As they cleared the end of the pier, she caught more of the light breeze, and by now the four boats had taken positions astern and were adding a knot or two to the increasing movement astern of the French ship.

Once or twice, Fergus, at the wheel himself, found the ship a little clumsy to steer when going astern, and he found it necessary to use the hooded lanterns to signal to the pulling boats to help steer a straight course for the opening between the headlands.

Still, there was no action in the embrasures. An enterprising French sailor on one of the French ships apparently found one gun still loaded and fired it as a warning. The boom echoed across the harbor.

"Damn!" Fergus said, "That should wake up some of those sleepy soldiers in the fortifications."

By now they were abeam of the headlands, and Fergus decided to bring the ship about and go ahead, towing the boats astern with the men resting on the oars. The wind outside the harbor was increasing, as he expected it would be, and the *Mystère* worked up to five knots.

Astern, lights on the ramparts became visible, and men could be seen running about the walls bringing the large guns to bear.

Suddenly a ragged salvo came out from the northern embrasure, but the shots fell well short.

"They're wasting their powder," Fergus said. "They can't even see us." He sat back in the after sheets of the boat with Captain Larsen, watching as the crew of the boat pulled them back to their ship. "See, they don't even seem to be tired."

Captain Larsen sighed. "But the marines are. So am I."

In an hour they were in sight of their four ships, and at dawn, after the boats had been unloaded, Fergus directed that the four boats be hoisted. He left Lieutenant Ballinger aboard and designated him as prizemaster. He left ten sailors and two marines with him.

"If you need help, lower the flag," he said. "Good luck."

CHAPTER 10

Promotion

THE NEXT MORNING Fergus decided to return to the Thames. He had been ordered to return about the end of the month, and the twenty-ninth would be close enough. Also, he felt the French might send out a strong force to take revenge for the humiliating loss of the *Mystère.*

Later that morning he knew he had guessed right. Astern were two sails headed right at them. From the cut and color of the sails Fergus knew the ships were French and he sent Poston aloft with a long glass to watch them. Soon Poston came down and confirmed that they were French and their superior speed would allow them to close by dark. Fergus brought the *Dashing* close aboard and when they were in speaking-trumpet range he shouted, "Puller, when the closing ships are just out of gun range, we will turn together on my signal and close them. They may be angry at us, but that won't help them much. I'll leave the sloops with the *Mystère* in case other ships appear ahead. Do you have any questions?"

"No, just let me at them."

Just before noon, Fergus judged that the French ships were close enough to be a danger to the *Mystère.*

"Hoist the signal to close," he shouted. "Right full rudder."

By the time they were steady on course toward the French ships, Fergus ordered the bow chasers, "Commence firing!" Puller did the same.

The French started firing their bow chasers also, but the English gunnery was better. Two or more balls could be seen to land on the forecastle on the ship being engaged by Fergus. He stole a glance toward the other ship. Their fore-course sail was badly torn.

"Damn!" he shouted. "Good for young Puller."

The action was not enough to deter the French ships, and Fergus ordered, "Right full rudder. Port battery stand by!"

Puller had anticipated Fergus's move, and the *Dashing* was about as fast in turning. The French ships stood on for a few minutes, obviously concentrating on getting at the *Mystère.* At least two broadsides fell on each French ship before they gave up and turned their broadsides toward the English ships. It was enough to allow them to be damaged badly, and their return broadsides were half-hearted and well short of the English ships. Fergus could see damage to the French sails and rigging and one or two guns on their sides. After a few minutes the French ships fell off and disengaged to the south.

"Damn!" Fergus said. "I'd like to go after them, but we may not have the speed to catch them, and I don't want to leave the *Mystère.*"

"Let the bastards go," Poston said. "I can imagine the explanations they're going to have for their admiral. They'll say we were a whole fleet."

Fergus brought the ship around and soon they were back in position ahead of the *Mystère.* As they closed, he said, "I wonder why the French admiral only sent two ships after us?"

Poston shrugged. "He must have thought we were only one ship. The *Mystère* could only see us and the sloop in the scouting line as they passed us to the north."

Fergus shrugged. "When they caught up with us they found they had to get through two English frigates and cope with two sloops. No wonder they quit and went home."

"Yes. They did all right to attack us at all."

"Oh, they'll have a good story for their admiral, and the former captain of the *Mystère* will get another hiding for misinforming the admiral. Maybe they'll give him the guillotine. The French don't tolerate failure lightly."

As they sailed north in the English Channel, Fergus kept a close watch astern, but no other sails appeared. The *Mystère* rode heavily in the middle of the formation.

The next day, about noon, Lieutenant Ballinger closed the *Daring* and picked up a speaking trumpet. When he was close enough to be heard, he began to shout, "Commodore, I've completed a search of the ship and report that three holds are filled with gold bullion. I can't estimate its value. It's too heavy to move at sea. I estimate it to be somewhere in the millions of pounds. You'll have to wait until we get into port to have it moved and valued."

The men, lazing about the deck, heard Lieutenant Ballinger's report, and the word was soon about the ship. One man said, "'Lucky Kilburnie' has done it again. That's why I signed on with him."

A second man nodded. "Maybe it's luck, but I still think it's because he always goes after what he wants. That's better than luck."

For a solid week a southwest wind blew down the channel. Fergus's flotilla tacked back and forth trying to make headway to the north, but at the end of the week they had only made a hundred miles northing. The two sloops, with their fore and aft rigs, loafed along, trying not to get too far ahead, but Fergus was getting testy. He was concerned that the French would send an even bigger force after them, but he reasoned that they had made their bid and failed, and now would stay in port and sulk.

On the eighth day the wind shifted to the east, and all ships stayed on a steady tack making good progress to the north up the channel.

Poston, checking the master's navigation, said to Fergus, "Only two more days to port if this wind holds. The sailing master is a good navigator."

On the third day, at dawn, they passed out of the Straits of Dover and rounded Margate Head. It was in plain sight in clear weather, and Fergus passed it as close as he could and headed due west for the mouth of the Thames. As he passed Margate Head he identified his ships to the signal station there and gave an expected time of arrival. The long signal arms began to move, and in the distance he could see the next set of arms repeating the message he had just sent. In half an hour it would be on the desks of the admirals at the Admiralty.

The strong wind pushed them ahead at about ten knots, and eight hours later the flotilla stood in to the Royal Navy dockyards. They were moored in a group before dark, and Fergus kept a strong guard of marines on the *Mystère.* He was sure word would get around to all the ships of the flotilla and even to the workmen in the dockyard, and such a large store of gold might trigger anything.

Early the next morning a carriage arrived with a summons for Fergus to appear at the Admiralty immediately.

The carriage ride was fast and rough, and after an hour Fergus poked his head out of the window and shouted, "Driver, are we really in such a hurry? This carriage is taking a beating and so am I."

The driver laughed. "Sorry, sir, my orders are to get you there as soon as possible. I would guess our arrival at about 11 A.M. Anything later, and I might get sacked, and I don't know what would happen to you."

"Am I in some sort of trouble with the Admiralty?" Fergus asked.

"Oh, no. Just the opposite. All I know is the gossip about the stable."

A few minutes later the horses clattered up to the entrance at Whitehall, and Fergus somewhat anxiously clambered down and trotted up the steps to the door. He knew the way to Jeris's office and in a few minutes knocked on the door. The familiar voice rang out, "Come!"

Fergus walked in. Jeris jumped up and ran out from behind his desk. "My lad, it's good to see you! I'm beginning to hear a little about your cruise, and Lord St. Vincent is waiting to hear it all from you. Now let's go."

Jeris strode so rapidly down the hall that Fergus almost had to run to keep up with him. He knocked on Lord St. Vincent's door, now adorned with a new huge brass plate indicating that Lord St. Vincent was "The First Lord of the Admiralty."

Fergus was puzzled. "What's this? He didn't used to have his title on the door."

Jeris rolled his eyes. "The king told him to do it. I don't know why. He didn't like it, but he did it."

The door was opened by an aide, whose eyebrows shot up. "Ah, gentlemen, the lord has been expecting you. Please come right in."

Lord St. Vincent looked up from a pile of papers. "Ha! Now I can leave this damned stuff. Welcome back, Kilburnie. Now tell me all. Start with that foul-up put together by Lord Greenway. You'll be interested to know he's back on his farm in Surrey. Maybe he can outsmart his damned cows. Now sit down and go to it."

Fergus and Jeris sat down and Fergus cleared his throat. "Well, I'm sure Captain Essex told you about the fiasco with the first landing."

Lord St. Vincent slapped the table. "He certainly did. I had Lord Greenway out of here in minutes. The traitor is under trial now. I'm sure he'll be hanged soon. If he isn't, I'll run him through myself with my sword. Now why do you call this the 'first landing'?"

"I couldn't let that first landing stand and not do something, of course. I took Monsieur Gervais and his loyal helper and their three bags of gold to the alternate landing. We landed them without incident. I haven't heard anything further. All was quiet, and they disappeared into the bushes."

"Well, that's a load off my shoulders. I have hesitated to inform the king. Now I can give him some good news, thanks to you."

Fergus smiled. "But, sir, I have more news for you, and I'm sure you'll like it as well."

Lord St. Vincent was beginning to feel his prelunch stomach rumble. He patted his middle impatiently and said, "Well, go ahead, young man, out with it."

"You may recall that your intelligence section told me that one or two

French frigates were bound for L'Orient from the Caribbean with valuable cargo. Your operations section ordered that I attempt to intercept one of them after I completed my intelligence mission. I set up a scouting line and eventually I intercepted the *Mystère*."

"You did? Wonderful! And you have her?"

"Well, not the way you think. I failed to capture her at sea the first time I encountered her."

Jeris squirmed, sensing that there might have been an embarrassing failure somewhere.

Fergus went on. "She came into the Channel too far north for me to intercept her. I was at the southern end of my patrol line. I chased her, but as your experts will find out, she was extremely fast."

Lord St. Vincent was having trouble following the narrative. "Lad, you lost her, but you have her? Go ahead." He looked at his clock. "Er, don't leave anything out, but finish as fast as you can. I'm very hungry."

Fergus smiled. "Yes, sir. She escaped into L'Orient Harbor, but I resolved not to let her get away."

Lord St. Vincent, now much more interested, said, "Well, go ahead, lad."

"I decided to cut her out."

Jeris frowned. "That would have been very difficult with the strong defenses of that harbor."

"Damned near impossible," Lord St. Vincent said. "But you must have found a way to do it. Go ahead."

"I reconnoitered the situation the first night, and I was sure I could do it. The Frenchies were sound asleep. The second night I took four boats in and landed alongside and across the pier at the same time. I cut her mooring lines and let down her courses. The French had left their sails at the yards in their haste to get ashore to celebrate."

Lord St. Vincent forgot all about his lunch and sat up straight. "And then?"

"I sailed her out stern first with my boats towing us."

"And they didn't discover you?"

"Well, a lone naked Frenchman burst out from below and avoided my marines. He managed to dive over the side and swim to another ship."

Lord St. Vincent laughed, his booming voice carrying out into the corridor. "Well, those Frenchmen will never cease to amaze me. I knew they slept naked with their women, but on board a ship? This is too much."

"We got up pretty good speed astern and were well clear before that naked

Frenchman managed to alert a ship to fire a warning gun. The shot was well short of us, but it woke up the sleeping soldiers in the embrasures around the harbor fortifications. They shuffled about for a while, shouting and hollering, and they managed to get off a few shots, but we had no trouble getting away."

Jeris said, "No one was hurt?"

"No. No shots fell aboard or even close. The next morning we sorted ourselves out and brought the *Mystère* home as a present for you," Fergus went on. "I was afraid the French would send out a group of ships to try to intercept us the next day, but nothing happened for several days. Then it happened, but we handled it all right."

St. Vincent smiled. "The French would have hanged you."

"She's got a good cargo of gold. The king, you, and the crews will all profit very handsomely. She herself will make quite an addition to the fleet. She's very fast."

Lord St. Vincent leaped to his feet. "My boy, you are to be congratulated. I will inform the king myself at dinner tonight. By the way, Captain Essex is well enough to go to sea and will take over the third sister ship to yours. In case you are interested, and I know you are, her figurehead is exactly the same size as yours."

Jeris cleared his throat. "Ah, yes, sir, you must tell Kilburnie the king's comment on this subject."

Lord St. Vincent guffawed, this time so loud the aide poked his head in the office door to make sure all was well. When St. Vincent had dispatched the aide, wiped his eyes, and recovered, he said. "The king told the story about the broomstick penis. The story had been told over every port after dinner session in town. Unfortunately the queen overheard the king, whose loud voice carries well, and later she told him such a story was not appropriate for such occasions."

"And then?"

"The king said if he couldn't tell it, no one else could either."

Jeris nodded. "I'm afraid it is history, and you'll have to tell Captain Puller not to let it happen again. By the way, it has been decided to let Captain Puller keep his command. Admiral Nelson would have been very irritated if he had not been kept there."

Lord St. Vincent was aware of his stomach again. "Gentlemen, will you join me for lunch?"

Fergus stood up. "Thank you, sir, but I must get back to my ship."

Lord St. Vincent grinned. "I don't think that's so vital. I direct that you stop by and see your wife for a two-day period. Then you can take her aboard with you."

After Lord St. Vincent had said goodbye and taken his departure for his long-awaited lunch, Jeris walked Fergus to his office. He said, "I will send for my carriage to take you to your flat. In the meantime we can talk a little. You know, of course, you have a new overall blockade commander in the Channel and Admiral Nelson has retired to Surrey."

"Yes, but will he stay there?"

"I don't think so. He retired on 22 October, while you were at sea. Here it is early 1802 already. I'd say he will be back to duty somewhere in early 1803. You will have a year of very boring duty in the Channel."

"Yes, but I'll be able to get into London occasionally and see my wife and children."

"You know, of course, that you are now entitled to be called 'Commodore' because you command a flotilla. There is talk of making you a full commodore, and your latest escapade should ensure it. As a full commodore, you will be able to come home to see your family whenever you are in port."

Fergus grinned. "I'll be waiting for the word. Now please send me home. I have only two days there, and I want to make the most of it."

The next two days were some of the best days of Fergus's life as he played with his son and visited his stepdaughters at their school.

On the third day he reluctantly returned to his ship, and Jeris was waiting to greet him. "Lad, let's stop on the quarterdeck. I want to correct an error. You don't have the proper flags flying."

"I don't understand."

"You are flying a commission pennant."

"Of course."

Jeris pulled a packet out from under his jacket. "Yesterday the king decreed that you are to be promoted to full commodore. He thought your gallant and brave action at L'Orient should be rewarded properly." Then Jeris laughed. "Not the least was the large amount of French gold your action put in the purses of the king, Admiral Nelson, and Lord St. Vincent."

"And some for me and the crews of my ships."

Jeris nodded. "Of course. There was plenty enough to go around."

"That's good."

"Yes, and now to the promotion. Of course you should be wearing the proper uniform." He opened the packet and pulled out a swallow-tailed pennant. "This is your commodore's pennant. Please fly it."

Fergus took it and smiled widely. "I am indebted to you, Lord St. Vincent, and the king, and I will always endeavor to honor it."

"Don't forget to think well of Lord Satterfield. He dropped many a good word in your favor."

"Oh, yes, I will always be grateful to him."

"Yes, I know you will, and we all will expect more of you in the future as you take over your new rank. Now remember what I told you. You can go home at your leisure when you are in port. Now hoist your pennant, and come with me in my carriage. I'll drop you off at your flat."

CHAPTER 11

Rendezvous with the *Diligent*

FOR A WEEK Fergus enjoyed his newfound privilege of leaving his ship in port and going home at night. He left Poston with the responsibility for the ship and appointed him flag captain.

"Is this legal?" Poston asked.

"Mister Fairlie says the Admiralty won't object," Fergus replied, "and, remember, Admiral Nelson carries Captain Hardy as his flag captain."

"But he still only wears the captain's uniform and gets the pay of a captain."

"You're seeing the point wrong," Fergus said. "You'd make a good Scot. The honor is important but the money doesn't hurt. When we come back from our next cruise and are every bit as successful as I think we'll be, I'll recommend that you be promoted to the rank of post captain."

"You will?" Poston said.

"I will what?"

"Both. We'll be successful and you'll recommend me for promotion?"

"Of course. If we expect it, we'll do it, and you'll get your reward."

Poston pulled at his chin. "You always seem to do something to make yourself successful. I'll just do what you do and see what happens."

Fergus laughed. "And what do you think I've done all these years?"

"Damned if I know, but you always succeed. Maybe I'll be successful, too."

After the second week Fergus went by the hospital to see Essex.

The chief surgeon shook his head. "Captain Essex? Oh, he's been out of the hospital for a week. And he's at the Royal Navy dockyards right now taking over his new ship."

"Damn!" Fergus said. "No one told me, and the ship is to be under my command."

The doctor laughed. "Maybe because, as we surgeons say, it hasn't been born yet. I think it is not to be commissioned until tomorrow."

Fergus dashed out of the hospital and leaped into his carriage. "To the

Royal Navy dockyards!" he yelled. "And don't spare those damned horses!"

Three hours later the gasping horses pulled the carriage up to the brow leading up to the gangway of the new ship. Once Fergus leaned out of the window of the carriage and saw the word "*Diligent*" across the stern, he pulled his head back in. He climbed out of the carriage, stretched his stiff legs, took one last look at the ship, and started up the long brow. At the gangway stood a grinning officer in a captain's uniform.

Fergus pretended to look stern. "Damn you, Essex, why didn't you tell me? I'm only your commodore."

Essex roared. "I almost put one over on you. I was going to present you tomorrow with a 'newborn offspring.' The surgeons at the hospital gave me the idea. Now I'll have to ask you to stay for lunch and attend the commissioning this afternoon, and it will no longer be a surprise."

"And I take it there'll be no funny business with broomsticks."

Essex feigned innocence. "Why, of course not!"

"I understand the *Daring* and your ship have exactly protuberant figureheads."

"Lord St. Vincent laid down the law," Essex said. "I'll be quiet. All you have to do is make sure young Puller accepts his role as the shortie."

Fergus nodded. "He already has. Now when will you go to sea?"

"In a month. I'm allowed that time for outfitting, and Lord St. Vincent says I can report to you for a month or less of shakedown."

"You won't need all of it. As soon as your gunners are ready I'll put you right in the middle of our formation."

Essex grinned and looked at Fergus's uniform. "The Admiralty tells me you are now a full-fledged commodore. You don't look like it."

"Yes, I haven't picked up my new uniform yet. This won't change our relations or the way we fight together. I hope to turn this job over to you very soon."

Essex looked at his watch. "Time for lunch. I swiped my father's personal cook for my steward. Father doesn't eat much anymore."

Fergus raised his eyebrows. "I knew he was getting up in years. Is his health going?"

"I'm afraid so. And so are my days at sea."

"I don't understand."

"My father's title is inherited. When he goes, I will become Lord Satterfield, and I feel an obligation to my father and the king to run my father's estates and to sit regularly in the House of Lords."

"And you will have to retire from the Navy."

"Oh, yes, I've always known it, but I have achieved my goal in the Navy of commanding a good ship, or will, if we finish a successful cruise."

Fergus sighed. "We will miss you. In the meantime let's get this old swab bucket in commission and get to sea. I figure on rendezvousing with you six weeks from now off the harbor of L'Orient."

"I'll be there, Kilburnie. Now let's go to the quarterdeck. We have important work to do. The Admiralty is having a big conference today so no one will be down here for the ceremony." Essex raised his eyebrows, mischievously. "Will you make the speech?"

Fergus swallowed. Making speeches was not his best accomplishment. "Er, I hope not. I'd rather hear your golden tongue."

Essex laughed. "Bollocks! But I'll speak first. I promised the crew I'd tell them a good story, and you'll be in it."

Fergus colored. "I hope it will be about one of my better times."

"Oh, yes, you'll like it."

The next two weeks of April were some of the best times Fergus had ever experienced. London weather was idyllic, and the girls were home on Easter vacation. Fergus and Shannon took them on daily picnics, walked in the parks with them, and young Strath seemed to grow daily.

On 20 April 1802, a date Fergus would long remember because Shannon informed him she was pregnant, he was standing at the front window contemplating the good news. Then he saw Jeris coming up the front stairs. As usual, he was using his good arm to steady himself, and now a brown envelope was tucked under his stump.

Fergus met him at the door. "Ah, Uncle, I see you bring news, but no matter how bad it is, I am happy. Shannon is newly pregnant."

Jeris beamed. "My boy, good news. Let's sit and have a glass of port to celebrate this happy occasion."

When they were seated, Jeris handed Fergus the brown envelope. Fergus asked. "What's this?"

Jeris shrugged. "Look at the address. It's from the Operations Section of the Admiralty and it's sealed. In this case I'm only a messenger. I asked for permission to deliver it to you. You forget. I write orders to officers to go to ships. I don't tell the ships where to go."

"And you don't know what's in it?"

"Certainly not. Well, I can guess from gossip at lunch. I suspect you and your flotilla are going to patrol the French Atlantic coast."

Fergus groaned. "Boredom for sure."

"But good spring weather."

Fergus opened the brown envelope with little enthusiasm, but with his usual Scottish thoroughness and thrift was careful not to destroy the envelope so the girls could have it to play with later. He took out the letter addressed to him and read it slowly. Then he pressed his lips together and handed the short letter to Jeris.

Jeris read it quickly. "I guessed as much," he said. "There'll be little excitement until Admiral Nelson gets tired of gardening in Surrey and goes back to sea. This puts you and your flotilla on patrol off the coast of France as I expected it would. However, don't give up. The replacement for Lord Greenway is Lord Silver. He's very dynamic, and rumor has it he will throw some excitement your way soon."

"You mean more agent-landing business?"

"Oh, no, he and the agents you landed have discovered something that will produce opportunities for you. This may take a month or so. Now may I go to the nursery and watch your children play?"

"You could, of course, but they are out in the garden now with Shannon."

Even before they reached the garden they could hear shouts of pleasure as the children chased each other around the garden. Jeris smiled. "I've been waiting for this. I don't see enough children in my job."

Fergus grinned. "The girls are here on vacation. You can see them all day. Do you think Aunt Martha might like it if you brought Strath home for a few days? Shannon hasn't been feeling well and she may like a little time off."

They entered the garden, and Jeris put his one good arm around Shannon. She kissed him warmly and returned his embrace. "Oh, Jeris, I don't see enough of you."

"I know."

"Please come to dinner tomorrow night about seven and bring Aunt Martha."

Jeris looked at Fergus and raised his eyebrows. "Maybe you should tell her, Fergus."

Fergus cleared his throat. "Dear, I go to sea in three days, maybe for six months."

Shannon sighed. "I've been expecting this news for some time, and we've been very fortunate in the time we've had together. It has been marvelous. You'll probably be home for the next birth."

Fergus said, "I think so. I've told Jeris the good news. If it's all right with you, we'll still have dinner together."

On 23 April Fergus led his flotilla out the Thames. As they got under way he waved at Essex, busy directing the movements of piles of equipment and supplies on the deck of the *Diligent.* Fergus noted that the *Diligent* was indeed an exact replica of the two other ships. He picked up his long glass and examined the figurehead in detail. It appeared to be exactly like the lady on his bowsprit, but then he started and focused the long glass more exactly. Then he laughed. He turned to Poston. "That son of a gun has done it again. Look at this."

He handed the long glass to Poston. Poston refocused it and examined the figurehead. "I don't see anything any different," he said.

Fergus said, "Look again."

Poston went over the figurehead again. Then he laughed so hard he could no longer see through the long glass.

"You see it, then?"

"Of course. The nipples on the figurehead are a good two inches long. Longer by an inch than on our figurehead. What are you going to do about it?"

"I'll congratulate him. Then I'll keep it very quiet and you do the same. I don't want to start another controversy and get the queen after me."

For a week they sailed south, holding drills and testing their guns and gun crews. When Fergus was satisfied with the readiness of his ships and their crews, he spread them in a scouting line and practiced maneuvering with signal flags. At night he substituted hooded lanterns. The lantern system, as expected, was slower, but it worked.

For the next month the flotilla chased a succession of small French ships that passed from port to port along the coast. All were small and fast and usually not worth the trouble of pursuing them, but Fergus believed in keeping his crews busy, and finally one was caught and taken as a prize. Fergus went aboard and examined the ship and her sparse cargo. When he got back, he said, "I gave orders to destroy her and send her crew ashore. She wasn't worth tying up a prize crew."

Poston nodded. "This is a useless exercise."

"Don't worry. Something interesting will come along."

On the first of June the lookouts shouted. "Sail ho!" They were at the rendezvous point for Captain Essex and the *Diligent.*

Fergus sent a midshipman to the foretop, and in a few minutes he was down. "Sir, it looks exactly like this ship."

Fergus grinned. "It should. She's a sistership—or almost like one."

Poston smirked, but kept quiet.

In a few minutes they were together, and Essex sent a signal: "Permission to call on the commodore."

When his head came up over the edge of the deck, Fergus looked at his grinning visage and laughed. "Essex, it is always good to see you. The whole world livens up. Now come on up that damned sea ladder and we'll go in to my cabin. I suspect you have good news, and I have a bone to pick with you."

Essex's eyebrows shot up. "And what could that be?"

"I congratulate you on the modifications to your ship, and I will never mention this subject again."

Essex laughed. "Agreed. It is better not talked about in public and certainly not in the palace."

When they were seated over port, Essex said, "Fergus, you'll never believe this. Our agents paid off. They sent back word that the French are sailing a good-sized force of four frigates, a two-decker, and a transport on the fifth of June."

"This is the second time Monsieur Gervais has done something to restore our respect for him."

"I agree. There was never any problem about him. He didn't like the replacement agent either. Lord Greenway was completely responsible for that."

"I'm glad to hear that. What are the ships going to do and where are they headed?"

"All the ships will be loaded with at least two hundred soldiers. The two-decker, named the *Sicily,* carries four hundred troops, and the transport will be loaded with the artillery of a regiment and the men for them. The force will be commanded by Rear Admiral François Cristo in the two-decker *Sicily* as his flagship. The landing force will be commanded by General Talisin, also embarked in the two-decker. The transport is named the *Saracen.* I don't know the names of the frigates."

"Where are they bound for?"

"A landing on a small island named the Grand Cayman. We hold it now, but I don't know exactly why they want it. I do know they are expected to join another force from one of the local nearby garrisons, and they expect to land together on the first of July."

"Are we supposed to destroy this force? It sounds formidable."

"Of course not. We are supposed to harry it and slow it so that they cannot make the rendezvous and land on time. If they can't, the whole landing won't be able to take place. It will either fail or be called off. By the second of July we will have reinforcements in place, and any size landing force won't be able to take it."

"That we can do. I'll call a meeting of all commanding officers at 9 A.M. tomorrow and set some plans."

"Sounds just like you. By the way, your beautiful wife told me to tell you not to worry. She is over her morning sickness and is glowing again. She sends her love. I am tempted to try this matrimony thing myself soon with her example."

"I keep telling you that you are missing the best part of life."

"I thought commanding a ship was the best part."

"Well, maybe so, but married life is right up there. I have both parts now."

Essex laughed. "I envy you."

"I'll spend the night planning and see you in the morning. By the way, I congratulate you again on your modifications to your figurehead."

"Well as you said when I arrived, we don't want any of this to get to the queen. It was bad enough last time."

"I certainly won't say anything. It is hardly visible even through a long glass. So far only Lieutenant Poston knows on my ship, and I have threatened him with keelhauling."

CHAPTER 12

Sneak Attacks

FERGUS PACED the deck throughout the night, muttering occasionally and shaking his head. At dawn he sent for a cup of coffee and directed his quartermaster to lay out charts on his table for the transit to the Grand Caymans. Then he sighed deeply. He had made up his mind, and he knew what had to be done and how to do it. Now he needed a large breakfast to prepare himself for the 9 o'clock conference. The hard decisions had been made.

Promptly at 9 A.M. Fergus made the signal to lie to and then the signal for commanding officers to report on board. He watched as the ships came into the wind and their boats approached the *Daring*. Since the weather was mild, the coxswains were able to make the sea ladder with ease. Poston, as flag captain, met the arriving captains and escorted them to the cabin. The steward, Radcliffe, had coffee ready, and when all had arrived, he diplomatically disappeared.

Fergus began with a no-nonsense summary of their mission and then a listing of the forces they would meet. "The French admiral, Cristo, flies his flag on the two-decker *Sicily*. She carries twelve 32-pounders and forty-four 24-pounders. She can make about nine knots. She's slow but powerful. The French Army general, Talisin, is also aboard. He will be in command of the landing force including the artillery battery.

"Admiral Cristo also has four frigates, comparable to ours in gun power, but I would think we can outmaneuver them, and even though they are French, our speed is still about two knots faster. Our two sloops can make about four knots above them. The transport *Saracen* is an old ship of the line and can make about eight knots. She has no armament, a mistake that I took advantage of in my early days when I commanded an armed transport."

Poston laughed. "You certainly succeeded. You captured two frigates that time."

Fergus grinned at the memory. "With a little help from a cargo of guns and some passengers."

"And a lot of cleverness."

Fergus returned to business. "General Talisin has an artillery battalion embarked in the transport and its attached artillery men and about 1,500 soldiers spread about in the other ships. Any questions so far?"

The captains shook their heads.

Captain Harley of the fast sloop *Hatchet* spoke up. "Don't forget the *Hatchet* and *Axe*. We can do a bit of damage with the 32-pounder we each carry mounted in the bow as a bow chaser. We also have six 12-pounders each. Our speed and maneuverability are great assets."

Fergus agreed. "I'm depending on you for many things, but wait until we talk about tactics. First, let's discuss our task. As I said, we have been given the responsibility of preventing this force from arriving at Grand Cayman by the first of July to join with another part of the invasion force. If we can do this, the invasion will fail or have to be called off. We are not charged with destroying this force, although I'm sure the Admiralty would be happy if we were able to sink or capture one or more of these valuable ships."

Captain Puller's young face broke into a broad grin. "That's for me, Commodore, just tell us how."

"Don't get in such a hurry," Fergus said. "First, a discussion of the playing field." He gestured at the chart of the Atlantic Ocean on the table. "We start from here, a hundred miles off the port of L'Orient, where we hope to intercept the force. They will come from L'Orient on the great circle course. However, they would be foolish to transit all the way on that course even if it is the shortest way.

"In a few days, they will head southwest toward the Canary Islands. The first part of the trip will be through the bad weather of the Atlantic, and it will hold them back. At the latitude of the Canary Islands they will enter the tradewinds bands and head almost due west. From then on they will have good weather and a following wind that will boost their speed by two knots. The Grand Caymans lie on the latitude of the tradewinds. They may run into tropical storms during the latter part of the trip.

"They will have to make about 3,600 miles in twenty-four days. That requires an average of 150 sea miles a day, or about six knots. Without our resistance they could do it easily. Our job is to slow them down seriously or cause them to divert from their course."

Poston shook his head. "A tough job."

Essex looked at him. "Not only *not* impossible, but a very interesting gamble on both sides."

"Do you think we will win?" Poston said.

Essex laughed. "Of course. It's a sure thing. Not even much of a gamble."

The comment reminded Fergus of Essex's younger days, when he had gambled away his mother's fortune before deciding that the life-or-death fighting with an enemy in the Navy was a bigger thrill. Essex had not gambled since, except against the enemy.

"Now, as to our job," Fergus continued. "I think they will be in a box-shaped formation with the two-decker and the transport in the middle of it. They will place two frigates in the van and in the front of each corner and the other two astern on the after corners."

Puller could hardly contain his youthful enthusiasm. "I have some ideas, Commodore," he interrupted.

Fergus didn't want to contain that enthusiasm but stuck to his plan. "I'm sure you do, but listen. I plan to put you in the *Dashing* with the two fast sloops in front of the French force, at least out of gun range to start with. The *Daring* and *Diligent* will take position to the rear.

"My general plan is to harass them day and night, but especially at night. Our goal is to damage the transport so that the whole force is slowed to her speed. If we can also slow one of the frigates, the admiral will probably stay with her or even turn around to come to her aid. In the process, we will attack suddenly to make each individual ship either change course to avoid our guns or bring their broadsides to bear. Then our attacking ships will pull out of range quickly to avoid any damage.

"We will start these attacks at odd times at night to keep their crews awake and each attack will be from a different direction. We will keep this up as long as we can. If it is not sufficient to slow them enough, we will have to be bolder and try different tactics in the daytime."

Essex said, "This will damage them, but it may also result in more damage to us. And individual attacks on the frigates won't by themselves slow the whole formation."

"You are right," Fergus agreed. "This is designed to get them ready for our next moves. Our last maneuver is to go by them and get at the transport. Even a few salvos will damage her sailing capability and eventually her speed."

Essex nodded. "I see. It should work. We just get her to come apart by small pieces."

Fergus turned to Puller. "Now, Puller, you come in. You will be in charge of the two fast sloops. Immediately when we sight the French force, without further signals move your ships up ahead of them. Then, each night, as many times as you can, all three of you make dashes back at the leading French frigates. You will coordinate the movement of the ships up forward. If you can, get past the van ships. My suggestion is that you make quick dashes toward them, and then when you get in gun range, fire your bow chasers, come about to bring your broadside to bear and fire a salvo or two, and then turn away. You will be across the bows of the defending ships, and they will only be able to use their bow chasers. By the time they can turn to open their broadsides, you can turn away.

"Some of your salvos will do some damage, and they will have to change course. With three ships, if one can slip by the leading French ships on the side and fire on the two-decker or, more important, the transport, they will have to change course and that will slow them a little. Many small losses of distance will add up to a lot of miles. They will have a lot of trouble making it up."

Puller grinned. "As you say, there will be three of us and the smaller ones are very fast and maneuverable. A potshot by their big gun falling on the decks of the transport will do a lot of damage. There should be hundreds of Frenchies on deck."

"Good. I'm counting on a lot of damage after several nights from those sloop attacks. They won't know who is attacking them and will have to turn away to open their broadsides of the two-decker even if their target turns out to be only a fleeting sloop."

Captain Harley said, "Our 32-pounder is rigged so that it can fire about 10 degrees off either bow. Any closer might damage the forestay or our jib."

"Burning powder?"

"Yes. But we should manage to get off one good shot on each pass. That's all we can count on at night. The gunners will lose their night vision."

Fergus nodded. "We will get in a few lucky shots, and then get away quickly."

Essex could hold himself in no longer. "You haven't talked about the heavyweights yet."

Fergus laughed. "The best for last. You and I have fought together so much we won't need many signals. We'll find ways to sneak up on them at night and harry all the ships. We'll try to attack the same one until we bring her down. Then the admiral will have to either slow the formation or leave her to be sunk or captured."

"Perhaps it's wise not to have exact plans for us," Essex suggested. "We can try several methods and pursue the most successful."

Fergus nodded. "I think that covers everything. We won't be able to signal much. I will depend on the initiative and courage of each of you. Now go back to your ships while the weather still permits. Our first task is to set up a search line with ten miles between ships fifty miles west of L'Orient. Fire a gun if you sight a large formation. Then we'll start to carry out our plan."

On 17 June, just as expected, the French fleet appeared on the horizon. The *Dashing* sighted it first and fired a gun. Without signal Puller headed west and the fast sloops followed him.

Poston laughed. "The French will think we've scattered like a bunch of scalded chickens."

Fergus said, "For once the Admiralty Intelligence Section was right. Our landing paid off."

As the French fleet passed, the other two frigates took a westerly course and dropped behind the French force. Fergus could see that they were in the box formation as he had expected. The frigates ahead were three miles in advance and the frigates in the rear trailed by two miles. While Fergus turned to take a following position astern of the French formation, he could see Essex doing the same on the other quarter. The French sailed on, ignoring the British ships.

At dusk, Fergus ordered Lombardi to crowd on all canvas, and the gun crews raised the gun ports and loaded and readied the guns.

Darkness closed in, and the lookouts searched the blackness ahead. They were heading up the wake of the frigate on their corner. In two hours the last remnants of the wake of the ship ahead became visible. Then a lookout shouted down, "Sail ahead. Two miles."

The bowchaser gunners soon reported that they could see the target.

When all was ready, Fergus shouted, "Bow chasers, commence firing!"

The explosion of the two bow chasers blinded those on deck, but the gunner had warned the gun captains to turn away and close their eyes during the firing.

Fergus shouted, "Lombardi, change course four points to starboard!"

The ship swung rapidly to starboard, and the port battery gun captains could see well enough to fire, but after one salvo their vision was too damaged to make it worthwhile to fire another.

Fergus shouted, "Cease firing! Lombardi, reverse course!"

In the distance Fergus could see Essex doing the same set of maneuvers. The flashes came and stopped abruptly as Essex turned away. The campaign had begun.

Two hours later the two British frigates repeated the attacks, and the starboard battery had their turn. This time they tried two salvos, and Fergus could see holes in the after-course sails.

"Damn!" he said. "They must have felt that, and any soldiers sleeping on deck must have suffered."

This time Fergus sheered off to port, and the French ship, now roused, changed course to starboard looking for the culprit. Fergus could see men scurrying on deck, and he held course until the Frenchman gave up and rejoined the formation. Then Fergus reversed course to close the formation from astern again and just before dawn repeated the attack.

Poston chuckled. "Those bastards aren't getting much sleep. They'll have to stay awake all the time, while our men can sleep between the attacks."

Fergus, refreshed by repeated naps, as was his crew, thought about the French crews. They had been up all night, never knowing when or where the attacks would come from. He resolved to press each attack deeper and deeper, realizing that the French would become increasingly fatigued.

Up ahead were several flurries of fire as Puller duplicated the attacks on the French frigates.

Just after dawn Fergus changed course to close the *Diligent.* He rounded up astern of the *Diligent* and paralleled her course within speaking-trumpet range.

"Good morning, Essex. How was the shooting?"

Essex replied promptly in his usual confident tone, "Good, I think, but I didn't start up any fires like you did. What do we do today?"

"Let our crews catch up on their sleep. Once or twice a day, close your frigate slowly to just in gun range. Let your crew sunbathe on deck with the bow-chaser crews hidden. Close very slowly. When you are in range, fire your bow chasers and reverse course quickly."

"I've got it. Next time I'll cruise along for several hours just outside of gun range with the crew sunbathing again. That will drive them crazy, because they'll have to stay at quarters and they'll never be able to rest."

"Yes. Your crew can rest and do light work."

"Sounds good to me. I suppose you have a new gambit for tonight you're building up to."

"Tonight we attack a single ship together and stay with her until the other ship is alarmed, closes us, and then we both leave."

"I suppose you have something else different for tomorrow night?"

"I'll talk to you again tomorrow morning. See what you can come up with, too."

The daytime sneak-up attack, as Poston called it, worked well. They could see a ball land on the quarterdeck, bounce once, and knock over soldiers like ten pins. Finally it came to rest on the forecastle.

"About ten casualties," Poston said.

Fergus shook his head. "They might be able to fire that ball back at us."

That night, about midnight, both British frigates came up behind the French frigate on the left rear corner. Four solid hits were made on her stern with the four bow chasers. The French ship turned to unmask her battery, expecting to engage a single British ship. Instead, both British ships turned in opposite directions to unmask their batteries and poured four salvos into the outmanned French single ship. After the last salvo, a second French frigate loomed out of the darkness and began firing. Both British ships left without damage, but one of the French ships had lost a mast and two course sails. Several soldiers could be seen lying on the decks, either dead or wounded.

Poston said, "The poor bastards are so crowded with all those soldiers many of them have to sleep on deck. I shudder to think what happens when several balls come flying out of the darkness into a crowded deck and the splinters of wood start flying around."

The next morning Essex shouted to Fergus as they joined, "That was great! Now we need to get at the transport and slow her down."

Fergus laughed. "We think alike, don't we? I see Puller is thinking the same way. Last night he sent his fast sloops after the forward frigates, drew them away, and slipped between them and fired a few salvos into the transport before the two-decker chased him away. The transport had to change course to escape further damage. They probably lost fifty miles along the course. That's what we want."

"That young man is learning. Now what do we do for a change tonight?"

"You close the French frigate on your side and give him enough trouble so the other frigate thinks we've doubled up on her again. This time I'll take a wide position and slip in behind the other and get several salvos into the transport before the two-decker can try to drive me off. Maybe she will change her course again."

"I hope that works. All we've done so far is prepare to slow down that pesky transport. Doing it will be the key to final success."

"Good luck."

About midnight Essex played his part just as planned, and both frigates came after him, apparently expecting the duplicate attack of the former night. Fergus came in between the after frigate and the center group of ships. The *Daring*'s bow chaser shots landed on the quarterdeck of the transport. Fergus turned to port to unmask the starboard battery. The gunners, now used to keeping their eyes shut, poured two salvos into the helpless transport before the two-decker could react. One of the 32-pounders landed on the gun deck of the *Daring* without doing any serious damage. Puller took advantage of the confusion in the French fleet and launched three attacks from ahead. The transport captain, now thoroughly confused and not wanting to lose the protection of her consort, reversed course, and lost precious distance toward their objective before the admiral could get her back on course again.

"They lost at least another fifty miles," Poston said, looking at the plot on the chart.

While the fighting was still going on, Fergus tried to assess the total effect of the multiple attacks. In the light of two small fires started in the fighting, he could see several sails in tatters and the bodies of several soldiers lying on deck. The battle was brief, but as the *Daring* drew off, Fergus could see that the sails, rigging, and two yards of the transport had also been damaged.

The next day Fergus saw that the transport had slowed to steerage way in order to make repairs and to let the other French ships catch up with her.

Poston looked at the large chart, now permanently laid out on the cabin table. "Damn! This is costing them valuable time," he said.

For the next three nights Fergus tried variations of the tactics to get at the transport, and each attempt either damaged her or caused her to turn off track.

On 25 June Poston plotted their morning position. "Here we are. We should feel the tradewinds any day."

Fergus, who had just come inside the cabin, said, "Go see for yourself. We're in the tradewinds now. The French have turned to due west. What does your plot tell us?"

Poston made a few calculations. "It tells me they have to make seven and a half knots. We've managed to add a half a knot to their problem. I'm not sure they can do it. The transport is laboring and one of the frigates is crippled badly."

"All right," Fergus said. "This means we have to keep up the night plan and take a few chances in the daytime, too."

He went back up on deck. The tradewinds were blowing steadily from the east. The color of the water had changed to a light blue, and he could see many flying fish gliding by. Although sailors always considered them good luck, now they were a bad omen because they confirmed that they were in the tradewinds area. On the other hand he knew that Radcliffe would be on deck early to pick up the few that might have flown too high and landed on deck. They would make a good breakfast.

He stretched and went below for a few hours of sleep before the next attack.

CHAPTER 13

The Battle Goes On

THE NEXT MORNING Fergus called all his captains to come aboard for a conference while keeping the French fleet just in sight ahead.

Poston started the conference by showing them a chart he had been using to track the enemy. "I make their speed of advance about seven and one half knots. The tradewinds have been helping them. Unless something happens they'll make their arrival at dawn on the first of July."

Fergus shook his head. "We can't let that happen. We have to keep up the night harassment and become bolder in the daytime. Tomorrow at dawn we will be in position as follows: *Daring* will be astern of the left rear frigate. *Diligent* will be astern of the right frigate. *Dashing* will be up ahead again with the two fast sloops. Create a fuss with the two front French frigates. *Daring* and *Diligent* will attack the two rear frigates full out.

"We will be approaching at dawn and will have the weather gauge. I expect them both to turn into the wind or at least across the wind to open their broadsides. In either case we will have the advantage and I expect to continue to attack them until one or the other is badly damaged. When that happens, one of the forward frigates will come to her aid, and I expect the two-decker will probably drop aft. If she does, the transport will either stand on with one frigate or turn around and drop aft, too. If she turns aft, they will lose valuable distance. If she stands on, our forward ships will attack her through the forward frigate.

"This may all seem complicated, but it will seem even more complicated to the French when they try to defend against it. Now are we all understood?"

There was a chorus of "ayes," and all of them stood up in order to get back to their boats and to their ships as soon as they could.

The next day the plan took effect. The *Daring* plunged in after her assigned target and scored several easy hits. Several balls hit on deck and knocked guns over. One ball hit something that caused a brief flash and some smoke. "Black powder smoke," Poston said, as the initial flash seemed to spread along the deck.

As Fergus was about to direct Lombardi to make a course change, the smoke became a large and brilliant flash.

Poston shook his head. "What the hell is going on up there? If they're not careful they can blow up the whole ship."

Fergus shook his head. "Something has gotten into the powder supply on deck. If the flames get into the powder train and move below to the magazines, there will be a hell of an explosion."

Everyone topside watched in fascination as the flash enlarged into a sunlike glow. In seconds the sound of a violent explosion rolled over them. The concussion took a few more seconds to get there but then it knocked everyone to the deck.

"My God!" Fergus shouted. "She blew up!"

"I knew it would happen!" Poston said.

The air was filled with pieces of gun carriages, whole guns, and sections of masts. Parts of sails with their lines still attached, sections of rigging, a whole section of one of the boats, and barrels of food rose and seemed to turn over slowly as they mixed with debris high in the air. When they reached the top of their trajectory they started down, mixing with hundreds of smaller pieces along the way.

When Fergus realized that his ship was only fifteen hundred yards away from the wreckage, and that soon this mass of detritus would come down on them, he turned to Poston. "Get everyone below. I'll take the wheel."

Poston ran forward and shouted to the officers and petty offices getting up off the deck. "Get below!" he shouted, and the deck cleared, leaving Fergus alone. He put the wheel over in an attempt to move the ship away from the fallout area, but without the crew to shift the sails only a small course change could be made, and the ship reached the limit of turn it could make quickly.

To Fergus the passage of time seemed like an eternity. The smoke around the disturbed water that marked the scene of the explosion shifted downwind, and all that was left of the frigate was an oily-looking lake filled with small pieces of wood. Fergus looked up, and the bigger pieces of debris were coming down fairly close to the scene of the explosion.

However, many pieces of smaller debris were coming down directly at the *Daring.* He knew there would be no chance of running out from under all of the falling debris, so he wedged himself between the wheel and the binnacle, hoping for some degree of protection from their structures. Then the rain of small pieces began to land. He put his arms over his head and crouched down. Suddenly he felt two blows. One piece of wood grazed his cheek, and the other lodged in his right thigh. The pain was excruciating.

When the rain of debris stopped, Fergus eased out of his meager shelter. He pulled out his kerchief and dabbed at his cheek. Blood soaked his shirt, but he knew it wasn't serious. He looked down at his thigh. His trousers bore a jagged six-inch rip, and he could see a large splinter protruding from the flesh under it. "Damn!" he said. "My best trousers."

He limped aft to his cabin and flung open the door. His steward was sitting quietly in the corner of the cabin with the cot drawn over him. "Radcliffe, go shout down the hatches for the crew to come back on deck and ask Surgeon Pollitt to come and tend to me."

Fergus went back to the wheel and steadied the ship until the regular helmsman returned and said, "My God! Captain, there's blood all over you."

Fergus shrugged it off. "It's not as bad as it looks. Now steer for the transport."

Surgeon Pollitt ran to Fergus and looked him over with a practiced eye. "Not as bad as I thought, but there'll be some cutting and stitching."

"It will have to be done here. I can't leave the quarterdeck just when we're about to get a crack at the transport. Send for some rum and a chair and get on with it."

Fergus sat down in a chair that Radcliffe brought up, finally admitting to some weakness, as he became light-headed from the shock. He asked the quartermaster for a long glass. With it he watched the two-decker and the transport for a few minutes, but they stood on. "Damn it, Lombardi, they're not returning even to pick up survivors."

"There aren't any," Lombardi answered.

Fergus said, "We'll have to do more than this to stay out of trouble. Bring her about. If we close them now, the two-decker will chew us up."

The next morning, after the usual night attacks, Fergus called another conference. "As you can see, we got a lucky break, and the number of frigates is now equal. We know now that we need to do more to lure the two-decker away from the transport. Tomorrow the sloops will stay up ahead as a threat, and our frigates will take on their frigates ship to ship. I hope that we can damage one of them enough to the point where the two-decker will have to come to her aid. Yesterday we passed that point too quickly and there was no point in her leaving the transport. Any questions?"

The next dawn they found the French formation altered somewhat. There were still two frigates astern, but only one ahead. Fergus picked the frigate on the right flank for himself, and again the approach from astern with the tradewind was a distinct advantage. Out of the corner of his eye he could see the other pairs of frigates hotly engaged, and he noted that so far the two-decker had stayed in her usual position.

Fergus also noticed that Essex, with the *Diligent,* had closed what he considered to be too close, but this was typical of Essex, and he resolved to warn him at the next meeting.

The weather gauge was the deciding factor in the engagements. Fergus could wear his ship easily to bring alternate broadsides to bear and the French ship had to tack.

It was an easy battle. Some French balls came aboard, but the damage they did was bearable. One overturned a gun and killed two members of its crew. Another created a cloud of splinters as it hit the base of a mast, but few splinters reached members of the gun crews.

After an hour, it was no contest. The French frigate had lost her foremast and had large holes in all of her course sails. Her rate of fire slowed, and Fergus ordered Lombardi to close her. "Shift to grape!" he shouted. "Kill as many soldiers as you can, but don't sink her!"

A lucky shot carried away her steering gear, and in a few minutes, the quartermaster, watching her closely, shouted, "She's struck her colors, sir!"

The quartermaster was not the only one watching the French flag flutter down. Fergus raised his long glass and focused it on the quarterdeck of the two-decker. He could see plainly the admiral and the general in animated conversation. The flag captain stood aside, apparently waiting for orders. The admiral pointed to the stricken frigate, and the flag captain seemed to give orders to his crew.

"Here they come," Fergus said to Poston. "We've been waiting for this opportunity."

The two-decker settled on a course for the stricken frigate and the transport stood on. Fergus could see Essex disengage and head for the transport, and Fergus stood by the French frigate as long as he could and then withdrew when the two-decker approached within range. In the precious interval Essex bent on every sail the ship possessed and soon was within range of the transport. For a while she was helpless, turning from side to side, trying to avoid the merciless fire Essex rained on her. One mast fell. Another tottered, and several sails split. She stood on, and still Essex pounded her.

Fergus continued watching the scene on the two-decker's quarterdeck.

Now the admiral and general were nose to nose, waving their hands. The admiral pointed to his wallowing frigate, and the general pointed at his stricken transport. Finally the general could stand it no longer, and he beckoned to an army officer with a sword standing nearby. There was no doubt in Fergus's mind what was going on. The army officer drew his sword and pointed it at the admiral's gut. A dozen armed soldiers stepped forward, and the group slowly herded the furious admiral to his cabin, and he disappeared inside.

Fergus laughed. "Damndest change of command I've ever seen."

The general turned to the bewildered flag captain and pointed to the transport. The flag captain shrugged and shouted several orders. The two-decker wheeled downwind and began to close the transport. Fergus closed her until the two-decker was in range of his bow chasers. The two-decker's stern chasers were the same size as the bow chasers of the *Daring.* Fergus began to pound the stern of the larger ship, but soon she began to return the fire and threatened to open up her larger broadside.

"Gunner, give her one last salvo as a calling card and we'll get the hell out of here," Fergus commanded.

The two-decker continued to close the transport, still bedeviled by the *Diligent.* In a few minutes the Frenchman was in range and began to fire on the *Diligent.* Essex knew he had done all he could quickly and well and turned and left the scene. The transport wallowed on as her sailors dashed about the decks trying to make repairs.

"Just a calling card," Fergus said. "Now, Lombardi, bring us back to the prize."

The stricken *Courtain* wallowed in the tradewinds under the watchful eye of young Puller and his fast sloops. Fergus came under the counter of the French ship and backed his sails. He turned to Poston. "Make a signal to the *Axe* to close me."

When the *Axe* was close enough for its captain, Harral, to hear what he was saying, Fergus related the conversation he had had with the French captain. Then he said, "Captain Harral, I have accepted the surrender of the French ship *Courtain.* Her captain understands that he is our prize, but that we will not board her. She is to proceed to Portsmouth on a direct course under your escort. There you are to turn her over to the prize court. After we have concluded our present business we will return to this location and run up the direct course toward Portsmouth until we find you. Do you understand?"

Harral picked up his speaking trumpet. "Yes, sir. Fortunately I speak French. I take it I will see you either in Portsmouth or along the course line."

"Good luck. Now carry out my orders."

Fergus returned the salute of the captain of the *Axe* and turned to Poston. "Rejoin the group ahead, Poston. I'm going to my cabin to get some rest. My wounds are acting up a little."

CHAPTER 14

Farewell to Lord Satterfield

THE NEXT MORNING the *Daring* had caught up with the rest of the flotilla plodding along behind the two-decker, the transport, and the remaining two frigates.

Essex was still well out of gun range of the enemy ships. When Fergus closed the *Diligent,* he came alongside and picked up his speaking trumpet. "I'd like to have breakfast, but my wounds are bothering me. Can you come over?"

Essex looked startled. "Didn't know you were knocked about, old boy. If you'll make a lee for my boat I'll be right there."

As Essex climbed to the top of the sea ladder, he looked Fergus over and said, "You look all right to me, Kilburnie, except for that damned plaster on your face."

Fergus laughed. "Just a scratch. I did, though, pick up a six-inch splinter in my thigh. Right now I don't climb ladders very well."

Essex said, "I had a little trouble myself. Took a ball or two. Lost six men and a gun."

Fergus frowned. "I thought you were a little too close at one point. I couldn't spare you if you were to catch one of those balls yourself. Be more careful. We'll get those bastards in due time."

"You know me," Essex said. "I'll have to do it my way. I still like the feeling of the big gamble. I do it better that way."

Fergus sighed. "I know you like to take chances, but do try to be careful."

At breakfast, Fergus brought Essex up to date on the prize. "I suppose you were too busy lambasting the transport to notice what went on over on the quarterdeck of the two-decker?"

"She was very quiet over there this morning, but I didn't know what it was. I just watched the transport trying to get herself back together. I don't think she'll make it on time."

"So you missed their change of command?"

"What? I don't understand."

"It was hilarious. The admiral insisted on leaving the transport to stand on alone, which put her in your hands and gave you the chance to deliver a knockout blow. He wanted to come back and save his precious frigate. The general, on the other hand, was obviously in favor of saving the transport and all his men and equipment. He got mad as hell at the admiral and finally had him removed from the quarterdeck with an armed escort. The admiral's shut up in his cabin under guard and the general is now both general and admiral."

Essex said, "It doesn't matter what the general does. He still won't make it, even though he sent over a couple of boatloads of army engineers to help. They're swarming all over the rigging and when a couple fell over the side the general wouldn't stop for them. We've picked them up. They're glad to rest in our brig."

Fergus had heard enough. "Before Radcliffe puts a good breakfast on this table, let's take a look at this plot." He sent for Poston. When he came in, he said, "Go over this plot with us. Let us know what it means and then stay for breakfast."

"Thank you. I'd be delighted," Poston smiled. "I'm happy with the plot. Right now they'd have to make ten knots to get there. An impossibility, from the appearance of the masts and rigging Captain Essex left with them."

Fergus and Essex inspected the plot and laughed. Essex said, "We've done it."

Fergus nodded. "I agree, but we should follow them until the first of July, two days more. Maybe the French general can pull off a miracle, but I'm sure they'll be a day late."

"No, he can't do it. When he gets there he'll have to take the French admiral over to see the governor and try to explain what happened."

On the first of July Fergus ordered the gunner to fire a one-gun salute in the direction of the French fleet. As the smoke drifted away, Fergus turned to the sailing master. "Lombardi, come about and head for the point where we took the prize and ordered her to proceed to Portsmouth."

The flotilla turned in obedience to signals and headed back through the tradewinds. Behind them the French fleet labored on, with all the undamaged canvas they could pile on.

Fergus looked back at the disappearing French fleet and said to Poston, "What a lost cause. Napoleon has taken all the starch out of the French navy. Fortunately for us, they aren't what they used to be."

Poston nodded. "You've done what you could to reduce the French fleet, and at little cost. I hope the Admiralty appreciates this."

"They will, but that's not why we do it," Fergus said. "Don't forget, we're part of Nelson's Navy. We do this for the king, country, Nelson, and the Navy."

Poston shook his head. "That sounds good, but a little approval by the Admiralty would help."

"What kind of approval would you like?"

"Maybe a week's leave for everyone."

Fergus laughed. "That sort of thing could never happen in our navy."

"They might just speed up the paying of our prize money."

"You'll get part of the prize money if we can find our prize. Let's concentrate on that."

Four days later, Poston, still monitoring the plot, said, "This is where we left the prize. Now we should follow up the course line toward Portsmouth."

"I hate to waste time doing this, but we have to do it," Fergus said.

"We should go through the motions. He might have made some repairs and speeded up."

Two days later Poston scratched his head as he put the morning plot on the chart. "This is where the prize should be at four knots. I recommend that we follow the course line for another day and then assume that the prize has diverted to head directly for his home."

"I agree," Fergus said. "The *Axe* couldn't do anything but follow her."

Poston gave him a course to take, and Fergus ordered the change made.

Two days later Poston's prediction turned out to be exactly correct, and the lookouts aloft sang out. "Sail ho! Dead ahead. Two sails."

They turned out to be the French frigate *Courtain,* still battered and missing her foremast but evidently repaired enough to sail. The *Axe* was still buzzing around her, like an angry bee. Evidently the *Courtain* still had enough guns to keep her at bay. The culprit was still making only about four knots, and in a few hours the *Daring* was under her counter. The *Axe* followed closely on the other side.

Fergus picked up the speaking trumpet and aimed it at the *Axe* first. "What happened here?"

The captain of the *Axe* took a deep breath. "The French bastard suddenly took off by himself. He wouldn't even answer me when I hailed her."

Fergus turned toward the French ship. "And what, Captain, is the meaning of this? You have violated your honor and the honor of your country and the French navy by breaking the word you gave me."

The French captain sneered and said in passable English, "I go my way, Captain. This is the revolution. I do not owe allegiance to anyone but to the common people of France."

Fergus said patiently, "Indeed it is not that way. Lower your sails immediately and prepare to receive my boarding party. If you do not, I will sweep your deck clear. My guns are loaded with grape."

The French captain turned red and gasped deeply, but he knew he had reached the end of the line. He turned to his senior lieutenant. "Lower all of our sails. Send all our soldiers below and disarm them."

When both ships were lying to, Fergus said to Poston, "This is your chance. Take ten men and ten marines with you. Take over the ship as prize, and follow us to Portsmouth. I will watch you closely several times a day and night to make sure those bastards don't violate the prize conditions again. Would you like to take my special cutlass with you?"

Poston laughed. "I don't think so. I might cut myself. I'll take my own."

Half an hour later Poston gathered the boarding party and followed them aboard the French frigate. The French captain was standing by the gangway, his sword in hand. Poston looked at him with venom in his eyes. "I suppose you are the former captain of the *Courtain.*"

"Yes, sir, I still am. I surrender her to you."

Poston was even grimmer. "You may give your sword to one of my marines. You do not deserve the honor of making a formal surrender."

"But, sir," the captain said, and he stepped forward and tried to hand his sword to Poston.

Poston took it as if it were dirty and threw it over the side.

"Now, Captain," he said, "go below with the rest of your crew."

"But, sir," the captain said, "I deserve the privileges of a captain."

"No, you don't. You have forfeited them. Now you will stay below with your crew, and I don't want to see you until we reach port. Then I will recommend that you be imprisoned as a common sailor."

The flotilla sailed steadily toward Portsmouth, and on the eighteenth of July entered the port and moored at a pier at the Royal Navy shipyard. Fergus had spent several days writing a report on the operation. He put the papers in an envelope in his pocket and went ashore to call on the commandant of the shipyard. The commandant asked Fergus to brief him on what had happened and was very interested in the narrative. "It's been the talk of the Navy as we waited to hear how you ended up. It was a difficult task."

The commandant volunteered to take the French captain off Fergus's hands and handle the negotiations with the local prize court for the prize. He also offered to speed the delivery of the report to the Admiralty. "They'll be very happy to get it," he said. "They were worried over the ability of anyone to delay or stop a force of that size."

Fergus left as soon as he could, and ten days later entered the Thames and moored his flotilla at the Royal Navy dockyard. The Admiralty sent word via a messenger to "commence a month's maintenance."

Fergus left promptly for his flat, leaving Essex in charge. His homecoming with Shannon and the children was all he had hoped for, but far too short a celebration. The next morning while they were at breakfast, a maid came in. "Sir, Mister Jeris is coming up the front steps. I don't like his looks."

Fergus rose and greeted him at the front door. "What is wrong, Uncle?" he asked.

"This is a very sad day. First let me sit down."

"Coffee, tea, or port?"

"Brandy, I think. You might need it, too."

When they were settled, drinks in hand, Jeris sighed deeply and began to talk slowly. "First, Lord Satterfield died two days ago. I went to the dockyard to inform Captain Essex and arrived just after you left. The Admiralty granted him leave until after the funeral."

Fergus shook his head and took a long draft of brandy. "Damn!" he said. "Essex has been expecting this for some time, and I know what he wants to do. We've talked about it at some length."

"Then you have guessed what he has already requested. He has submitted his request for immediate retirement. I returned to the Admiralty with it, and it will be granted, effective on the day after the funeral."

"I don't like to bring this sort of thing up so quickly, but who will be sent to take over the ship?"

"We will have somebody there the day when he retires."

"I have always known this would happen. Essex said he would have to retire immediately after his father died. As you know, he will be the new Lord Satterfield and will have to manage his father's estate and concentrate on his duties as a member of the House of Lords."

"There is something else you don't know. Lord St. Vincent has been anticipating this, too, and will appoint him Lord of the Admiralty for Intelligence."

"Good. He is well qualified for that position, and he will do a wonderful job."

"The funeral will be in two days. I hope you and Shannon will accompany me."

"Of course."

"My carriage will pick you up."

The funeral was held in Westminster Abbey and was attended by hundreds of Lord Satterfield's friends. Fergus dragged out of Shannon's closet his full dress uniform and for once wore his ceremonial sword instead of the cutlass he preferred to wear at sea.

As it was a sad occasion for Jason Essex, it was also one for Fergus Kilburnie. He had come to know and like Lord Satterfield. He knew well the close relationship between father and son, even though it was not always exhibited. They had been separated for years because of Essex's long time at sea. Even when he was in port he could not always leave the ship.

But already Jason Essex was becoming the new Lord Satterfield, and his intimates in the Navy were missing him. Then the new position was announced, and his total responsibilities began to close in.

After the funeral, there was an elaborate reception in the rooms of the House of Lords in honor of the deceased Lord Satterfield.

Fergus was amazed at the number of guests he knew. Now he realized that his associations with Lord Satterfield and Admiral Nelson had made him well known. He recalled the times he had been requested to narrate the Battle of the Nile at balls and receptions. Now at least a hundred guests, high-ranking naval officers, Lords of the Realm, and members of the government came up to him, met Shannon, and thanked him for past services, and commented on his speeches.

During one lull, Fergus said behind his hand to Shannon, "Looks like I could run for some office."

Shannon gave him a dig in the ribs. "Don't get off your level. You are a Scot and nothing more."

Fergus lifted his eyebrows. "I heard talk that I am to be the next clan chief of the Clan Kilburnie."

"That doesn't get you much in England. Scots of any Scottish rank are just Scots to the English. So are Irishmen just Irishmen."

Fergus shrugged. "And I'd rather be what I am—just a plain Scot."

"Wouldn't you like to become a rear admiral in the Royal Navy?"

"Of course, but they'd still think of me as just a lucky Scot."

Shannon and Fergus rode home in Jeris's carriage and stayed for a light supper. When Jeris and Fergus were comfortable in front of the fire, Fergus said, "Uncle, I don't like to bring this up so soon, but has the Admiralty selected a relief for Essex yet? I know you said they would get to it, but the time is getting close. I'd like to get to know him as well as possible before we go to sea."

Jeris laughed. "Of course. Candidates are running through the halls of the Admiralty like hounds after a fox."

"Well, who is going to catch the fox?"

"They have already caught the fox because he lives in their den."

"I don't follow you."

"Forgive me for trying to be humorous. I know this is serious for you."

"Uncle Jeris, if you don't stop talking in circles, I'm going to limit your brandy."

"Well, I guess I can talk to you plainly. After all, he will be one of your flotilla captains."

"And?"

"He was made a post captain two years ago, but was sent home with some strange ailment after only two months in command in the Caribbean. The surgeons say he's cured now, but I'm not so sure. I suggest you watch him carefully. Anyone who likes paperwork can't be normal."

"And what of it?"

"He was an assistant to Lord Entwistle. Entwistle swears by him. Says he knows instantly the positions of every ship in the Navy."

"Is that bad?"

"No, but he seems to sneer openly at anyone who doesn't know as much as he does about any subject. This amuses Lord Entwistle, but I think it puts Lord St. Vincent off, and he wants to get rid of him diplomatically."

"Well, why doesn't he just order him out?"

"He's a member of the aristocracy. Related to the queen. She dotes on him."

"You have given me a bad recipe for future trouble. Believe me, I'll watch him like a hawk when he gets here. Essex's ship is the among the best in the Navy, and I'd like to keep it that way."

Jeris sighed. "I doubt it. He will report to you tomorrow to relieve Essex."

"And the name of this paragon of paperwork?"

"Captain Anthony Hardcastle."

"Oh, no, I've heard something of him. I was in the Caribbean when he took over his first ship. There was some joking down there that the crew would have pushed him over the side some dark night if he hadn't become ill. And all that in a two-month tour."

"And what was the trouble with him?"

"The same as now, I guess. It was said that he was a paperwork nut and a martinet."

Two days later there was a knock on Fergus's cabin door. "Come," he said.

The messenger pushed open the door and said, "Sir, there's a post captain coming up the brow."

Fergus pushed back his chair and walked out to the quarterdeck. The newly arrived captain was standing on the quarterdeck, looking up at the rigging. As Fergus strode over to him, he could see him shaking his head, obviously with disapproval.

Fergus cleared his throat loudly, and the captain turned toward him, came to attention, and saluted him. Fergus could not read his expression, but he was sure it indicated disapproval of the state of the rigging.

Fergus returned his salute. "Welcome aboard, Captain. I am Commodore Kilburnie. I assume you are Captain Hardcastle."

"Yes, sir."

"Please follow me to my cabin." Fergus turned on his heel and walked aft to the cabin door. Hardcastle followed him, still gazing at the rigging.

In the cabin Fergus turned, "Please sit down. We should discuss the arrangements for your taking command of the *Diligent* tomorrow."

Captain Hardcastle sat down. So far he had not uttered a word except to acknowledge that he was Captain Hardcastle.

Fergus looked at him. "Well, it seems you do not approve of the rigging of my ship."

Hardcastle cleared his throat. "Sir, we can discuss that some other time? Now I am anxious to assume my command."

"That's better," Fergus said. "I was beginning to think you had other matters on your mind."

"Oh, no, sir, I am most anxious to get back to sea."

"Oh, yes, I can see that. Then I suggest you put up tonight at the hostelry just outside the dockyard gate, and come aboard the *Diligent* at 9 A.M. tomorrow morning. I will arrange with Captain Essex for the ceremony of the change of command to begin at that time." Fergus rose and held out his hand. "I wish you a successful command."

Captain Hardcastle took Fergus's hand and shook it, but there was no warmth in it, nor was there any in his eyes. Fergus muttered, "I'll have to do something about this right away."

Hardcastle looked at Fergus closely. "Did you say something, Commodore?"

"Nothing, Captain. I was just going over in my mind the procedures for the ceremony."

"Sir, I hope it will be short. I have a lot to do here."

Captain Hardcastle turned on his heel, left the cabin, and went down the brow, throwing a quick salute to the officer of the watch and the colors.

The officer of the watch returned the salute. "Damn!" he said. "I don't envy the *Diligent* getting that one."

CHAPTER 15

Essex's Retirement

THE NEXT MORNING Fergus rose early, shaved closely, ate an excellent omelet prepared by Radcliffe, left the *Daring* promptly, and at five minutes before nine walked aft to the brow of the *Diligent,* where Captain Hardcastle was waiting for him.

Hardcastle came to attention and saluted his commodore smartly. For the first time he smiled slightly. "Good morning, Commodore. Ready to go aboard and assume command."

Fergus returned his salute. "Good morning, Captain. Please follow me aboard."

At the top of the brow, after saluting the colors, Fergus stepped down on the deck and held out his hand to Essex, who was waiting for him. "Good morning, Essex. May I present Captain Hardcastle, who is to relieve you."

Hardcastle bowed slightly, but said nothing.

Essex was in a hurry to get on with the ceremony, and his smile as he offered his hand to Hardcastle was perfunctory. "Let's go to my cabin for some refreshment while my first lieutenant musters the crew. We should be ready for the ceremony in just a few minutes."

In the cabin, when Essex offered refreshment Captain Hardcastle raised his hand, declined, and looked about the cabin. Fergus and Essex ignored him and asked the steward for glasses of port.

Fergus said, "Well, Essex, this ends a wonderful adventure for us at sea. I will miss you, but I know the Admiralty will be the better for you."

"Oh, yes, Kilburnie, I will miss you, too, but now I will be able to keep an eye on your family, and I'll like that. You might like to know I am now engaged."

Fergus smiled broadly. "Wonderful! And who is the lucky lady?"

"Actually she is a Lady—Lady Pamela Hairston—but she's still down to earth. She knows Shannon."

"Well, if she knows my wife . . . " Fergus smiled.

Essex beamed. "I was lucky to find her."

"Will I be at your wedding?'

"I don't think so, old man. I wanted you to be my best man, but I'll have to delay the wedding for a reasonable time after the funeral. You'll be at sea by then, I'm sure." He smiled knowingly and grinned. "If your tour is long enough, you can help christen our first child."

Fergus shook his head. "What a change from the Jason Essex I used to know, who gambled all his money on the turn of a card, strode up and down the bulwarks of an enemy ship when we were alongside, cutting grapnel lines, and landing special agents on a hostile shore. Now all you can chat about is weddings and children."

Essex blushed. "Pamela is a wonderful woman, and you'll like her. I love her very much."

Captain Hardcastle cleared his throat, obviously becoming impatient at the turn in the conversation and at being ignored.

Fergus said, "Captain, you are about to take over a wonderful ship. Do you have any questions of Captain Essex?"

Hardcastle said without hesitation, "No, sir, I know all I need to know about this ship."

"That's fine," Fergus said.

Hardcastle sniffed. "And I know what has to be done to bring her back to excellence."

Essex looked at him with an expression that bordered on anger. "And what specifically are you talking about?"

Fergus interrupted, trying to ease the situation. "I know the ship well, and there is nothing that needs to be done to improve her."

Hardcastle seemed to realize the he had gone too far. "Well, Commodore, I apologize. I just know that I want to do all that I can to make the ship one of the best in the flotilla."

Fergus frowned. "She's already the best, including my command, and I hope you can keep her there. Now let's get on with the events of the day."

With a knock on the cabin door, the senior lieutenant poked his head in. "Captain Essex, the officers and men are assembled, and the ceremony is ready." He turned to Hardcastle. "I assume, sir, you have your commission pennant."

Hardcastle nodded and pulled a commission pennant out from under the edge of his jacket. "Yes, I have it here. I picked it up this morning at the office of the dockyard superintendent." He handed it to the lieutenant.

Fergus rose. "Well, Jason—I guess I should call you that now—we seem to be ready. Please lead on."

Essex nodded, rose, and walked out to the quarterdeck and took a position next to the binnacle. Fergus and Hardcastle stood behind him, facing toward the officers and men who were lined up in ranks facing aft.

The senior lieutenant handed the commission pennant to the senior quartermaster, who took position next to the halliard from which the present commission pennant was flying.

Essex looked fondly at the officers and crew and up at the rigging. Fergus noted that Hardcastle followed his eyes and didn't seem to be bothered this time. He hoped that Hardcastle had sensed his disapproval of his conduct and was taking it into account.

Essex said, "Before the change, possibly the commodore would like to say something."

Fergus, not at his best at extemporaneous speaking, colored slightly. "Ah, yes, of course." He stepped forward to the binnacle and Essex stepped aft. Fergus cleared his throat nervously and began. "I know you are used to seeing Captain Essex climb up the rigging every morning."

Someone in the crew snickered loudly in a friendly manner.

Captain Hardcastle allowed a small sneer to flicker across his features.

Fergus looked at Hardcastle. "Maybe Captain Hardcastle won't continue this custom."

Hardcastle again smiled thinly, and the crew knew he would stay on deck.

Fergus went on. "I want to congratulate Captain Essex on a very successful cruise. His ship has performed superbly, and I will miss him. He tells me he will be driving horses around his farm instead of driving his men here."

There was another friendly snicker, and Hardcastle rolled his eyes upward.

Fergus turned to Essex. "Captain, I turn this ceremony back to you. I will miss you." The faintest of tears appeared in Fergus's eyes as he clasped Essex in his arms and patted his back. Essex's eyes were moist, too, and many of his men bore expressions of genuine regret.

Hardcastle suppressed a grimace of disapproval and resumed his inspection of the rigging.

Essex stepped back to the binnacle and waited for his eyes to clear. Then he took a deep breath and began to speak slowly. "Officers and men of the *Diligent,* I leave you with great regret, and I leave you only because I will have to assume greater responsibilities. I think you know I am leaving this ship and the Navy because my father died and left me the responsibility of carrying on his duties as Lord Satterfield. I have no other choice. I am honored to do it, but I still will miss you and this fine ship. I will remember you always, and I wish you smooth sailing and good luck." Essex turned to Captain Hardcastle. "Sir, I am ready to be relieved."

Hardcastle stepped forward and saluted. "Sir, I relieve you and I assume command of his Majesty's Ship *Diligent.*" He turned to the senior quartermaster. "Please hoist my commission pennant."

The quartermaster hauled down the pennant flying and at the same time hoisted the new one, bent on to a similar set of halliards.

Hardcastle turned to Fergus. "Commodore, I report to you for duty."

The ceremony was over. Fergus returned the salute and said, "Very well, sir." There was little warmth in his mien as he turned and headed for the gangway. Essex followed him, seemingly anxious to get on with his new life.

At the bottom of the brow both officers paused and looked back at the ship. Fergus said, "Jason, I don't feel that we gave you much of a ceremony."

Essex nodded. "I agree, but this wasn't the time for it. When you fired the one-gun salute at that sorry French fleet back in the Caribbean, I knew it marked the last phase of my seagoing career. I called my crew together then and made the speech I wanted to make to them. I told them that my father wouldn't last out the cruise and I would be leaving them when we got back. On the cruise I had an opportunity to talk with each officer, petty officer, and each individual man. This meant more to all of us than this ceremony. I only ask one thing of you. Take good care of my ship and crew. I worry about what the new captain will do, but I trust you will keep an eye on him."

Fergus nodded, barely able to speak. "I promise you that I will have that ape up there off in three months. Now let's get in my carriage and go to my flat. I have a large bottle of Scotch waiting for us there. Maybe we can put our feet up, hoist a few, and talk about old times."

"I'd like that, but I want you to remember that as soon as I learn the ropes of my new job, I want to share lots of time with you and my new wife."

"We will. Shannon and I will be looking forward to it."

In the carriage Fergus put out his hand and signaled to the driver. He flicked his whip gently over the horses and picked his way carefully between the piles of supplies on the pier. At the gate he snapped his whip, and the horses took off in a flurry of dried horse manure.

On the quarterdeck, Hardcastle, who had been fidgeting while waiting for the senior officers to leave the area, turned to the senior lieutenant, "Dismiss the crew and come to my cabin in five minutes." He turned on his heel and strode confidently toward the cabin. Then he stopped and looked back over his shoulder at the rigging. "And bring the boatswain with you. We'll get a good start on doing the rigging job right away."

The senior lieutenant frowned. "But, Captain, our rigging was just tarred in anticipation of the ceremony. It's the best in the flotilla now."

Hardcastle turned back to him and said, "You haven't seen a good tarring yet. One more comment like that and you'll be tarring along with the crew in your dress uniform."

"But, Captain."

"That's enough. You will stay in your room for four days."

The lieutenant with the watch muttered to himself, "The bastard is crazy. Commodore Kilburnie will have to rescue us."

CHAPTER 16

Dinner with the King

FOR OVER A MONTH the ships of Fergus's flotilla remained at the piers of the Royal Navy dockyards, conducting much needed maintenance and repairs to the rigging and equipment showing the strain of the many hours of rough weather they had encountered in the channel.

Fergus spent the days getting reacquainted with his pregnant wife. He was sure he would not be present when the next child was born, and he might be in the Mediterranean for the next year or two.

From the conversations in White's, where he was now a member, apparently reliable high government officials were openly predicting Napoleon's next push would be in the Mediterranean basin, and, of course, they all agreed that the Royal Navy would have to meet it. One garrulous but widely respected old gaffer loudly predicted, "Of course it will be to the south. Where else would it be? And who will meet it but our own Admiral Horatio Nelson, of course."

One younger man said, "But he's out in his garden with his flowers going to seed in Surrey. Lady Hamilton will make him into a has-been wimp."

"Never!" the old man bristled. "When the king calls for him, he'll get out of her fat, velvet clutches, put on his boots, and get back to sea. He came into town to buy some clothes the other day."

"How did he look?"

"Fine."

"And his eyes?"

"He could recognize everyone he met and his bad eye was only a little red. I'm sure he can see the enemy."

"Well, I'll take care of him if his aide has to point out the nearest Frenchman."

Fergus chuckled and said to his dinner companion, who happened to be Jason Essex, now totally immersed in his duties as the new Lord Satterfield, "Jason, does this make any sense to you? Do any of these noisy old men know what they are talking about?"

"Of course. That old man is Admiral Minter, or used to be. He knows more about political and military strategy than all the old fuds in the Admiralty put together and that includes us and maybe Admiral Nelson."

"Then I may be in the Mediterranean for some time?"

"Yes, or in some other area, such as the Caribbean. It may keep you away for a year or two. They are saying in the Admiralty that Napoleon is getting crazier every year."

"And I may not see my next child for some time."

"Probably, but I'll see that he is well cared for. By the way, you and Shannon are to be invited to a formal dinner to be given in my honor by Lord St. Vincent in the halls of the Admiralty. The king is going to honor us with his presence."

Two weeks later a footman arrived at Shannon's flat with a heavily engraved envelope addressed to "Commodore and Mrs. Fergus Kilburnie."

She opened it excitedly and read it. She put her hand to her mouth. "Oh, Fergus, I can't go in this state. I have no gown that will fit me anymore." She patted the obvious swelling in her middle.

Fergus laughed, leaned over, and patted her, too. "Do you think your newest child should miss dining with the king?"

Shannon picked up the invitation again and read it carefully. "This doesn't say anything about the king. It says given by Lord St. Vincent in honor of Lord Satterfield. I know Lord St. Vincent is the head of the Admiralty and Jason is the new Lord Satterfield. But it says nothing about the king."

"Jason told me a few days ago that the king would be there. Such information is never put on invitations and I am not allowed to pass it on when told in confidence, but I am sure it is all right to tell you. After all, you have to prepare. I'll take you to your dressmakers tomorrow for a new gown, but you can't tell her why you need it. The fashion right now is just the thing for pregnant ladies. High fashion dictates full skirts. I think every lady in London and on the continent is pregnant now, or if they aren't, they certainly all look like it."

After a flurry of visits to the dressmaker and tailors, both Shannon and Fergus managed to have themselves turned out in time for the dinner.

The designated date found them in their carriage and later at the Admiralty after a ride through downtown London. Both drivers were on the box for safety. Shannon shook her head in wonder as they drove up through the large colonnades of Admiralty Headquarters. "I've never been inside the Admiralty building and never met the king. Now tonight I do both. Do I curtsy when I meet the king?"

"Of course. Nobody will know what you're doing anyway under those full skirts."

"Don't be droll. I'll do it right. Besides, Aunt Martha showed me how."

"And she met the king?"

"Not this one. The one before. But she says it was the night of her lifetime and she remembers it well."

"Well, just do what she told you."

At the Admiralty entrance, Fergus handed Shannon down carefully. "Don't be so obvious," she said. "I won't break. I've been pregnant before, and I've even ridden a horse before and climbed out of a carriage by myself."

Fergus frowned. "Fine. But just be careful. I wouldn't want you to fall on your face in front of the Admiralty and particularly the carriage drivers. They wouldn't know what to do."

"What do you mean?"

"They wouldn't know whether to laugh or to help you smooth down your skirts."

Shannon giggled. "I think you worry more about such a spectacle instead of what it might do to your child."

Fergus said patiently, "Stop baiting me and concentrate on those entry steps."

At dinner Jason was seated next to the king. Fergus was opposite to him with the queen on his left and Shannon on his right where they could hear the king's conversation. Lord St. Vincent, on the other side of the king, began the conversation by regaling him with a recital of Jason's exploits. When Jason began to fidget, Lord St. Vincent relented and said, "I am sure you know of his more serious exploits and adventures than I can tell you."

"Oh, yes," the king said. "He and young Kilburnie over there have contributed a lot of prize money to my treasury. I am grateful to them and am well aware of their histories. I hear the events start back with the Battle of the Nile and end with their splendid actions against the invading French fleet. I understand they not only prevented the invasion of friendly territory but also destroyed a French frigate and captured another. All against a superior force. If you, Lord Satterfield, had stayed in the Navy, I would have had the pleasure of making you both admirals."

Shannon drew in her breath and said quietly to Fergus, "Did you hear that, dear?"

"Yes. But don't count on it. He'd like to promote all of his friends and relatives, too."

The queen couldn't hear too well, but finally interrupted. "What was that, young man?"

"Ah, nothing important, ma'am. My wife was just suggesting a good school for our son."

After dinner, the ladies retreated to a drawing room. The conversation among the gentlemen, fortified by several rounds of port, became political and vocal. At one point the king looked at Fergus. "Kilburnie, I hope you have got this wooden penis thing straightened out. Personally, I delighted in telling my friends and guests about it. I think you know the queen overheard my recital on one occasion and gave me perfect hell that night. Seems she thought the tale should be put on the banned list."

"Oh, yes, sir, it is taken care of. I have the figureheads on my ships made all the same size."

"And you have altered the, er, protuberances?"

"Yes, sir, I have cut down the, er, breasts of two of them and have added to the muscles of the male warrior's chest."

The king guffawed. "Gad!" he said. "Now there is a new story I could use. I'll try it on the queen first."

The groups of men shifted about and the king and Lord St. Vincent moved to a private corner to carry on some state business.

Fergus found himself with two men he had met before at one of Lord Satterfield's dinners. The taller one he remembered as Fletcher Howard, who had held forth for some time on the affairs of what he called the "Irish French problem."

"What, sir!" Satterfield had said. "You mean the Irish revolutionaries when combined with a substantial French landing force could cause Great Britain serious trouble?"

Fergus laughed as he remembered the interesting exchange. Now he said to Howard, "Have you changed your views about the capabilities of the Irish revolutionaries?"

Howard rolled his eyes. "I'm afraid I'm too old for that anymore. Now I just try to clean up the loose ends." He nodded toward the dark-visaged gentleman standing with them. "I am sure you remember Monsieur Pierre

Reynaud. He is of French descent, but he is an Englishman legally, just as I am. Both our mothers are French."

Howard turned to Reynaud, "You will remember Commodore Kilburnie."

Reynaud bowed. "Certainly."

Fergus said, "Ah, yes. We met at one of Lord Satterfield's dinners." He turned to Howard and said, with a gleam in his eye, "But he was more subdued than you were."

Reynaud laughed. "With a French name I had to be more careful. Now I just help Howard with his cleanup chores, as he calls them."

Fergus said, "I don't understand this expression 'cleanup' chores. I thought your Irish blood would flow forever."

Howard sighed. "Let me lead into the subject a little differently. Lord Malin was your present wife's former husband at the time they were living in London. He was a representative of the Irish government. His work was so recognized that—had he lived—I think he would have exchanged his Irish title for an English one. I knew his views well. If he could have safely taken some part in the Irish revolution, he would have accomplished a lot for the cause. I met Shannon, but I never asked her feelings. I don't think she would have participated either."

He paused. "Now to my point. I know Shannon is putting together an organization to raise and run racehorses. She is the largest employer in Donegal and needs more help than she can find."

Fergus was puzzled. "I don't see why this is of any interest to either of us."

Howard continued. "As I said, we are involved in a cleanup operation. We no longer try to foment trouble or make revolutions happen. It is over for us and almost over for the former revolutionaries, unless Napoleon rises again."

Fergus's jaw clenched at the thought. "Well, he won't get far. The Royal Navy won't let him. Now let's get back to the cleanup business. The ladies will be coming back soon."

Howard nodded. "I think you know that most of the important former revolutionaries have been rounded up and confined."

Fergus nodded. "I've heard that. Donegal is peaceful again."

"It is. That's why I'm making this proposition. We have a hundred or so Irish revolutionary veterans. Some are slightly wounded. Others were former minor participants who can't go back to their former residences. Most of them can wield a pitchfork and many of them can ride well."

Fergus caught on. "And you want Shannon to employ them?"

"Yes. It would be a patriotic move, and no one would ever be embarrassed.

I understand it would help her a great deal. Labor in Ireland is getting more and more scarce."

Fergus said, "I'll talk to her and let you know of her decision. Now I see the ladies returning." He nodded to both Howard and Reynaud. "I am glad to have made your acquaintances again. I wish you good luck. You seem to be more peaceful than when we met last time."

On the ride home, Shannon was quiet at first. Then she said, "I don't see why the queen was concerned about that story. After all, the sailor who performed the act was very resourceful."

"Yes, dear, let's drop the subject. I've heard too much about it. I'd rather talk about the way we tricked the French invasion fleet."

Shannon laughed. "We ladies did talk about that."

"And what else?"

"We argued about who was the most handsome man there, you or Jason."

Fergus colored with embarrassment. Then he recovered. "And who won?"

"Neither. We decided that Lord St. Vincent was the most handsome, although some of us thought he was a little past his prime."

The next morning Fergus paused over his heaping dish of Scottish porridge. "Shannon, last night I met a Mister Fletcher Howard and a Monsieur Pierre Reynaud. I had met them before, at a dinner given by Lord Satterfield. They left no doubt they were friends of the Irish revolution."

"But why would the king have them at dinner?"

"Times have changed. Most of the open revolutionaries have long since been rounded up. Howard and Reynaud have regular occupations and have become just barristers again. They do a lot of business with the government."

"And what did they want with you?"

"They wanted me to ask you if you would employ up to a hundred wounded veterans of the revolution who had not been rounded up by the government."

"Why can't they be employed at home?"

"They will be well known at home and might be added to the persons already rounded up."

"How do I know they won't make trouble again?"

"Mister Howard guarantees that they won't, and some of his men would supervise them. I think it is something you patriotic Irish ought to do."

Shannon poured another cup of tea and pondered deeply. "All right. I'll take a chance. Your brother, Ennis, has been telling me that he can't get enough people to work on the estates. All the young men are going to the United States to find work."

"Well, there is certainly an opportunity on our estates. Ennis says the manure is piled very high."

The succeeding weeks were wonderful for Fergus and Shannon. Although the threat of Fergus having to leave hung over them, the fall days passed by in endless pleasure with their children.

On the first of November, 1802, the idyllic fall ended when a messenger arrived at the flagship as Fergus was inspecting the workmanship of the yard. He opened the embossed envelope and read the orders he pulled out of it.

Poston, standing nearby, asked, "Is this it?"

Fergus nodded and handed the orders to him. "They say I have a week to get the flotilla in shape and we are to depart on the sixteenth for the Mediterranean."

"Just what are we to do there? Admiral Nelson is still resting in Surrey. If he's not with us, then there won't be any action there."

"True, but it won't be long before Napoleon stirs things up down there, and he'll come down to take over. Besides, Admiral Collingwood is there, and Admiral Nelson thinks very highly of him. If Admiral Nelson thinks highly of him, then we do, too."

During the final week of preparation, Commodore Kilburnie made a thorough inspection of all his ships, including the *Daring.* Poston had been left in charge of the overhaul, and he had done the excellent job Fergus had expected of him.

The two sloops were commanded by Navy captains who were well qualified and were in line for bigger commands. Fergus spent a minimum of time inspecting the smaller ships, and left well satisfied.

The *Dashing,* with young Puller now in command, was inspected more thoroughly. His youth and inexperience warranted a thorough check. From the moment he stepped aboard, Fergus knew she was in excellent shape. Puller brimmed with confidence and insisted on informing the commodore about each man responsible for its condition. To Fergus, the confident, happy expression on each face made him decide that Puller would be an admiral some day.

Fergus saved the *Diligent* for last. He had not seen much of Captain Hardcastle during the overhaul. The *Diligent* was moored astern, and from the *Daring*'s quarterdeck he could easily see the activity on deck. The outward appearance of the ship was better than his own ship. The paintwork gleamed under new varnish, the rigging was taut, and where it was recently tarred, that showed, too.

But something stirred in Fergus's gut. On the days when he had been aboard and had been walking on his own quarterdeck, he noticed that when his own men had been painting and tarring, they wore old paint-stained clothing. Those on the *Diligent* doing the same work were wearing spotless uniforms, and he wondered how they could work well under such conditions. Something was clearly wrong.

The week before Radcliffe had come back from shopping with a strange tale. The steward was one of the few sailors allowed to leave the ship and had been ashore filling the captain's larder for the forthcoming cruise.

"How did your trip ashore go?" Fergus had asked.

Radcliffe frowned. "The provisions part of it was all right, but I ran into the *Diligent*'s steward ashore on the same mission."

"And?"

Radcliffe sighed. "Sir, maybe it's not right that I should be telling you this."

Fergus said, "I'd say it's something important. I'll hold anything you say in confidence."

Radcliffe sighed and began. "Well, Sasser, Captain Hardcastle's steward, was very unhappy." Then he paused.

Fergus encouraged him. "Go ahead."

"It seems the crew hates Captain Hardcastle and that seems to rub off on Sasser."

"Why does the crew hate him? I haven't seen much of him, and I must admit he's not a very pleasant person. What does he do to irritate them?"

"I think he does more than irritate the crew. He says that unless they do what he says and do it right now, he'll have them all on the grating as soon as they get to sea."

"Does the crew believe this?"

"Sasser says they do, and they hope you'll do something about him."

"Give me some examples."

"Well, I heard you comment on the fact that they always did dirty work and painting in their best uniforms. Sasser says having to wear good uniforms like that cuts their work production in half."

"And that's bad?"

"Yes, sir, some say they have to work slowly, trying to save their good uniforms, and they have to work twice as long. Even in port he cuts their rum and food rations."

"Well, thank you, Radcliffe, and I'll keep a close eye on the *Diligent.*"

Radcliffe paused. Then he said, "You know, sir, the crew calls him 'the Ferret.'"

"Why so? I didn't notice any particular resemblance to an animal."

"You don't see him in action, sir. When he's going around the ship his eyes squint and his nose seems to stick out further and quivers."

"But it's not that long."

"The crew thinks it is. He pokes it into everything, and they hate it."

"Now I'll have to look a little closer. When he's on my ship his eyes are usually on my rigging."

"And his nose, sir?"

"Well, it is long, I guess, and his hair is a little too long, too."

"It's the times you don't see him and when he's not on guard that he looks most like a ferret. You can't miss the resemblance."

Fergus went to the quarterdeck and began to pace up and down thinking about what Radcliffe had just told him. Now and then he glanced over at the *Diligent.* He shook his head. There might be trouble there. He knew he had been spoiled by having such good captains in the past.

Fergus spent his last three days ashore with his family, trying to forget his new troubles. There would be plenty of time at sea to take care of such things. Now, as he spent as much time as he could with Shannon and the children, he wondered how he could stand being away from them for a year or more. Maybe it was time for him to think about retiring. After all, Jason Essex had done it, and he was as happy as he had ever seen him.

CHAPTER 17

Deserters

FERGUS SAID GOODBYE to his family and had the carriage driver drop him at his ship at 8 A.M. Their departure had been scheduled for a favorable tide at noon, and after a frugal lunch at 11 A.M. Fergus came to the quarterdeck to observe the preparations for getting under way. All was quiet on the *Daring* and *Dashing* as the crews checked the furling of the sails that had been hoisted and set the day before.

On the *Diligent,* however, the crew ran about, seemingly without purpose. Captain Hardcastle strode up and down on the quarterdeck shouting commands. He was too far away for Fergus to understand what he was saying, but Lombardi, giving orders in a near operatic tenor, stopped and laughed. "Her sailing master is very good. Soon he'll stop listening to his captain and give the orders he knows have to be given to get the ship under way. You can rest assured, Commodore, the ship will get under way."

Fergus couldn't stand watching the *Diligent* very long, so he concentrated on watching the changing tide, the medium offshore breeze, and the traffic in the channel. Unless Hardcastle panicked completely, all he had to do was take in his lines and hoist his courses. The tide and breeze would carry his ship out into the channel following the *Daring.*

Poston laughed. "An easy job. Any midshipman could do it. Maybe he'll forget to cast off his lines."

Fergus relaxed a little. "Well, Poston, let's let Midshipman Searles take us out."

Poston sent for Midshipman Searles, who trotted up and saluted. Poston said, "Searles, take the ship out. I'll give you the course when you have her fair in the channel."

Searles's eyes widened, and he stuttered slightly, but he took a deep breath and said, "Aye, aye, sir." He looked at the chronometer in the binnacle. "At noon, I believe, sir."

"Good. You took the first step right, to confirm the time. Now, what is the second step?"

Searles was getting confident. "When the quartermaster strikes the bell eight, I order the lines taken in."

"Good. Now I'll stop bothering you. Mister Lombardi will get you out safely. Just remember to give him the order to hoist sails."

Fergus was so entranced listening to Poston break in the new midshipman that he forgot to look aft at the ships getting ready to follow him. Five minutes later he looked aft at the *Diligent.* She was under way all right, but her decks looked like they were covered with ants as the crew ran about, apparently trying to escape Captain Hardcastle's lashing tongue. Amidships a mooring line still trailed in the water. "Damn!" Poston said, "This won't do."

Fergus shook his head. "Not for long, anyway."

On the first night Fergus had his officers in to dinner in his cabin. The room was crowded, but the atmosphere was pleasant and the conversation spirited. Poston, on Fergus's right, was a constant source of light stories, almost all of which were about himself, or at least he was the butt of them, but he didn't hesitate to bring his captain down with a humorous riposte. No longer the young man who had been a fellow quartermaster with Fergus, Poston was now slightly gray and bulged a little in the middle. The commodore, with daily exercise, had maintained his physique, but Poston was gradually going downhill toward old age. Both, however, were growing slightly bald.

Lieutenant Ballinger, an older man, kept up with Poston, but Lieutenant Harrall, the younger by far, said little unless Poston prodded him. When one of Harrall's answers revealed an erudite streak, Poston was curious enough to ask, "Have you been to university?"

"Yes. A year or two. My parents couldn't afford any more." Harrall had a high forehead and a retiring manner. When prodded by two rums, he could manage a reasonable baritone that made him sound enough like Lombardi that they managed a passable duet.

The three midshipmen, who had reported on board just before the ship left, were seated at the other end of the table and kept a discreet silence until Fergus, at dessert time, began to question them in a friendly manner. They put down their forks and responded well, sensing the friendliness in the commodore's tone. Searles, still savoring his triumph, as least in the eyes of the other midshipmen in bringing the ship out, spoke up freely, but Nottingham and Briscoe talked very little and then in hushed tones. Fergus had sensed some potential in Searles and had chosen him over the others to conn the ship. Perhaps it was his slim, muscular figure and his keen look; the other two still carried a lot of baby fat.

Near the midshipmen sat the surgeon, boatswain, and the gunner, and at mid-table was the sailing master, Anthony Lombardi, his rank really the equivalent of the lieutenants. His pleasant voice carried the conversation at his part of the table, his dark face typical of Southern Italians. On his left, Gunner O'Farrell, a dark-visaged Irishman, perhaps was a descendant of the Portuguese or Italians who had been shipwrecked on the west coast of Ireland years ago. There was an affinity between the Italian and the Irishman that neither could explain, but they got along very well. O'Farrell was an expert with explosives and a gunner par excellence.

Boatswain Belltron was a pot-bellied older seaman, a veteran of twenty-six years at sea. His hands were like leather after years of handling rough lines, and his face was equally leathery from sun, wind, and saltwater. Fergus depended heavily on his warrant officers and Lombardi and the surgeon, Pollitt, sitting at the middle of the table. Now he included them all in his conversation and took the opportunity to praise each of them.

The dinner was very pleasant, and when it broke up Fergus found himself wondering if like gatherings were taking place on his other ships. He was sure Captain Hardcastle was dining in solitary splendor and would continue to do so.

For the next week the flotilla cruised south down the English Channel and along the French coast bound for Gibraltar. Although the officers and men were mostly veterans, Fergus knew they were rusty after weeks in the shipyard. He started the crews with single gun firings and worked up to broadside salvos. Between times he ordered loading exercises, designed to check safety precautions and to speed up the rate of fire. He maneuvered the ships by flag hoists and at night by hooded lanterns.

At the end of two weeks, he thought his ships were ready to meet and beat any French ship they might meet. As they sailed east along the Spanish coast, on the last leg of the voyage that led to Gibraltar, the smell of orange blossoms wafted out on the land breeze, and Fergus remembered visits to Gibraltar in his early days as a lieutenant and as a ship captain. Now he was older, and his thoughts turned to plans for topping off the supplies of the flotilla in a short port visit before proceeding to Toulon and reporting for duty to Admiral Collingwood.

On the morning of 20 December, on the flood tide, the flotilla stood in and was ordered to berth alongside a long jetty. Fergus, his ship leading the way, took aboard a pilot and gave him the conn. "Morning, Captain," he said. "She's yours. Treat her decently."

The pilot tested the steering by taking the wheel himself for a few minutes. Then he turned the wheel back to the regular steersman, stepped back, and looked aloft. "She's a beautiful and fast ship. You're a lucky man. And you have three just like her."

The pilot conferred with Lombardi for a few minutes. Then Lombardi made the sail changes the pilot asked for and the pilot headed for the far section of the jetty. The tide and the light offshore wind seemed to be just what he wanted, and he waved away the pulling boat designed to act as a tug. The ship moved directly into the berth, and when he judged she had just enough way to arrive, he ordered the remaining sails taken in. Almost miraculously the sails fluttered down and the ship coasted into the jetty. At the last minute the pilot called for a change of helm, and the ship eased gently alongside. The men on deck threw over heaving lines followed by the mooring lines picked up by black Moors waiting on the pier.

Even before the ship was secured, the pilot saluted Fergus and headed for the sea ladder and into the waiting pulling boat. He was off for the *Dashing* with a wave and in a few minutes brought her alongside the *Daring* without a scratch.

The *Diligent* was berthed by the ever-present pilot behind the first two ships, and the fast sloop captains, with their better maneuverability, waved the pilot off and brought their ships astern of the *Diligent.*

Radcliffe came up to Fergus as he stood on the quarterdeck watching the other ships. "Commodore, I hear we're to stay here over Christmas. May I go ashore and get some Christmas provisions for a Christmas dinner in your cabin?"

Fergus called Poston over. "Radcliffe, take the cook and purser with you and tell them to buy enough provisions to make a splendid Christmas dinner for the crew." Then he turned to Poston. "Don't we have a butt of brandy that we requisitioned for the surgeon?"

"Oh, yes, for medical purposes."

"Well, we'll use it now. A mug for each man after Christmas dinner and a double ration of rum before dinner."

Poston scratched his chin. "Commodore, if I may go with them, I know an innkeeper well. For a few pounds, I can induce his six waitresses to wait on us, so to speak. They sing well, too, and I can round up Lombardi's singing group for a little entertainment after dinner."

"This all sounds first-rate," Fergus said. "Send word to the other ships that they may do the same. I'll give you some personal funds for the waitresses and anything else you need. Just remember, the ladies have to get ashore by the next day. We sail at 1 P.M. on the day after Christmas. Now off you go, all of you."

Fergus left that afternoon to call on the port captain and was invited to stay for dinner. When he returned, the ships of the flotilla seemed to be settling down. Fergus knew they would be working hard for the next two days loading provisions and supplies, and he hoped the other captains would follow his example and give their crews a hearty Christmas dinner and a full holiday. It might be months before they could afford to take that much time off.

The next morning, as Fergus was shaving, the messenger knocked loudly on the door.

"Yes," Fergus called.

"Commodore, Captain Hardcastle is here and he says it is urgent."

"I'm dressing. Tell him I'll be with him in a few minutes and tell Radcliffe to get coffee ready."

In a few minutes Fergus opened the cabin door. Captain Hardcastle was pacing up and down outside. "Good morning, Captain," Fergus said. "Come in, sit down, and we'll have coffee in a minute."

Hardcastle was grim-faced. and he threw himself into a chair without even saying good morning.

Fergus sat down slowly. "This seems to be serious. What's the trouble?"

Hardcastle burst out, his voice trembling, "Commodore, I've just completed a careful muster, and I have to report I have six deserters."

"I suppose you searched all of your ship."

"Thoroughly, sir, and they are gone. They have deserted, and I want the local authorities to apprehend them and return them as soon as possible. I'll have them court-martialed right away for desertion." Hardcastle paused, waved away Radcliffe's offer of coffee, and started talking again.

"Whoa!" Fergus interrupted. "I need some coffee even if you don't. I don't understand why you have that many deserters if the other ships don't have any."

Hardcastle gritted his teeth and took in a deep breath. "The crew I have must be the dregs of the Navy. I think I have more than they have of bad ones, and I expect to sort out more. I'd like permission to send an armed search party ashore to apprehend and return them."

"Of course you can't," Fergus replied. "The army won't let you because they think they'll start an altercation with the local police. You don't seem to realize that Gibraltar is garrisoned with a very strong army force designed to keep the Spanish and French out. They certainly can keep your men from getting out to Spain. I'll wager they'll bring your men back by tomorrow."

Hardcastle rose, his lips grimly set. "Good morning, sir. I see I'll get no help here, but I won't leave my ship. Neither will anyone else. I'll double my sentries."

Fergus sighed patiently. "Hardcastle, I remind you that Christmas is just a few days away. All the other captains are making arrangements for Christmas festivities aboard. I suggest you relax a little and do the same."

Hardcastle shook his head. "No, sir. They haven't earned it. Good day, sir."

About noon the next day, in the middle of loading operations, Poston knocked on Fergus's door, poked his head in, and grinned. "Commodore, come on out in a hurry. You've got to see this first hand."

Fergus pushed back his chair and strode out to the quarterdeck. Poston pointed to an army officer in full dress and sword, marching down the pier. The officer turned, climbed the brow carefully so as not to entangle his dangling sword sheath, saluted the colors and officer of the watch, and said, "Your commodore, if you please."

The officer of the watch returned the salute and pointed at Fergus. The army officer turned on his heel carefully, clanking his sword, and saluted smartly. "Major Kilmer," he said. "I have a delivery to make to you."

Fergus looked puzzled, and Poston pointed up the pier. "There," he said.

Fergus was still puzzled. "And what on earth are they doing?"

"'Frog marching,' or more accurately being 'frog marched.' I've seen it done before."

"But what are those other soldiers doing? I take it those four men are some of our deserters. They look like they are running a few inches off the ground. And why are they being followed by a squad of soldiers?"

Poston laughed. "Frog marching is hard work. You'll see that every hundred yards some of the soldiers will move up forward and take the places of the men holding up the deserters."

"And what is happening to our men?"

"Each soldier puts one hand on the culprit's collar and the other hand on his buttocks and lifts."

"And then?"

"Lifts him almost off the ground and marches him forward with his feet hanging down."

"My God! That must hurt."

The British officer laughed and interrupted. "It most certainly does, sir. Their butts will be raw for days."

Fergus let out his breath. "I take it they are our men. If so, please turn them over to the frigate aft of us, the *Diligent.*"

The army officer raised his hand to get the attention of the sergeant in charge and pointed to the *Diligent's* brow. The sergeant nodded and changed the direction of the group toward its proper destination.

Fergus said, "I'm afraid to look at Captain Hardcastle."

"I'm not. He looks like he's lost his last friend."

Fergus turned to the army officer. "Major, I think we had six deserters. Can you tell me what happened to the other two?"

"All of them must have been very desperate. They had no chance of crossing the border, and they should have known this. Even Napoleon and all his armies couldn't do it on the way in."

"And our men tried anyway?"

"The fastest got by the first of our sentries and was shot down by the Spanish. They returned him to us. The second we shot in the leg. The rest saw the light and gave up."

"And what happened to the bodies?"

"They weren't killed. It is customary to shoot deserters in the legs. They are in our hospital and will be put in our brig after they have recovered. They will be dealt with pending your instructions."

"I'd rather you turned them all over to the port captain. They'll all end up there for court-martial."

"I thought as much. I'll send our paddywagon for them tomorrow, and I'll deliver them. They won't be able to walk for a while."

The next day Fergus went aft to the *Diligent,* boarded her, and asked Captain Hardcastle to be allowed to see the prisoners. "Alone," he added.

Hardcastle followed him to the brig and retired a reasonable distance. The four men were lying on their stomachs. Fergus clasped the bars and started talking to the nearest prisoner. "I'm Commodore Kilburnie. May I ask why all of you did such a stupid thing?"

The prisoner stirred. "Sir, it may have seemed stupid, but to keep on staying in this hellhole with that slave driver over there was worse."

Fergus tried to get the others to talk, but they turned their faces away and remained silent. After a few minutes he gave up and went back to the quarterdeck. He left, grim-faced and stiff-backed, not even bothering to return

Hardcastle's salute. When he returned to the *Daring,* he sent for Poston and Searles, who had been appointed as the commodore's secretary because of his education and skills at speaking and writing.

When the two arrived, Fergus, still grim-faced, said, "We have a long-time bad situation here. I'll have to prefer charges against Captain Hardcastle eventually. I'll need written evidence. Lieutenant Poston will dictate the events of this incident. I'll fill in later with my observations of past incidents, and from time to time in the future we'll add to the written evidence. When we reach our senior flag officer, I'll take the necessary action."

CHAPTER 18

Interrogation

FERGUS HAD RECOVERED from his distress over the problems on the *Diligent* by Christmas Eve and took pains to assist in arrangements for the crew's Christmas dinner. The cook, Radcliffe, and the purser came back from shopping with several crates of chickens, bags of potatoes, and a dozen pans of plum duff. Also in the wagon were crates of oranges and bags of nuts. Fergus watched them come aboard and was struck by the physical differences in the three men. Even so, when they went ashore they worked together like three brothers. The purser, Mustafa, who was in charge, wore a black coat, hat, and knee breeches and lent dignity to their dealings with the shore-side merchants. He was a slightly dark Levanter who had been in the Royal Navy for about twenty years. His Mediterranean features made those who saw him ashore think he was Jewish. Actually he was a devout Muslim and played his presumed characteristics against the merchants he dealt with. The cook always came back from a trip ashore with some new tale about how Mustafa had driven yet another bargain with a merchant.

The cook was a burly Londoner, probably sixty years old and slightly rheumatic, but his warm galley kept his joints limber. Few members of the crew knew that his name was Stafford, and he was always known as "Cook" or, to his friends, "Cookie."

Radcliffe was strikingly different from the other two. Where they were dark and fierce, or fat and doughy, he was slim, dark, and handsome—so handsome, in fact, that rumors flew about the ship that he might be homosexual. It was not true, and the culprit who started the rumor received a late-night visit from the purser. It was soon discovered that the culprit now bore a thin crescent carved on his forehead by a small razor-sharp knife carried in the bootleg of the purser. He had placed a strong hand on the face of the culprit and neatly incised the figure before the man could cry out. When this failed to quiet the culprit, a second visit was made by the cook. His two strapping arms, strengthened by years of kneading dough, put a painful knot in the neck of his patient. Rumors flew no more.

Radcliffe innocently walked about the ship, little knowing that no one dared to question him in any way. His dark black hair, brown eyes, and fair Welsh skin made his twenty-five years look like twenty.

Fergus liked the trio who were so important to well-being of his ship. Mustafa saw to the purchase of the best available provisions. The cook did his best to transform those provisions, plus the dried supplies they always carried, into palatable food. His task was unusually difficult because the provisions purchased and furnished by the Admiralty were known for having countless weevils. The cook had tried to pass them off as miniature crawfish once, but that had been his only failure. Mustafa was able to find spices, strong molasses, flavorings, and other additives that allowed the cook to succeed regularly.

Radcliffe was allowed to purchase additional canned and preserved food for the commodore. Fergus lived in relative splendor until the additions ran out. Then he lived on the fare produced by the cook and fancied up by Radcliffe.

In some way or other, the three contrived to keep the captain, officers, and crew reasonably happy, and Fergus appreciated it.

Radcliffe reported after their trip ashore that all ships except the *Diligent* were getting ready for a large dinner.

"And the *Diligent* cook?"

"I didn't see him ashore."

"And the waitresses?"

"Lieutenant Poston got the best waitresses in town, but the other ships won't be left out completely. They each have a few."

Christmas dinner started with the double rum rations promised by the commodore. By dinner time, the crew was ready to eat anything that didn't move; by dark, the kitchen was cleaned out. Radcliffe brought aboard several candles to illuminate the weather deck. After the crew had finished their dinner in the lower deck spaces, they came topside and waited for the issue of mugs of brandy.

Fergus, who had hosted a dinner for the officers in his cabin, came out to preside over the issue of the brandy. As he came on deck, the crew cheered loudly, and the crew of the *Dashing* alongside joined in. Fergus raised his hand and pointed to the keg of brandy. A line formed in front of it, and in a few minutes it was nearly empty, as was the keg Fergus had sent to the ship alongside.

Lombardi gathered his choral group, and they ran through all the carols they knew. Lombardi arranged with the *Dashing* to borrow the piper they had uncovered, and Lombardi broke out his flute. The boatswain improvised a drum out of the empty brandy barrel and a broomstick.

The combination soon had the crews of both ships and the waitresses dancing. Those not lucky to await a turn with the waitresses danced by themselves or stood by and clapped. As usual with sailors, several turned out to be able to dance a respectable hornpipe, and the purser, when urged, gave a Turkish version that drew cheers. Soon the decks were a whirling mass of dancers that kept going until midnight when Fergus called a halt and sent them below. As the last man disappeared down the hatch, Fergus turned to Poston, "Where are the waitresses?"

Poston rolled his eyes. "I'm not sure you want me to find out."

Fergus smiled. "Remember, they have to be ashore by noon tomorrow."

The next morning there were several foggy heads, but the flotilla would be ready to leave on the evening tide.

Fergus asked Radcliffe, "What happened on the *Diligent* last night?"

"Nothing, sir. They didn't even come topside to dance to our music."

Fergus sighed. "Well, just one more incident to put in our Hardcastle log."

Even though it was Christmas Day, Fergus went to the port captain's office to make a farewell call, and to ask for his advice about where to report to the commander-in-chief for duty. Fortunately the port captain had come into his office to pick up some documents, and he asked Fergus to come in.

Fergus asked, "Captain, I have orders to report to the commander-in-chief of the Mediterranean Force. Where do you suggest I go first?"

The captain laughed. "He's been blockading Toulon for a long time. I'm sure you'll find him there. By the way, I'll be trying the six deserters soon."

"Thank you. I hope you'll treat them with compassion. The captain of the *Diligent* has given them a hard time."

"That's what I understood when I talked with them. I'll take that into consideration. I suggest you consider getting him replaced."

"I will. Thank you for your help. My men and I had a very merry Christmas."

"I understand you are leaving on the evening tide."

"Yes, I've already stretched my orders."

"I suggest you conduct a search of the area on the way to Toulon. You might pick up a stray French warship or a merchant ship sneaking between ports."

"I will, Captain. Again, thanks for all your help."

At 4 P.M., the flotilla got under way, with the first two frigates conned out by the same pilot who had brought them in. He was a little grumpy at being called out on Christmas Day, but a tot or two of Fergus's leftover brandy soon brightened his smile. He took the *Dashing* out first, then came back for the *Daring.* When he climbed up the sea ladder, he grinned and said, "That was hard work, Commodore. Would you have any more of that brandy?"

"Of course. The steward will bring it up to you. As a matter of fact, he'll make it a double because you have to take the *Diligent* out next. There won't be much Christmas spirit over there."

"I noticed an unpleasant atmosphere over there when I brought her in. Do you know what's wrong? Some strange disease perhaps?"

"I know what's wrong," Fergus said, "and there'll be some treatment for it in the next port."

Before dark the flotilla was on an easterly course, bound for Toulon, and Fergus formed them in a scouting line, ten miles apart.

For two days they sailed with a moderate westerly wind. Fergus let them alone to cure their hangovers.

On the third day, the wind shifted to the east, and it was necessary to tack into it. All night long, Fergus tried to order them to tack into it at the same time every four hours.

Poston approved of the plan. "This way we work the sails with both watches and they lose a minimum of sleep."

For two days the plan worked well, but on the third night something went very wrong. Just after midnight, when the tacks were ordered and should have been made, Fergus heard loud shouting on the quarterdeck. He grabbed his trousers and ran out, adjusting them rapidly as he went. Just as he arrived, he could see the bow of the *Diligent* looming in the darkness on the starboard side. "Good God! Wear ship!" he shouted. "Left full rudder!"

The ship began to swing, and then came parallel to the closing *Diligent.*

Just as the ships were about to collide, the *Daring*'s bow continued to swing, and the distance opened.

"Damn!" yelled Fergus. "That was close!" He turned to the midshipman who had the watch. "Why didn't you take avoiding action?"

The midshipman stammered, "Well, sir, I thought the other ship was about to take the action that had been ordered."

"Well, young man, you learned a valuable lesson. Of course you had her on your starboard bow and she legally had the right of way, but never trust the other ship. Always remember to take care of yourself."

"But, sir, she was supposed to tack at midnight. We made the proper signal, and she answered."

"Of course. I'll find out what happened in the morning. In the meantime we'll stay on this course the rest of the night. Now think over your sins for the rest of the watch."

After breakfast the next morning, Fergus hoisted the signal to lie to and then called for his gig to be lowered. Poston was startled. "But, Commodore, why don't you order the guilty party to come over here?"

"I'd like to talk to some of the other witnesses over there. If I bring the captain over here, a lot of the truth will be left behind."

Fergus sat glumly in the stern sheets of his gig as it was rowed over. Once alongside the *Diligent,* he climbed the sea ladder and saluted the colors and the officer of the watch. He turned to Captain Hardcastle, who was waiting for him on the quarterdeck with his usual glowering expression. "Captain, I'd like to see you in your cabin."

Fergus followed Hardcastle into his cabin, and both entered stiffly. Without even saying good morning, Hardcastle motioned to a chair. Fergus sat down quietly, and Hardcastle remained standing.

Fergus said, "Please sit down. This is just a call so far and not necessarily an inquisition."

Hardcastle pursed his lips. "Sir, I'd prefer to stand."

Fergus shook his head, and in a firm voice said, "I said to sit down. Now sit."

Hardcastle frowned but sat down gingerly.

Fergus took a deep breath and began. "Captain, about midnight last night I gave the flotilla by hooded lantern the order to tack to port, but apparently your ship failed to tack. Twenty minutes later we almost collided. Can you give me any reason for this near disaster?"

Hardcastle sniffed. "I don't remember getting any such signal."

"Where were you at midnight?"

"I was expecting to receive your signal, and I was on the quarterdeck."

"And you didn't hear the officer of the watch repeat the signal to you?"

"Well, no, I don't think that he did."

"What were you doing at the time?"

"As I remember it, I was occupying my time by writing a report by the light of the binnacle."

"Well, Captain, you have stated your case clearly."

"As I remember it, I had you on my port bow and therefore had the right of way."

"Of course. That's why I took avoiding action to prevent a collision, but you seem to have no clear understanding of what happened. Now please send in the officer who had the watch when this happened. Please wait outside."

"But if you are to interrogate him, I'd like to be here when you do it."

"You should already have interrogated him before I got here and have all the facts. Apparently you don't. Now please carry out my orders."

Hardcastle rose stiffly and stalked out. In a few minutes a young lieutenant came in, saluted, and removed his hat. "Lieutenant Roscoe, sir."

Fergus nodded at him pleasantly. "Please sit down. Now tell me the events of the near collision last night."

Lieutenant Roscoe cleared his throat nervously. He was apprehensive facing the commodore, but he wanted to tell his story. "Sir, at about midnight last night, just after I relieved the watch, I observed two hooded lanterns in the flagship. I directed the quartermaster to answer them and reported the facts to the captain."

"Where was he at the time?"

"He was leaning into the binnacle writing a long report by its light."

"Did he acknowledge your report?"

"As well as he ever does when he's writing a report. He mumbled something about not disturbing him. I knew I was not supposed to tack without orders from him as long as he was on deck. I reported again, and he mumbled something again and said clearly, 'Don't bother me.'"

"I thought about carrying out your orders to tack anyway, but I'd taken independent action before, and it didn't work out too well."

"What happened?"

"I was ordered to my room for four days."

Fergus chuckled. "I can see your reasoning for your actions. Please do not repeat this conversation to anyone. I will correct this problem as soon as we join our commander-in-chief. I will see that you do not suffer for your frank testimony or for your actions."

Back on the flagship, Poston asked, "What happened?"

"Just as I expected. The captain was knee deep in his damned papers."

"Are you going to discipline him, sir?"

"Not really. He's too far gone for that. I'm going to get rid of him in Toulon."

Fergus was careful to tack only in the daytime for the rest of the trip. He always kept a wary eye on the *Diligent,* day or night. In a week the flotilla arrived off Toulon. As they approached, Fergus could see a forest of masts in the harbor, which he judged to be French warships under blockade. Off the entrance a half dozen British warships sailed slowly up and down, obviously ready to react if any of the French ships came out of the harbor.

Fergus looked over the large ships and found one at anchor. Admiral Collingwood's flag was flying from her. He anchored nearby and directed his other ships to anchor at their pleasure. Meeting with Admiral Collingwood would be a new experience for him, and he hoped it would produce new life for the *Diligent.* Her crew had taken about all they could bear.

CHAPTER 19

A New Captain

As his gig made its way to the flagship, Fergus fingered the envelope containing his report on Captain Hardcastle. He wondered how he should approach the commander-in-chief on the Hardcastle matter. Certainly he should not open his call with a negative matter. First he would have to report the arrival of his command for duty, and ask for instructions, and then get to know his admiral a little. Then, as a last matter, he could bring up Hardcastle.

Fergus stirred on the hard thwart to ease the pain in his muscles. He shifted his buttocks and then eased his back, but neither movement helped.

He remembered all he could about Admiral Collingwood. He had never met him but had seen him across the room at social affairs. Collingwood was short and blockily built, bordering on plump. His features were heavy, and his eyes large and black. His dominant feature was his eyebrows, thick and black. Those who knew him described him as very intelligent, quick in conversation, and a strict disciplinarian. Fergus wondered if that meant he would take his side in the Hardcastle matter, or might not and would stand up for Hardcastle, but he guessed that Collingwood would be on his side.

Fergus stirred again on the uncomfortable thwart and remembered that Admiral Nelson had described Collingwood as a "superb tactician. One you would like to have on your side in a battle." Well, that was something else in his favor, and it was enough for him. He would have to expect the best.

The coxswain brought the gig smartly alongside, and Fergus rose, walked forward in the boat, and mounted the ladder. He did not expect Admiral Collingwood to be on deck to meet him, but the officer standing there in an admiral's uniform could be none other. Fergus recognized him readily, saluted, and walked over to him. Collingwood grinned in a friendly manner and held out his hand. "Welcome," he said. "Admiral Nelson has told me a lot about you and your flotilla. Please follow me into my cabin for some refreshment."

The cabin was large and well appointed with thick drapes and heavy furniture. On one side table was a very large silver bowl of oranges. Collingwood ordered his steward to bring port and invited Fergus to sit on one of two ornate leather chairs. He walked over to the sideboard and picked up a plate, knife, and fork, and a large orange. "Will you join me?" he asked.

Before Fergus could open his mouth to answer, the admiral sat down, plunged the fork into the orange and began to peel it. "You should eat an orange or a lemon at least once a day. It will ward off scurvy."

Fergus was so preoccupied watching Admiral Collingwood that he forgot to answer.

Collingwood raised his eyebrows inquiringly at the silence.

Fergus colored slightly and said, "Er, no, thank you. I have already eaten my lemon for today. My steward is waiting on my quarterdeck with four crates of oranges we picked up in Gibraltar. He will bring them over to you when I return."

"Ah, thank you for your thoughtful gesture. You will soon appreciate such small events as your visit and your thoughtful gifts. They help the monotonous days pass. I have been on this ship for almost a year without having been ashore, just staring at the masts of the damned dagos over there."

Fergus cleared his throat. "I have another small gift as well. One of my sloops captured a small fishing vessel yesterday. We paid the captain of the vessel for his catch. I will have most of it sent over to you."

"Good. We want to treat the small people both at sea and ashore in a friendly manner, and the fishermen are a good source of intelligence. You are learning the blockade art very rapidly. Let me give you some instructions as to your routine. I'll send you on patrol tomorrow. Your area will be from here to Gibraltar. I suggest you spread your ships along the south coast of France, but try not to fall into a routine that they might anticipate. I will send you either to Gibraltar or Sardinia every four months to water and provision. Frankly, the days will pass very slowly. Learn to be patient."

Fergus sensed that Collingwood had finished his part of the business and decided it was time to bring up the Hardcastle matter. He drew the folder containing his notes out from under the edge of his jacket. "Sir, I must bring up a very unpleasant matter. I ask that you remove the captain of the *Diligent,* a Captain Hardcastle. I have in this folder the particulars of his continuing misconduct." Fergus rose and handed the folder to the admiral.

Collingwood opened it, glanced at it quickly, and tossed it on the sideboard next to the large bowl of oranges. "Thank you, Commodore, but I'd prefer a quick oral briefing. Go ahead."

Fergus cleared his throat. "Sir, Captain Hardcastle was assigned by the Admiralty just before the beginning of this cruise to relieve Captain Essex.

Captain Hardcastle had been assigned for several years to the administrative section of the Admiralty. I am afraid his poor performance of duty reflects this lack of sea duty."

Collingwood raised his hand. "Enough. I know him." He got up and paced up and down. Then he stopped, and a grin flitted across his heavy face. "Ah, I have just the solution. He is an excellent writer and administrator. I can use him on my staff."

"But, sir, I don't want to burden you."

"You won't. You will be solving a problem for me, too. I have a Captain Sherrill who has been acting as my chief of staff for six months. Frankly he can write his name, but not much else. Captain Sherrill had been wounded, removed from his ship, and was waiting to recover before being shipped home. My chief of staff was invalided home six months ago. It seemed only natural to use Sherrill as my chief of staff. It was a huge mistake. My records and reports are in a shambles, and I think the Admiralty thinks I have ceased to exist. Hardcastle could straighten all this out in a week."

"But, sir, what about Captain Sherrill?"

"You will like him. His crew worshipped him, and he's a superb shiphandler and a courageous fighter." Collingwood smiled. "Beside, he's your only choice. If you aren't satisfied, stop by again in four months."

Fergus suppressed a sigh. "Yes, sir. Thank you, sir."

"I'll send him over to the *Diligent* tomorrow. In the meantime please prepare Captain Hardcastle."

"Aye, aye, sir. I'm sure he'll want to appeal to you. He's been saving up reams of reports to give you."

Collingwood also sighed. "Send him over, reports and all. I'll solve the problem. In the meantime, I suggest you talk to him tonight and prepare him. Maybe he'll realize the arrangement is the best for all. Once again, thank you for the oranges and fish."

Fergus rose and took his departure. The trip back was shorter and easier, and the uncomfortable thwart didn't seem so hard at all.

When Fergus returned to the *Daring,* Captain Hardcastle, large portfolio under his arm, was pacing the quarterdeck. As soon as Fergus had saluted the quarterdeck, Hardcastle said, "Sir, I request permission to call on the admiral as soon as possible."

Fergus rolled his eyes. "Well, Captain, before you go over there, come into my cabin first." He turned and headed for the cabin door. Hardcastle followed him and sat down without being invited.

Fergus eased into a chair and looked at Hardcastle. "Captain, I know why you want to see the admiral. Let's talk for a few minutes first. As you can guess, I did ask the admiral to have you relieved."

"Yes, sir, I'm sure you did."

"But before you jump to conclusions, let me tell you what happened. I did make my report and he decided to order you to his staff as chief of staff."

Hardcastle swallowed hard and his eyes blinked. "I don't understand, sir."

Fergus avoided his eyes. "He needs your services urgently to straighten out his correspondence, files, and administration. I think you should go over and confer with him in a friendly manner. He can arrange a relief for you tomorrow. I think this change would be for the benefit of all."

Hardcastle smiled for the first time Fergus had ever seen him. "I still request permission to call on him."

"Of course, and after you call, please drop by and tell me what happened."

Two hours later the *Diligent* gig pulled alongside the sea ladder of the *Daring*. Captain Hardcastle leaped up and climbed the ladder. Fergus was waiting for him. Hardcastle beamed. "Commodore, I'm in a hurry to get back to my ship. It was as you said, and Captain Sherrill will relieve me tomorrow. It will be a quick and informal ceremony. I need to get over to the flagship right away."

Fergus interrupted. "That was very quick. Did he take the time to read all of your report?"

"Oh, no, there wasn't time for that. He just tossed it over on the sideboard on top of another report lying there next to a large silver bowl of oranges. He said he'd have plenty of time to go over it later."

Captain Sherrill took over rapidly. In days the crew seemed to be resurrected. Radcliffe came back from a quick trip to trade supplies with the *Diligent* steward with word that the crew was smiling and hard at work in their painting clothes, but were not tarring the rigging.

Fergus sighed. "Well, that's a load off my back. I'll sleep better now."

Two days later Fergus's flotilla left for the patrol area and formed a patrol line along the French coast. The three frigates were fifty miles apart, with the *Diligent* farthest to west. The two sloops accompanied the other two ships. The individual ships were to remain within sight of the coast so that no ships could pass between them and the French coast.

Poston plotted the patrol stations on a large chart placed on Fergus's dining table. Then he stood back and looked at his handiwork. He shook his head. "Neat," he said. "But what the hell is all this for?"

Fergus laughed. "The line curves just like the coast line. What we are doing is trying to prevent French ships from escaping from Toulon and going to Barcelona or any other Spanish port, or even entering the Gibraltar straits and running up the French coast."

"Dammit! I suppose we can capture or destroy a small ship but what about a 60-gunner?"

"We'll have to find a way to gang up on her. Our sloops won't help much except to take information back to Toulon and ask for help."

"There's one thing they'll be able to do. Don't forget the stingers in their bows."

For almost four months the ships of the flotilla patrolled monotonously without sighting a single ship. Then, almost out of the blue, one morning the lookouts yelled down, "Sail ho! And a big one. Maybe sixty guns!"

Poston, who had the watch, gasped. "That's more than we wanted and more than we can handle."

When he was notified by a panting messenger, Fergus came running up on deck, still adjusting his clothing.

Poston pointed to the large ship, looming ever larger and headed their way.

Fergus whistled. "Now what do we do?"

Poston looked puzzled. "I'm supposed to ask you that. The only thing I can think of is to shadow her and send a sloop to report to Admiral Collingwood."

"Right, but not yet. We need the sloop now."

"How so?"

"If I guess right, the French ship came out of a small French port and is now attempting to escape to the Atlantic and join one of the French fleets based there."

"But we can't stop her."

"Oh, yes we can. We've got two more frigates along her line of escape. I'll send the *Hatchet* up ahead to make controlled attacks on her bow and stern. When she turns to unmask her batteries, we'll make attacks on her bow or stern. When she turns back to attack us, we'll drop out of range and let the sloop have at her again."

"Sounds like what we did to the French ships out in the Atlantic."

Fergus nodded. "And it worked, too. Now call the *Hatchet* alongside and we'll set up the maneuver."

When the captain of the *Hatchet* had been instructed, he left at his best speed to take position ahead. He could make about five knots more than the clumsy two-decker, and about noon she was in place to begin the attacks.

"Commodore, are you planning to bring this big ship down all by yourself?" Poston asked.

Fergus laughed. "Like the dogs and the bear. Just a bite or two. Soon she'll bleed to death."

Poston shook his head. "That'll take a lot of bites."

"Don't forget. We'll run into the *Diligent* and Captain Sherrill in a few hours. Then there'll be two biters."

"Now I see your game," Poston said. "By tomorrow morning there'll be another biter. We'll catch up with the *Dashing.* We'll chew her to death then."

"Now you have it. In the meantime, let's take some more bites. This time we're going to move right up her tail and let her have it."

In a few minutes the two-decker was in range of the *Daring's* bow chasers and Fergus shouted, "Commence firing!"

The two-decker returned the fire from her two stern chasers. They just about matched the weight and range of the *Daring's* bow chasers. The two balls crashed on the foredeck of the *Daring* and destroyed a gun carriage. Splinters flew up in the air, and Fergus felt a blow on his head. Then all was black.

Fergus came to slowly to the sound of gunfire ahead at the bow. He recognized the boom of his bow chasers, and he raised his head and looked around. Surgeon Pollitt pushed his head back down on the hard deck. "Commodore, rest for a while. You had a concussion."

"But I've got to get up. We're in danger."

"Lieutenant Poston has it well in hand. He has fired two salvos, and now he's turning away."

"What happened?"

"We took two hits. There is some damage, and four men were injured. I'll take care of them in just a minute, as soon as I'm sure you'll rest on deck for a while. Radcliffe is here. Ask him if you want anything. When I get back I'll probably let you get up slowly."

"What the hell hit me?"

"A piece of gun carriage."

Poston came over to him. "How do you feel, Commodore?"

"I've got a hell of a headache, but I don't seem to be bleeding."

"Right. The surgeon says you'll be up soon."

"What happened to the French ship?"

"We put two balls on her quarterdeck, but I think we got a little too close to do it."

"And the *Hatchet*?"

"She got in a couple of good shots up forward on the Frenchy. Her fore course sail is in tatters."

"Good, but we need to harry her more."

"As you said, in a couple of hours the *Diligent* will be with us, and we'll really go to work on her."

In two hours, Fergus was up and mentally alert, but still nursing a headache.

Then the lookouts sang out, "Sail ho! Dead ahead."

Fergus said without bothering to look at the newcomer through the long glass, "That's the *Diligent.* Now we'll see if her new captain knows how to fight."

Almost as if by instinct, Captain Sherrill took position on the port beam of the French ship. The two ships took turns closing the French ship from astern until she turned to counterattack them. Then the ship on her bow closed into range and pounded her with broadsides until the French ship got wise to it and turned back.

Then the sloop got in a couple of 32-pounders before she had to turn away.

The French ship grew more and more battered as the day wore on. Fergus said, "I like the way Captain Sherrill joined in without instructions."

At daylight the *Dashing* showed up earlier than expected, apparently alerted by the gunfire.

"My God!" Poston exclaimed. "Where will we put her?"

Fergus laughed. "There's always room for one more. We're only fifty miles from Gibraltar, and we need to put her away before we get there. Hoist a signal to attack."

All three frigates closed to maximum gun range and began to fire broadsides at the French ship. With all this firepower falling on her, she could not concentrate on any one ship. They could close her at will and withdraw the same way. When she swung to fire on one ship, that ship withdrew and the other ships closed her. Slowly her sails became tatters and her rate of fire slowed as more guns were put out of use. Finally she slowed to a knot or two.

Fergus, looking through his long glass, said, "She has to strike any minute."

In an hour it was all over. The French ship's fire fell off more, stopped, and her sails were down. Then it was apparent that she had lost steering control. Her colors came tumbling down.

Fergus turned to Poston. "You will have the honor of taking her in as a prize. Take the necessary men with you to repair her steering control and some marines and notify me when you are ready to proceed. We'll escort you right into Gibraltar for provisioning and upkeep."

Poston laughed. "This will be the shortest command on record. Maybe Midshipman Searles should take it."

"Fine. Call him up for instructions."

"I'll get him right away."

Lombardi had been giving orders in a strong wind for days and his voice was giving out. He grinned, "I'll have to use hand signals soon. Lieutenant Poston, you don't have anything to do now. Will you take her in?"

Poston laughed. "I think you're pulling my leg, but I'd be glad to."

CHAPTER 20

Nelson's Return

AS HE ALWAYS DID, Fergus went to call on the port captain as soon as the flotilla was moored. Captain Stark was glad to see him and rose to greet him. "You always bring excitement. What are you up to this time? By the way, I'm sending your six deserters back to their ship. The members of the court-martial thought there were extenuating circumstances and four months at hard labor was enough punishment for them. Apparently your Captain Hardcastle has become well known throughout the Navy."

"Thank you. Their ship has been resurrected by a new captain and will need them. Hard-working sailors are hard to find at sea. By the way, I'm having a celebration on my ship tomorrow night."

"I'll tell the local police not to bother you. What are you celebrating?"

"Ah, Saint Lombardi's Day."

"Never heard of him."

"Well, come down to the ship this evening, and you'll hear him sing."

"I think you're pulling my leg, but enjoy yourselves. Time in port is short."

"I'll want a day for the hangovers to wear off before we begin to provision."

When Fergus got back to the ship he called Poston in. "Poston, we're going to have a flotilla-wide celebration tonight. Please get the word to all captains that we're going to have a dinner in honor of Saint Lombardi."

Poston looked puzzled. "Never heard of him."

"It will come to you soon enough. In the meantime get the word out. It will also be in honor of the capture of *Saint Christophe,* your recent command that you gave away."

"I understand that, but are you pulling my leg about Saint Lombardi?"

"Of course. It's our Lombardi."

"Well, sometimes I don't think he's any saint. He doesn't talk like one."

"You don't speak much Latin or Spanish. Otherwise you'd hear him call on all the saints in heaven in several languages when the foretopmen don't move around fast enough up there to suit him."

Poston shrugged. "I thought it was just good old swearing."

"Let's not worry about the finer points. The goal is to give the crews a big dinner like we did at Christmas. Also tell the captains to issue a double ration of rum, and I'll pay for a keg of brandy for each ship."

Poston grinned. "I think I get it. I'll start the wheels going right away. I'll also include some friendly waitresses for us, but the other ships will have to make their own arrangements for their ladies."

"Tell them the day after will be a holiday in honor of Saint Dominic."

"Isn't that Captain Puller's first name?"

"You are beginning to learn the system just fine."

The special dinner went well, and two days later provisioning began. When the crew was halfway through, Stark, the port captain came aboard to call.

When Fergus and the port captain were settled over port, Stark said, "I have a surprise for you, Commodore. You'll have to stay in port for five more days."

Fergus smiled. "An unusual and pleasant surprise. What happened?"

"Well, I know you've been at sea continuously since you arrived in the area and are out of touch with your country's affairs. Napoleon is planning new moves, most of them toward the Mediterranean. Even his admirals are getting ready to go to sea."

Fergus leaped up and began to pace the deck, banging his fist on the woodwork. "Damn!" he said. "That means that Admiral Nelson will be at sea soon."

"You are clairvoyant. He is. As a matter of fact he is on his temporary flagship, the *Amphion,* and is just passing the entrance to Gibraltar. He wants his trip to Toulon to be kept quiet. That's why the harbor is closed, but I thought you deserved to know the reason. I assume that after the ban is lifted, you will be free to report to him in Toulon, or wherever you may find him. The messenger, a frigate captain, said Nelson might go to other ports first. You know him well, and you'll know where he might go."

Five days later Fergus led his flotilla out of port and made all speed to return to Toulon.

When they arrived on 8 July at the anchorage off port, Fergus could not see Admiral Nelson's flagship in the anchorage. Obviously Admiral Collingwood had been relieved and had departed.

Fergus called his gig away and had himself rowed over to the ship flying the flag of an admiral.

Rear Admiral Bickerton met him at the gangway. "Good morning, young man, I know you're looking for Admiral Nelson. Everyone in the Mediterranean, except for the French and Spanish, is looking for him. As a matter of fact, he's embarked in the *Amphion,* and a crowded flagship it is."

Fergus frowned. "And where might the *Amphion* be?"

"Try Palma and Sardinia and a half dozen other places," Bickerton answered. "I suggest you take a leisurely cruise looking for him. He promised to be back here at the end of July. The *Victory* will be here then, and I know he wants to get settled aboard her. Will you come to my cabin for a little refreshment now?"

"No, thank you, sir, I want to be off as soon as possible to find Admiral Nelson."

"Suit yourself." Bickerton shrugged. "He'll be a hard one to find."

Fergus lost no time in getting under way and decided to go to Palma first. By the time he got there, Nelson was long gone, and the port captain thought he might be bound for Sardinia. "Maybe Naples," he said, raising his eyebrows. "He has a lot of connections there, if you get my drift, but he's a close one, and I'm just guessing."

Fergus decided to pursue his guess, but no one in Naples had seen Nelson. "Try Sardinia," the port captain there suggested. "The *Amphion* was here, but I didn't see Admiral Nelson. Only a Captain Hardy came ashore."

Fergus nodded. "Of course. Captain Hardy is his flag captain, but obviously Admiral Nelson didn't come ashore. There was no sign of him."

Fergus started for Sardinia, but on the second day a terrible nor'easter overtook him.

"Damn!" Poston said. "This is awful." He struggled to keep his feet in the face of the vicious wind. "The seas are so short the ship seems to whip back and forth."

Fergus blew the spray out of his mouth. "You should read more."

"How so?"

"You'll find out that there is a typical storm peculiar to this area. Quick, vicious, and dangerous. The Greeks call it 'Poseidon's Tears.'"

"I didn't know the gods ever cried."

"They don't. This means the god Poseidon gives the sailors tears."

Poston wiped his streaming face. "I see what you mean. I've got a lot of them."

They fought the storm for two days, closely reefed, and on the third day resumed course for Sardinia.

When Fergus ordered the flotilla to anchor in the lee of the port normally used by the fleet for provisioning, it was vacant.

"Missed again," Fergus said. "We'll provision here and catch him at Toulon."

Poston came up. "What are your plans for provisioning? Five ships won't find much."

"Let them all try. There will be more than you think. The moment the natives ashore see us, they'll beat the bushes for miles around."

"Maybe so, but I don't fancy eating bushes."

"You won't have to. They'll produce some vegetables, fruit, and, if we're lucky, a bullock and some pigs. If not, a lot of scrawny goats."

"Good. I'll go round up the purser, the cook, and the boatswain."

"Send Lombardi. They will need an interpreter. And don't forget to send over all the empty water butts you can round up. Lombardi says they have the best water in the Mediterranean."

Within the hour, both pulling boats set off, the crews pulling strongly and thinking about the cold Italian beer they might find while the big wheels were in the hinterland looking for provisions.

Three hours later, Poston called Fergus to the quarterdeck. "Damndest procession I ever saw!" Poston said, pointing at the column of boats headed for the ship.

Fergus looked at it and broke into laughter. "One boat is full of water butts, and I expected that. The other is half full of vegetables and fruit, and it is towing a barge of some kind full of goats, tended by four Sardinians."

"Yes, I think they're trying to keep the goats from jumping over the side. If I were a goat, I'd certainly try, and they aren't succeeding."

In a few minutes the pulling boats came alongside, and the boatswain climbed up the sea ladder, followed by the purser, Lombardi, and the cook.

"My God!" Fergus said. "What's that smell?"

"Goats," Lombardi said.

"And Sardinians," the boatswain added. "I think they smell about the same."

Lombardi bristled. "If you had to herd the damned things all day long, you'd smell like them, too."

Fergus said, delicately holding his nose, "There seems to be space in one of the boats for them. The boat with the vegetables is only half full. If you had put the goats in there you would have saved the cost of the barge."

Lombardi laughed. "The purser wanted to, but the head Sardinian herder said the vegetables would all be inside the goats before the boat got here. If we did that, he wanted to be paid for both the goats and the vegetables before we left the beach. The purser refused, so we compromised. Now we have spent a little extra money."

Fergus could stand the smell no longer, and he moved the group forward. "What can we do about the smell? The manger won't keep it in even if we go downwind."

The boatswain said, "I'm going to bring the beasts aboard by a lifting sling rigged to go around the belly of each goat. I'll lift it off the barge and dunk it several times before I hoist it into the manger."

Poston scratched his chin. "What's with this 'dunk'? I've never heard it before."

Lombardi laughed. "A German word for pushing something under water."

"Oh, I understand, but I don't think it will work. The only alternative is to eat the goats as soon as possible." He turned to the cook. "Will the crew eat goat?"

"Better than salt horse," the cook said. "When they get hungry they'll eat anything."

Lombardi said, "They tell me Sardinian goat meat is so thin and tough it can be made into leather without skinning it before tanning it."

"I don't believe it," Fergus said. "I'll tell Evan to try some goat soup on me first. If I can eat it, the crew can, even if they don't like it, and the cook will empty his spice boxes into it if he has to."

Poston said, "If I'd been there I'd have tied lines to each goat and made them swim out. By that time they'd have been clean."

Lombardi said patiently, "Sardinian goats can't swim. They don't have enough fat to keep them afloat. They'd all have been dead by the time they got here."

Poston shrugged. "They'd smell the same either way."

Fergus laughed. "Enough. Let's get going with the loading. I want to get under way. How did the other ships make out with provisioning?"

"About the same as we did," the purser answered. "The *Diligent* didn't take any goats. Said they smelled too bad. They might smell up the ship."

Five days later, after dodging another storm, the flotilla arrived at Toulon. Fergus searched the anchorage impatiently, scanning the ships through a long glass. Finally he relaxed and lowered the glass. "The *Victory* is in. As soon as we are in range, hoist a signal asking permission for me to call on the admiral."

The answer came back promptly.

Fergus called away his gig and was soon on his way to the flagship.

As the boat neared the *Victory*'s stern, the coxswain looked up at the great structure towering above them. "My God!" he exclaimed. "It looks like an apartment in Soho. But there ain't no guns sticking out astern like we have. Any ship could sneak up astern of her when she wasn't looking and let her have it right in the poop."

Fergus laughed. "Not so easily done. When battle is imminent, all those fancy windows come down. There are two good-sized chasers behind them. Anybody trying to fool with her would get badly hurt."

"I'd think the admiral's rugs would get trampled on when all the gun crews ran about in their dirty boots."

"No, they'll all be rolled up and taken below. The flooring is made up of painted canvas squares and is very durable. The admiral has the top apartment, as you called it, the ship's captain the middle, and the chief of staff the lower. Altogether a cozy arrangement, but not the kind I'd like. I like smaller and faster ships."

In minutes the coxswain brought the gig alongside the accommodation ladder. Fergus thought he was climbing up forever, but after a while he reached the top and paused for a breath.

The aide met him and escorted him to the great cabin. He knocked on the door and announced that Commodore Kilburnie was calling.

"Ah, come in," said the familiar voice, and Fergus went in, looking around at the plush accommodations of the cabin as he went. Nelson rose from his desk and came forward to meet him. "Welcome, lad, I've missed you. I'm glad we're together again. Like my digs?"

"Beautiful," Fergus said.

Nelson laughed. "Not bad for at sea."

Fergus smiled broadly as he shook Nelson's hand. "Sir, I'm also glad to be with you once more. It has been a long time. What chores do you have for me and my flotilla?"

"Well, I always keep in mind the best quality of your ships is their speed, and I intend to use it. Now, first, I have a letter for you from your Uncle Jeris. Read it, please, while I sign some letters. Then I have some more detailed directions for you."

Fergus took the letter, sat down, and opened it carefully. When he finished it he looked up with a broad smile.

Nelson asked. "What's this good news you have there?"

"I have a second son. He's fine."

"I'm glad to hear this. I'm sure he'll be as handsome as his mother is beautiful. What's his name?"

Fergus hesitated. "I hope my wife has not been too presumptuous. His name is Horatio."

Nelson slapped his thigh. "Good! I am honored. May you have many more, but it will be very difficult with your long tours at sea."

Fergus sobered. "Yes, but now I have four children. This may be enough. Now, sir, you said you have some directions for me."

Nelson got up from his desk again. "First, let's go topside. We'll take a little sun."

When they arrived above, Nelson said, "Sit with me. This is my time for sherry and a cake or two. Some of my staff will join us."

On the area of the quarterdeck reserved for the admiral, several chairs were drawn up in a circle. Nelson pointed to two large leather ones. "Take one of those over there. It belongs to my flag captain, Captain Hardy, but he won't be here today. He's ill."

Fergus said, "I'm sorry. What's wrong?"

Nelson laughed. "Italian stomachache. I sent him over in Naples to deliver some documents to the ambassador. Hardy likes to eat, so he stopped in a favorite restaurant. Now he wishes he hadn't."

Fergus nodded. "My sailing master is from Naples. He says it takes a lifetime to build up immunity in Naples and even the Italians have trouble."

As they talked, some of the staff officers drifted by and sat down. Nelson introduced them. "This is Doctor Scott. He's not a surgeon. He's a learned secretary who keeps my foreign papers in order. He speaks a dozen languages. I have another Mister Scott on my staff who is my real secretary."

Doctor Scott said, "I heard what you were talking about. I may not be a 'sawbones,' but if you follow Admiral Nelson's daily routine you will be as healthy as he is. But then, if you go ashore in Naples, nothing will work."

Fergus laughed. "I plan to, but right now we cleaned out all of the vegetables and fruit in Sardinia. However, I have several crates of oranges left from Gibraltar."

"Good. You'll be all right then."

Doctor Scott said, "Actually I am the *Victory*'s chaplain. I hold services every Sunday. I hope you'll attend whenever you are in port."

Fergus said, "Thank you, but I'm seldom in port."

Nelson interrupted and began a discourse. "I expect you to be busy keeping track of the French forces, and soon the Spanish forces we cannot account for. It will mean a lot of sailing in the Mediterranean for you. When you locate a ship or force, send word to me by one of your fast sloops. A negative report that a harbor is vacant is also valuable. Come back to see me every three months."

Fergus nodded. "A pleasure, sir."

Nelson cleared his throat. "One other thing. French Admiral Tremaine is trying to entice our forces into combat under conditions where his French force is superior. He will only fight under these conditions. Your purpose is to provide information, not to fight. There will be an opportunity to fight later. Am I clear?"

"Yes, sir. Now I'll take my departure and get my flotilla ready for sailing tomorrow."

"Permission granted. When you have an opportunity to write next, please give my regards to your beautiful wife, and thank her for honoring me. I hope your latest son will follow in your footsteps and mine, too."

"Thank you, but I don't think there is much future for a Scot in this Navy. I have been very fortunate."

"You have done well, but Scots are increasing in numbers in our Navy. Duff is one of my best captains. Captain Cochrane is another."

Fergus said, "Sometime the Royal Navy will decide that Scots make good naval officers."

Nelson's one good eye twinkled. "And also good captains of our ships. You are one of our best."

"Thank you, sir, but I seem to be an exception."

"Maybe it's because your country is concentrating on other things."

Fergus said, "I don't understand."

"Scotland now leads Great Britain and even the world in educational institutions. Think of Edinburgh University."

"Thank you, sir."

"From these universities flow lawyers, doctors, and engineers who can be found around the world now improving the health, legal systems, and architecture and engineering of the countries they have gone to."

Fergus frowned. "Sir, I am sorry you had to remind me. I am very proud of the accomplishments of my countrymen, and now I might do a better job of planning the educations of my sons." He rose and said, "Sir, I must return to my ship. This has been a fascinating and rewarding day for me."

Nelson nodded. "Smooth sailing. I look forward to our next meeting."

The next morning the flotilla got under way and sailed to the southeast for Sardinia. A week later they cruised around its coast clockwise and searched its periphery to Cagliari and then to Terranova.

As they passed by, Poston shuddered. "I can still smell those goats. When we finished eating the ones we took aboard, and in soup, I might add, I had to send extra duty men below to the manger to clean it out. Good thing the cook's loyal, or he might have left the ship."

When there were no French ships anywhere, Fergus sent the *Axe* back to Toulon to report to Admiral Nelson. *Axe* was ordered to rejoin them off Palma after the flotilla had completed its reconnoitering of Sardinia.

Again, the results were negative, and the *Hatchet* was sent back to report.

"Damn!" Poston complained. "This is nothing but an expensive tourist's tour."

"Don't squawk," Fergus said with a smile. "At least you are getting plenty of fresh fish and fruit, and you don't have to go ashore and get some strange Italian disease like Captain Hardy picked up."

"Oh, yes, the fish is good, but this is very boring. We can't fight the Italian and Greek fishing vessels."

The reconnaissance continued to Cyprus and Crete, and then they returned via the ports at Cairo and Malta. By now the four months had passed and Fergus decided to report in person to Nelson at Toulon.

He brought his flotilla to anchorage off Toulon in early November.

Nelson received him but gave him little hope for immediate action. "Maybe a year," he said. "But think about me. I'm stuck off this miserable port. At least you are having a tour of the Mediterranean that our countrymen would pay thousands of pounds for."

Fergus nodded. "Thank you, Admiral, for making it as easy as possible. But do you have any hope for a change in the political scene?"

"Not really. My spies and the information I get from the Admiralty all indicate that Napoleon is doing everything he can to build fires under his French admirals. He wants them to leave port and find action."

"And no luck?"

Nelson shrugged his shoulders. "So far they find excuses not to go to sea."

"And the Spanish?"

"We'll be at war with them within the next year."

"And your best prediction?"

"Early in 1805 Napoleon will force his senior admirals, or new ones, to break the blockade and move to the Caribbean."

"Well, sir, please put me at the head of the force that is ordered to pursue him."

Nelson laughed. "You can count on that. I'll need speed and young eyes to find them, and you have both."

Fergus continued his leisurely tour of the Mediterranean until January 1805, when he arrived in Gibraltar for a five-day overhaul and provisioning stay.

Poston, leaning on the rail, watched the stevedores begin to bring provisions aboard and said, "Commodore, can you think of some reason to send me ashore for a few days? I'm getting a little stir-crazy."

Fergus looked at Poston's handsome, rugged face, and said, "I can see that your hair is growing a little gray. I think you need to see a little action on the social level before it all falls out. Come into the cabin with me."

In the cabin, Fergus went to his desk and pulled out his journal. He looked back to an area near the beginning of it. "My God!" he said, "I didn't realize that it was ten years ago when I first visited Gibraltar."

Poston laughed. "Oh, yes, I remember that visit well. You spent a week ashore."

Fergus colored. "Yes, I did. Carlita," he sighed. "I stayed with her for five days."

"And I persuaded the port captain not to send a search party after you."

For the first time in ten years Fergus called Poston by his first name. "Tom, the time has come for you to meet Carlita. Here's her address. Come back in five days. She will cure what's wrong with you if you are man enough to cure a little of her loneliness."

Poston shook his head. "I am lonely for something other than a prostitute."

Fergus laughed. "She's not one. She works for our government as a spy. Most of her time she lives in Gibraltar, but she travels around on her business. In person I find her hard to describe. She is beautiful and charming, but that's only the start. Tom, I have known you since we were quartermasters together, and I know you to be a charming man yourself. Only those who know you well know that you are a vicar's son. Well read, well educated, and a great conversationalist. I think Carlita will uncover all these qualities that you keep hidden so well most of the time. Now get ashore. By the way, you should call her 'Carla' when you first meet her. That's her real given name. Carlita is the Spanish diminutive for Carla. She will call you Tom, or even Tomas, which is Spanish for Thomas." Fergus grinned. "Who knows? She may even get to calling you Tomasito."

Poston shook his head. "That's too much to hope for in five days. Tom will be fine."

Fergus handed Poston a piece of old paper, well worn. "Here's her address."

Poston grinned. "Now as I remember you weren't married then."

CHAPTER 21

Carlita

AN HOUR LATER, Lieutenant Tom Poston trotted down the brow, carrying a small brown portmanteau. Since he was on leave, he was wearing civilian clothes. Fergus had helped him dress, getting spots of mildew out of his clothing, which had been stowed in his sea chest for several years. A small skillet heated over the cook's fire was used to press out the bigger wrinkles. In the town of Gibraltar, and at most restaurants, the outfit was acceptable among the members of the varied citizenry walking the streets.

Poston looked back and waved at the commodore leaning on the rail. Fergus raised his hand, grinned, and returned the wave.

Poston fingered the notepaper in his pocket and walked rapidly up the street. After a few false turns, he stopped at a police box, pulled out the note, and asked the British policeman for help.

The policeman looked at it and then pointed up a winding street. "Up there some place. Go up for about half a mile and then stop and ask in a small store. They know everybody in their neighborhood. I'm not from the area, of course." He grinned. "As a matter of fact I don't think anybody in the bloody country has lived here very long."

Poston increased his stride and climbed the steadily rising street. He followed the policeman's instructions and stopped at a small store, piled high with a collection of dried foods and mixed vegetables. The clerk looked at his note and called back over his shoulder. An old woman said, "Two blocks more up the hill. Over a clothing store."

Poston found the store without trouble since it was the only store on the block. He climbed up an outside stair leading to an entry door. He knocked, wondering if he were still young enough to take on such an adventure. He decided to take the commodore's advice, and he knocked again, this time more forcefully. He sighed. It had to be now or never. Soon he would be too old and too sea worn to care.

After a few moments the door was opened by an older woman, wearing a long, colored gown and a white cloth over her head. "Yes?"

Poston was disappointed. The face was obviously not that of a beautiful young woman, but he did not come all this way to back down. "Carla?" he asked.

"Ah, no, senor," the woman said in a strong Spanish accent. "I will get her."

Poston was reassured. He looked in the open door but did not step inside. The furniture was handsome, the odor wafting out of the open door was attractive, and his spirits rose.

Then another face came to the door. His spirits rose even further. "Yes?" a pretty woman said. She had sparkling brown eyes, long black hair to her shoulders, and a face as beautiful as Fergus had described it.

"Are you Carla?" Poston asked.

"I might be. Who are you?" Her eyes twinkled, and she was obviously sizing him up.

"I am Lieutenant Tom Poston of His Majesty's Frigate *Daring* in the harbor here."

"And who is her captain?"

"Commodore Fergus Kilburnie."

The woman's face broke out in a beautiful smile. "Ah, yes. I had heard that he might be here, and I had hoped to see him again. Please come in."

She stepped back and ushered Poston in. "Please sit down and have a drink with me. I want to know all about Fergus. I understand he is married."

"Yes. Several years ago. She lives in London with their four children. That's why he sent me to see you."

"And for what purpose?"

Poston colored. "I, ah, asked him to let me come ashore for a few days of leave, and he suggested I come to see you." Poston hesitated for a moment, realizing that he had been awkward. "Er, I think he thought that you might know someone I'd like to spend time with."

Carla laughed. "I think I get the picture. I unravel unusually odd situations in my business. Besides you look like as handsome and as nice a man as Fergus was. I hope you'll visit with me."

Poston was in deep water again. He protested, "But, Miss, I didn't mean to intrude."

Carla's tinkling laughter came again. "Don't be embarrassed. I am sure Fergus told you I am not a prostitute, but I cannot tell you exactly what my business is. Now give your portmanteau to Maria. She will take you to a room in the rear. When you are settled, come back and we will have some sherry before lunch."

The room he was shown to was airy and sunny, and Poston felt comfortable. When he came back to the living room he resolved to stay as long as she would let him. He sat on a comfortable couch, and Carla handed him a glass of sherry and sat down beside him. He could smell the scent of clean soap and good cologne, and when she moved closer to him he began to feel sensations and urges he had ignored for years. Clearly, if she liked him, this could be a wonderful visit.

It started with a good sherry, and then another, and after that a superb lunch.

After lunch, Carla said, "I have some business to attend to. If you will take a nap, I will be back for you in about two hours and take you for a walk up to the summit. We will be able to see your ship from there. It is just up this street. Then we will come back for some good Scotch and an even better dinner."

By the end of a delightful dinner, and a second glass of port, Poston had recited his whole life. "Not much of a life, after all," he said, "and I suppose it doesn't compare with the exciting life you must lead. By the way, Fergus said I could call you Carlita if you liked me and would permit it."

Again the tinkling laugh came, and Poston felt it penetrating his very vitals. "Of course," she said. "I think we will get along very well together. I will call you Tomasito."

Poston laughed and took her hand. "You make me very happy," he said. "You were about to tell me something about the life you led."

Carla laughed, and he was always hoping to hear that laugh again. "Well, my life is a bit more humdrum than you think. I have to entertain a lot of people I don't like. Now I can spend time with you, and I think we will both enjoy the few days we will have."

Poston was out of practice with the art of love making, and it started when she gently took his hand. After another brace of ports, he dared to take her in his arms. She responded as he hoped she would, and the night that followed was the best experience he had ever had.

As he held her in his arms, sleeping peacefully, he thought about all the long nights he had spent at sea, pacing the deck, looking at the stars, and wondering if he would ever hold a woman in his arms. He had though it might never happen, and he would grow old at sea, finally retiring as a worn-out husk. Now he felt vigorous and potent as he looked at Carlita. He remembered earlier in the night when he had held her with increasing passion. He had never made love to an experienced, mature woman, except for occasional prostitutes, and he had felt increasingly awkward at his lack of skill and experience. Carlita had helped him get over the awkwardness, and he then had moved with increasing confidence. He felt a force that almost caused him to explode, and she was able to accommodate all of his force. Now he was anxious to preserve all this happiness for him forever, and he resolved to ask her to marry him as soon as she woke up. With only a few days of leave left, he could not afford to waste a single hour of it. He reached over and began to caress her. Her eyes opened slowly and then widened, and she reached back and folded him in her arms. In a few minutes he was in ecstasy again, and he could hardly wait to press his offer of marriage.

In a few minutes, as they lay back in the warm bed, he asked her, "Will you marry me?"

Again the tinkling laugh. "Don't ask me something that serious before I give you coffee."

He asked her again, and this time there could be no misunderstanding of his feelings.

But she put him off, and he asked her again as often as he could. Still, he knew from her reactions that she loved him. He did not think she had to tell him so. He felt it in the way she looked at him and in the softness of her caresses.

After the days that followed, he never wanted anything else, but he knew he had to go back to the ship. He asked her if she was ever going back to England.

She became pensive. "I think so. I am losing my effectiveness here. The enemy knows me too well."

"Where will you go in England?"

"I have a small farm and house my family left me. I'd like to teach music."

"Would you marry a retired naval officer?"

Again she laughed. "Are you really asking me to marry you?"

"Of course. I'll retire in a year or two, maybe as a captain. Then I'll ask you again. Please write to me so I will know where you are. I promise I'll come to find you the day I retire."

For the first time she initiated the love play, and now he was sure she loved him.

The last day of his leave was beautiful, and still an agony. He did not want to leave her. He was sure his feelings for her would last, but he was afraid hers would not survive. However, Fergus had said that he could trust her, and that was enough for him.

Poston left his Carlita before sunset on the fifth day with a tentative promise from her and walked down the winding street to the Royal Navy dockyard. At first his step was slow and reluctant, but by the time he could see the bottom of the brow he had recovered his good spirits, and he was sure of his future. It would be good.

He could see Commodore Kilburnie leaning on the railing, awaiting his approach. He smiled to himself, wondering what Carlita had called Kilburnie. "Fergusito?" Or "Fergie," as he had heard his wife call him. Should he ask him? Hell, no. It would not be proper. Kilburnie would always be Commodore to him.

He reached the bottom of the brow and started up, two treads at a time, barely touching them and with his portmanteau banging against his legs. Life was vibrant again. In one last leap he landed on the deck and saluted the officer of the watch, the colors, and Fergus with one sweeping salute.

Fergus returned his salute, as did the officer of the watch, wondering what had come over his senior lieutenant. Fergus said, "Well, how was your leave?"

Poston grinned. "Marvelous. The best time of my life, and I thank you."

"And you two got along all right?"

"Got along! I asked her to marry me."

"My God! What a Lothario."

Poston shrugged and walked below, remembering to read about Lothario.

Fergus watched him go and shook his head and said to the bewildered officer of the watch, "My God! He was better than Lothario."

Poston walked into his small stateroom and threw his portmanteau into a corner. Without even bothering to take off his civilian clothes, he threw himself face down on his cot. As he drifted rapidly off into sleep, he said to himself, "Who is this Lothario anyway? Even he must have needed some sleep." Then he was gone, off in a deep and untroubled sleep.

CHAPTER 22

On Patrol

On the last day of their stay in Gibraltar, Fergus paid his usual departure call on the port captain at his office. This time the port captain was depressed instead of his usual ebullient self.

"What's wrong?" Fergus asked.

"We've just got word that Admiral Villeneuve left port, passed by us in the night, and headed for the Caribbean, or at least intelligence thinks so."

"Then I'd better find Admiral Nelson as soon as possible and ask for orders."

"Maybe you should sail west and look for Admiral Villeneuve."

"No. Others will be doing that. Admiral Nelson has specific orders for me."

Fergus returned to his flotilla as soon as possible and sailed for Toulon. En route he spread his flotilla in a scouting line, not expecting to encounter a French foe, but more hoping to encounter Admiral Nelson passing toward the Straits of Gibraltar and the Atlantic.

Nelson was not at Toulon, and Fergus searched the eastern ports for weeks. Finally he found him at Palma on the last day of March. When he called on Nelson on the first of April, Nelson said, "Villeneuve actually escaped from port in the last days of March, and I must assume he is headed for the east. The intelligence about his passing to the west is probably wrong. I can't leave this area until I'm sure what he's going to do. Take your flotilla and put a screen to the east of Alexandria. When I'm sure he's not coming here, I'll shift you gradually to the west. Keep in touch with me with your fast sloops."

On 18 April, off Toro, a frigate arrived with the news that the French fleet had passed Gibraltar and into the Atlantic eight days before.

When Fergus heard it, he said, "Then the first information we were given about Gibraltar was wrong. I was fortunate not to have gone off into the Atlantic on a wild goose chase."

Nelson's fleet battled terrible weather attempting to make distance to the west, and Fergus stayed in place, just to the west of Nelson, hoping for better weather.

When the weather moderated, Nelson and his fleet passed Gibraltar and sailed for Barbados. On the trip, Fergus maintained a screen ahead, but never encountered any French or Spanish ships. The fleet arrived off Barbados on 25 May.

For weeks Nelson pursued Villeneuve from port to port, always finding out that he had just left. Grenada, Tobago, and other ports were vacant. In late June he gave up and sailed for Gibraltar, arriving 20 July.

Fergus's flotilla was released by Nelson as he proceeded north to England. Although Fergus hoped to be sent home for a much-needed overhaul, Admiral Nelson reluctantly told him, "You are sorely needed to patrol the coasts of France and Spain until this is settled."

By mid-August, Fergus learned that Nelson had returned to England, and he withheld the news from his officers and crew, thinking they would feel as abandoned as he did. The memory of two years of hard sailing and fighting without an opportunity for repairs rankled in him, and he put his men to work in calm weather trying to do whatever work they could on the battered ships.

On 20 August, almost by chance, Fergus reached the southern limits of the patrol area. The port of Cadiz was nearby, and Admiral Collingwood with a small force was lying off the entrance. When Fergus approached Collingwood's flagship, the *Royal Sovereign,* he asked permission to come aboard. While he was waiting for an answer to his request, he paced the deck with Poston. They could see a forest of masts in the harbor.

"Could that be that damned scoundrel Villeneuve?" Poston asked.

"Possibly. I'll know soon."

When Collingwood gave him permission to call, he ordered Poston to bring the ship under the flagship's counter and asked to have his gig called away.

Collingwood received him warmly and invited him into the cabin. "Lad, I'm glad to see you again. Now that Nelson is gone, you come under my command. As you can see, I have great need of you and your force. I had no frigates. Suddenly I have three and two fast sloops."

Fergus sat back in a comfortable chair and sipped a glass of sherry. "I take it those are the masts of Admiral Villeneuve's fleet over there."

"Oh, yes. I hear Napoleon is pressing him to come out and attack. My problem is not to let him know how weak my force is. Now that you are here, I will leave you to patrol the entrance. I will withdraw about fifty miles to the south and await reinforcements. I expect the Admiralty and even the king to decide to send forces soon, and I expect Nelson to take over soon."

"And what am I to do?"

"By all means don't get in a fight. If he comes out, shadow him, staying to windward. Send one of your sloops to inform me. If you let him get out and then lose him, you might as well jump over the side."

Fergus laughed. "I'll be careful, but I'd have to resist the urge to pick off stragglers."

Collingwood frowned. "By all means remember the urgency of your intelligence mission. It would be worth ten times the value of a single ship."

After Fergus returned to his ship, Collingwood retreated slowly to the south.

Poston said, "I feel naked as hell trying do the job of a whole fleet."

"We have to just watch them and report their movements. We won't fire a shot."

"The crew is unhappy and grumbling. They want either to fight or go home."

"They will have to be patient, and it is up to you to lead them. Admiral Nelson will be back in a few days, and I think there will be a quick climax."

By the end of August Admirals Bickerton and Calder and their forces had joined Admiral Collingwood. Now twenty-five ships were available to face Villeneuve's thirty-four.

Fergus learned later that Admiral Nelson, still at Surrey, heard on 2 September that Villeneuve was still bottled up at Cadiz.

By now Fergus had lost his patience, beating up and down the rocky coast, trying to keep the entrance to Cadiz in sight and still not being blown ashore by the changing winds and heavy seas.

On one particularly calm day, he called the *Axe* alongside and raised his speaking trumpet. "I am going to send over a packet of letters. After you have them, depart at best speed for the Thames. Deliver it to my wife, and, when you are ready to leave, drop by her flat and pick up any mail she may have for me. The main purpose of your trip is to call on Captain Essex, now Lord Satterfield, and Lord of the Admiralty for Intelligence. He will tell you in confidence what he expects Napoleon to do with regard to forcing his fleet to fight and when. When you ask him, he will also know when Admiral Nelson is coming back to duty and leaving Surrey. When you have the answers, or in a week at the most, return and report to me."

The *Axe* was soon a mere speck on the horizon, all sails set. Fergus watched her go, wondering what news she would bring back.

On 20 September, the *Axe* reappeared and came under the stern of the *Daring*. The captain said, "What I have to tell you is confidential. I request permission to come aboard and report to you."

When they were settled over coffee, he said, "Here is a large packet of letters, and your wife expects you home soon, or at least she hopes so."

Fergus's eyes widened. "Does she know something you don't know?"

Captain Harral laughed. "No. She's just smart, and she keeps her ears open."

"You are right," Fergus said. "Most women just keep their mouths open."

Harral nodded, apparently thinking about his own wife.

"Now what did Lord Satterfield say?"

"He said in confidence that Napoleon is unhappy with Admiral Villeneuve's performance of duty and lack of courage. He openly calls him a chicken, or whatever the French word is, and now has a replacement on the way for him. Lord Satterfield says he thinks Admiral Villeneuve will sail in a month or so in order to avoid his relief."

"Good!" Fergus exclaimed. "It won't be long."

Captain Harral rose. "Please excuse me. I am supposed to deliver some important official mail from the Admiralty to Admiral Collingwood. I suppose he is still somewhere fifty miles south."

"Yes, just off Point Trafalgar. Thank you for your excellent performance of duty."

"It was a pleasure. I was able to see my wife, too."

"And what about Admiral Nelson?"

"He was recalled by the king and left on the *Victory* on 12 September. You should see him soon. I estimate the *Victory* will go by here in about five days, She is as slow as a three-legged horse."

Captain Harral stood up, took his leave, and hurriedly climbed to the quarterdeck. He got into his waiting gig and was off to his ship, without stopping on his quarterdeck, while his watch officer quickly raised the sails.

Fergus estimated Nelson would pass by about the twenty-fifth of September, and he spread his force out in a scouting line to intercept the passing flagship.

On the first of October, the *Dashing* came in to report that the *Victory* had passed. Admiral Nelson had asked for Admiral Collingwood's location and was headed for him.

Fergus said, over the speaking trumpet, "Puller, I am going to leave you in charge of the patrol off Cadiz Harbor. I will leave you both fast sloops. Do not under any circumstances let Admiral Villeneuve and his fleet come out without immediately sending a fast sloop to report the fact to Admiral Nelson. Tell him what direction the fleet takes. Now listen carefully. You are not to attack any of the ships that come into the harbor or leave it. Do you understand?"

Puller slumped visibly, but he raised his hand. "Yes, sir, I understand."

"And stay upwind at all times and always follow the French fleet."

Puller laughed. "I couldn't help but obey that order. The damned wind always blows from the west. And when, sir, may I rejoin you?"

"I am going south to join Admiral Nelson and taking the *Diligent* with me. I will leave both sloops with you. By now Admiral Nelson will have taken over from Admiral Collingwood, and I will need new orders."

The next day Fergus found the fleet, now under Nelson, sailing slowly off Point Trafalgar, midway between Gibraltar and Cadiz.

Fergus asked for permission to call, but instead he was called under the *Victory*'s counter. Captain Hardy was on the quarterdeck holding a speaking trumpet, balancing himself on his sturdy legs against the swells from the south. When the *Daring* was in speaking range, Hardy said, "The admiral is a little under the weather and asked to be excused. He sends you his compliments and is glad to have you under his command again. He asks that you form a scouting line about ten miles to the southwest with your two ships. Keep him informed of approaching warships, and if there is action later, prevent stragglers from escaping in that direction. He knows that one of your ships is off Cadiz and awaits word from it. Our other frigates are in a similar scouting line to the southeast. Good luck."

Fergus raised his hand to indicate he understood his orders and saluted. In an hour he was on station with the *Diligent* to the west. The long wait was almost over, and he began to think about his future. He went to his cabin and reread the letters he had received from Shannon.

Obviously she was in good health and in good spirits, but was she becoming disillusioned? She had always been happy in London, but she and the children still liked Scotland more. Somehow he knew that he would have to retire and they would want to settle in Scotland. Why delay this final move?

How much longer could he withstand the rigors of the naval life? True, he was a naval officer, and this was his profession, and he was good at it. But the few moments of satisfying excitement and fighting were interspersed with years of grueling sailing in terrible weather. His ships, once new, were now worn out with constant use with minimum maintenance. In four years they were literally falling apart. Their bottoms were foul, the rigging was starting to rot, the wood they were made of never was meant to last over five years before it rotted. The sails were now one big patch from catching hurtling cannonballs and from winds of hurricane and gale force.

Fergus steadied himself against the heavy Atlantic swells and tried to write a letter to Shannon, but the inkwell shot across the desk, took off into space, and splattered all over the floor. He cursed silently, crumpled the paper, and threw it and the pen after the inkwell.

He pushed back his chair, angrily grabbed his hat, and walked up to the quarterdeck where he tried to calm himself with rapid pacing. After a while he sighed, went below, and tried to salvage the inkwell and pen. He straightened out the piece of writing paper and read what he had written. He began to write again. As he formed the words and then the paragraphs, he was convinced that retirement was not too far off.

CHAPTER 23

The Battle of Trafalgar

On 17 October the *Axe* appeared from the north, all sails set. She passed as close as possible to the *Daring* and, her captain raised his hand and circled his fist. Fergus was puzzled. "What does that mean?" he asked Poston.

"I think that means that Villeneuve is getting ready to leave port. He probably could see the ships in the harbor, raising their yards, rigging their sails, moving about, and shifting anchorages."

Fergus nodded. "I think you're right, and he's right about not stopping here. He needs to get this information to Nelson as soon as possible."

On the eighteenth, the *Hatchet* sped by from the north, the captain raising his fist the same way and pointing to the south.

Fergus laughed. "This time I get it. He means the French fleet is finally out of the harbor and is headed south, right into Nelson, just as Nelson planned it."

"Right," Poston said. "Could we move a little farther south and see the action?"

"By all means, as soon as Villeneuve passes."

That evening the *Axe* came back, headed north, and Fergus stopped him. "I'll send you right back as soon as the French fleet is in sight," he told him.

Late the next day, the French fleet was in sight, first on a westerly course. Fergus was concerned that his ships had reported the French as sailing in the wrong direction, but soon a near-gale caused Villeneuve to change course again in the direction of Nelson, southeast.

Early in the morning of the twentieth the weather changed again.

At 8 P.M., Nelson wore his fleet, changing course with his stern to the wind and now was on a parallel course with the French, but still out of sight.

Poston said, "Now he'll have to do something soon to bring the battle on."

He did. At 4 A.M. the next morning Nelson wore the fleet again, and he was now heading directly for the middle of the straggling French-Spanish battle line.

Fergus and his ships were in an excellent position to observe. Visibility was good, and all the ships of both battle fleets stood out clearly.

Soon after dawn, while the British fleet sailed toward the French-Spanish battle line at a leisurely pace of about two knots, Fergus stood beside his quartermaster on the quarterdeck. The quartermaster raised his long glass and then lowered it. "Sir, the *Victory* is flying a signal for the captains of all frigates to report aboard. This means you, sir."

Fergus shook his head. "Coolest thing I ever heard of. The battle is about to start."

He turned to Lombardi. "Lay us under her counter."

When they arrived close aboard, six other frigates were sailing close to the *Victory.* Most of the captains were obviously already on board, and Fergus and Sherrill boarded their gigs and came aboard the lowered brow in a small chop with little difficulty. The flag lieutenant ushered them below. Admiral Nelson greeted them and offered them his good hand. "Ah, Kilburnie, I see you are here, and I know you had the farthest to go. We are now complete. The last two nights I had my battle-line captains here for dinner in two groups. I had to leave you all out in the outer reaches of the fleet for our safety. Now I want to see you young ones and to tell you how much I appreciate all you have done for your Navy. You will be spectators while the big ships beat each other to death. After we are through, I want you to chase down any of the enemy that escape. I want to take them prize or sink them, all of them. Is that understood?"

There was a chorus of "Aye, aye, sir."

Blanchard, the senior captain, raised his glass of sherry. "To the king!" he said, and the group drank part of their sherry. Then the next senior raised his glass and said, "To the queen!" More sherry disappeared.

Fergus, waiting until the last since he was the senior flag officer, raised his glass. "To victory!" he said in a strong voice, and they all drained their glasses.

The flag lieutenant, obviously nervous, came in. "Admiral, we should get ready. The enemy is in plain sight."

The frigate captains took their cue from his words and moved toward the door in quiet good order, but obviously in a hurry to get back to their ships. Nelson shook each captain's hand as they left.

Soon they were headed back for their stations. As they were being rowed back, Fergus could see the French fleet still struggling to form for battle.

The coxswain, whose young eyes were better than Fergus's, said, "They are in a big crescent, sticking out to leeward, from north to south."

Back on board, Poston said. "I thought the admiral was going to keep you on board to be a cheering section or a gun captain. I was hoping to get command of this ship and to fight the battle myself. We're about to start over there."

Fergus laughed, "No thanks, I didn't want to stay. That ship will soon be a slaughterhouse. Now tell Lombardi to move us a little closer to the French fleet. I want to see that action, but not in range of those murderous 32-pounders."

When they were in position, Fergus and Poston picked up long glasses and climbed to the foretop platform for a better view.

Fergus noted that the big ships in the British line were jockeying for position. "Looks like the *Temeraire* wants to lead the force that is about to break through the line. That's Admiral Collingwood's flagship."

Poston, gripping a ratline to steady himself in the freshening breeze, said, "Don't bet on it. Captain Hardy won't let the *Victory* be outdone or maneuvered while Admiral Nelson is on board."

The head of the British line was now pointed directly at the middle of the still-spread-out French line. The large ships were almost bunched.

"A hell of a powerful punch," Poston shouted over the freshening breeze as he tried hard to steady the long glass against a vibrating ratline.

The wind began to freshen even more. The forenoon light winds made it difficult for all ships to maneuver, and ships of both lines straggled badly as they trimmed sails and tried to comply with the admiral's signals or just to stay in their assigned positions.

Fergus and Poston went below in a lull to find a snack to eat.

About noon, the quartermaster came aft to report to Fergus, who had come back from his cabin and the snack Radcliffe had put together. "Sir, a signal is flying on the *Victory,* made in several hoists. It is hard to read it, but I think it says 'England expects that every man will do his duty.'"

Poston nodded. "Of course."

Fergus was displeased and frowned. "That signal will become famous in history. Don't mock it."

Poston stammered, "I didn't mean to. It just seemed to be, er, different."

"Nelson *is* different. That's why he is so successful in everything he does."

In a few minutes it was evident that the battle was about to start, or at least the prebattle maneuvering was over.

The British line of battle in two columns was about to break the French-

Spanish line in two places. To the north the left-hand column, headed by the *Victory, Temeraire,* and *Euralyus,* was heading for a group astern of the *Santa Ana* and next to the giant *Santissimo Trinidad.*

To the south, the *Royal Sovereign,* with Admiral Collingwood embarked, was headed for a group ahead of the *Indomitable.*

Then firing broke out in both groups. Gradually the ships of both lines closed each other. The gun smoke rose in large clouds, and Fergus shook his head. "I can't see much now. We'll have to wait until the smoke clears."

Poston said, "Let's take long glasses and go aloft again. We should be able to see better."

The smoke did clear enough to see what was happening to the large ships nearest in the battle. Fergus focused his long glass on the after deck of the *Victory,* where he had sat with Admiral Nelson not so long ago. Now the once-peaceful quarterdeck was covered with sailors and marines running in all directions. Several figures, either dead or wounded, were lying about the deck. Fergus remembered that Admiral Nelson had told him that he had put planking over the center skylight to give him more room to move about in battle. Now several of the figures had been pushed aside to give even more room to move about the large deck. One large gun was on its side with the carriage mangled. If the quarterdeck was this bad, Fergus wondered how the fore part of the ship and her lower decks were faring.

Fergus shifted his long glass to the *Royal Sovereign.* She was more broadside to them, and he could see the whole upper decks when sudden shifts of winds blew the smoke away. Each salvo created a new heavy veil of smoke, but in intervals Fergus could see the shambles on her decks. He thought he could see Admiral Collingwood striding about, but he wasn't sure. Too many other figures got in the way.

Fergus shuddered. "My God!" he said to Poston. "We are lucky not to be over there. Battle on a small ship like this is much more bearable. Over there the whole scene is complete chaos."

Poston nodded. "It's bad enough when the balls are flying over here, but over there you never know who or what is shooting at you."

Both of them trained their long glasses along the battle line, trying to make sense out of the other individual engagements. It appeared that large clots of half a dozen ships had formed. The light wind would not let them maneuver much, and they just hung together. Where it was possible, one ship would throw grapnels over to the bulwarks of an adjacent ship, and an attempted boarding would take place. Fighting on the bulwark then was hand to hand and furious, but most of the time the marines in the foretops would pick off the boarders and the survivors would fall back and cut the grapnel lines.

Fergus shifted his long glass to the *Victory.* Now he could see a little better. "The *Victory* is afoul of the *Redoubtable,*" he said. "They collided and then fell apart, but their rigging is entangled." He concentrated on his glass. "I don't like this," he said. "The *Redoubtable* is a smaller ship, and her reputation is for filling her tops with marines. The level of her tops is about the same as the quarterdeck of the *Victory,* and right now she appears to be peppering them."

Poston shifted his glass to the *Victory.* "I see what you mean. There's a gaggle of men about a figure on their quarterdeck."

Fergus swore. "I hope that's not the admiral!"

Poston said, "Whoever it is is being carried below."

Then the smoke rose again.

Fergus said, "I've seen enough. The smoke is getting heavier all the time. Let's go below."

For an hour after they came down, the thunderous salvos continued, but about 2 P.M. the firing slackened as the gun crews killed each other and many guns were destroyed.

The smoke began to drift aft, and Poston began to count. "I can see at least twelve ships with their colors struck or no colors in sight."

"Any British?"

"None. Many of them are badly beaten up, but they aren't surrendering."

Just before dark the firing stopped, and individual ships began to herd their prizes toward Gibraltar. The wind, fickle all day, began to increase in velocity rapidly, and by dark it was a full gale.

Fergus and Poston, on deck, sent for their oilskins and doubled the lookouts. "Look out for escaping ships," Fergus warned.

At dawn the gale persisted, and Fergus could see that some enemy ships, badly damaged, had failed to weather it. Most enemy ships still afloat were under British escort, but one was headed south of Gibraltar, and none of the damaged British ships could keep up with her.

"Our game," Fergus said, and sent a signal to the *Diligent,* cruising nearby. "Engage."

Poston asked, "Will he know what to do?"

"Watch him. He'll circle to take position astern of her and from that vantage point will fire at her stern. We'll come for her from ahead and fire at her bow. She'll try to change course and uncover her broadsides. She'll roll so much she won't have much accuracy. We'll keep circling her to maintain our position on her bow or stern. The *Diligent* will continue to do the same thing."

The two ships maneuvered for thirty minutes, pecking away at the damaged third-rater, and gradually she appeared to subside. Her firing stopped. Fergus got overconfident and closed her. Three 32-pounder balls came crashing aboard. Fergus knew he had been hit by several splinters and fell to the deck, but after a few minutes began to recover as Surgeon Pollitt helped him up. "I'll take you below," he said.

Fergus shrugged him off. "Not until this is over," he said gruffly.

Poston had taken over command and brought the ship out of the Frenchman's firing range. Fergus asked, "What's she doing now?"

"About ready to strike," Poston said.

The quartermaster corrected him. "She has just struck," he said.

Fergus, feeling faint as the blood streamed from several wounds, said, "Order the *Diligent* to take her into Gibraltar and turn her over to the prize court. Then rejoin us."

The *Diligent* started off, carefully herding the prize in the right direction.

The lookouts yelled down, "The *Axe* is approaching."

The *Axe* came under their counter and the captain picked up his speaking trumpet.

Fergus, looking at him closely, said, "There's something wrong."

The captain of the *Axe* tried to speak but couldn't. Finally he wiped his eyes on his sleeve and tried again. "Commodore, I regret to report that Admiral Nelson is dead." He broke down and turned away. Then a low moan spread throughout the ship as the news filtered down below decks.

Fergus shook his head as he tried to avoid understanding the awful news, but he couldn't. "That's enough. We don't need to do anything else. Head for home and get the word to our other ships. We'll rendezvous at Cadiz and pick up the *Dashing*."

Suddenly the loss of blood and the penetrating sense of the tragedy overtook him, and he fell against Pollitt. Two men moved forward to help him below, and Pollitt said to Poston, "You'll be in command for quite a while until I get him back in shape."

CHAPTER 24

Future Plans

POLLITT WAS PREPARED to start work on Fergus while he was still unconscious, but Fergus regained consciousness and insisted that the surgeon work on the other wounded first.

"I can wait," he said. "Maybe the others can't."

Pollitt shook his head. "The others have been taken care of. The dead will be buried tomorrow. The sailmaker is preparing them for burial. You were lucky you didn't get it worse. Now be quiet and take this laudanum. It will dull most of the pain. I've got a lot of splinters to take out, especially in your left thigh."

"Will I lose it?"

"Not unless a serious infection sets in. I can take care of minor infections easily and I will soak your wounds every day. Others would put you in the hospital."

Fergus gritted his teeth, took a long pull on the cup of laudanum, and laid back on the chest that was acting as an operating table.

"Go ahead," he said.

"Drink enough," Pollitt said. "You won't know what I'm doing anyway."

After two hours Pollitt stepped back and looked at the pile of splinters in a basin nearby. "Got them all," he said to his assistant. "Throw them all over the side. He won't want to see them again."

Fergus could see nothing for a long period of time. Then he could see through a red haze. When it grew into white, he opened his eyes. Radcliffe was leaning over him. "Do you know me, sir?" he asked anxiously.

Fergus sighed as the physical pain came back. "I know you, Radcliffe. I'm all right." Then the meaning of the loss of Nelson came back, and he groaned.

Pollitt came over. "Is the pain worse?" he asked.

"Yes, but it's nothing that you can help with. Have you heard anything about how Admiral Nelson died?"

"Not much. It seems he was shot by a foretop marine, and it took a long time for him to die."

"Terrible!" Fergus said. "I think a man in the foretop of the *Redoubtable* shot him when she was alongside the *Victory.* We probably saw it happen."

Pollitt tried to reassure Fergus. "He didn't feel much pain, because his spine was severed. All the time he lived, he knew he had won the battle and his friends were all around him as he faded away. It seems to me that's a fine way to die."

Fergus sighed. "Thank you. He was a professional Navy fighter, and that's the way he wanted to die."

"That's right," Pollitt said.

Fergus sighed. "Maybe I'm not in his class. I'd rather die at home in the presence of my kin."

Pollitt turned to Radcliffe. "Try to get him to sleep a while."

Poston eagerly took over the flotilla, setting a course up the northern coast of Portugal. The weather was mild, and they made good speed. Just as they cleared Cape Finisterre the lookouts sang out, "Sail ho! On the port bow. Three merchantmen and a frigate."

The ships kept coming, seemingly unafraid of the imposing force of the flotilla of British warships. Poston could tell that they flew Spanish flags, and that the frigate carried thirty-six guns. He went below and talked to Fergus, who insisted on being carried to the quarterdeck and put in a chair. "I'll leave you in command, and I won't bother you, but I'd like to see this. What do you plan to do? Surround them and start shooting?"

"No. I plan to stop the frigate and find out what he knows. He acts like he doesn't know that Spain is at war with us. I'll take precautions."

"Good. Go back up on deck, and I'll join you."

Poston took another good look at the convoy, still sailing serenely along. He turned to Lombardi. "Can you speak Spanish well enough to interpret?"

Lombardi shrugged. "Sure, and I can use some of my Italian to fill in."

"Take us under her counter and with a speaking trumpet tell the frigate to lie to. He'll have to obey us with five ships surrounding him."

"What if he starts to shoot?"

"He'd be crazy. He should know that we'd sink him in minutes."

Poston gathered Lombardi, Ballinger, and the marine captain on the quarterdeck. "Lieutenant Ballinger, I will leave you in command. If the Spanish captain tries to capture me and my party, be ready to use maximum force. Sink her if he resists and never mind my party."

Lieutenant Ballinger raised his eyebrows. "That's a little tough. Are you sure?"

"Yes. This won't happen. The force he is facing is overwhelming."

Lombardi shook his head. "You don't know the Spanish like I do. They have a way of committing suicide when they are faced with a situation like this."

"Do you think this captain will?"

"Let's wait until we've seen him close up."

"All right." Poston said to the marine captain. "Captain Larsen, when we get aboard, face your men outboard around us. Stay in the middle of the group with me. If I give the word, tell your men to shoot the captain and all their officers. In the meantime, do not threaten to shoot and keep your arms lowered. Are we all agreed?"

No one spoke up. Poston said, "Let's go."

The Spanish frigate stopped, and Poston, Lombardi, Larsen, and the marines boarded her. On the quarterdeck the captain was at first angry and then bewildered. He used broken English. "Why you stop me? You have no right to stop a neutral warship. The only reason I stop is because you have so many ships, and I see you have surrounded me with armed marines."

Poston, now happy to be able to converse in English, asked him, "Do you know our countries are at war?"

The Spanish captain's jaw dropped. "No. I do not. The admiral in the Caribbean who sent us here a month ago didn't know. What happened?"

"I think your country got drawn in by Napoleon. Now your fleet and the French fleet have been destroyed by Admiral Nelson, but the war is still on. As a consequence, I have to inform you that you and all of your ships are now my prizes."

The Spanish captain's eyes glowed with hate. Poston watched him carefully, noting that his hands were tightly clenched, a bad sign.

Captain Larsen was equally tense, continuously scanning the officers and crew, looking for signs of trouble.

Only Lombardi was calm. He kept talking to the Spaniard with a continuous stream of soft language, almost musical. It was a combination of Spanish, Italian, and English, although Poston knew by now that the captain understood English. Poston could follow only parts of Lombardi's speech, but by now he could tell it was having the desired effect on the captain. Poston took a deep breath and tried to keep his hands unclenched, but he couldn't. He was nervous, and he expected the Spaniard to explode at any moment.

Poston stole a look at the crew, gathered facing the quarterdeck. They were dressed in a variety of clothing like that worn by all sailors of all navies of the time. They did not know the subject of the conversation and were not aware of the problems they were facing. They could expect to have the ships released any moment and be allowed to proceed to their home port. They conversed among themselves in low tones.

Poston thought about how he would have his party leave the ship. It would be better to withdraw his whole party now and leave the Spanish captain to have a short interval to let his crew know what was happening. Then he would send over a full prize crew well armed and ready to board.

Poston looked back at the Spanish captain. Lombardi was still talking softly but now there was a subtle change in the Spanish captain's eyes. No longer flashing, they were duller, and unhappy, but not dangerous. His hands were slowly unclenching and, like Poston, he was wiping his sweaty palms on his trousers.

For the first time, Poston felt he might pull off the affair without bloodshed. If they did, it would be due to Lombardi's diplomacy, and he resolved to give him due credit if they returned safely.

The Spanish captain's shoulders slumped visibly and he nodded. Lombardi turned to Poston and grinned.

Poston took several deep breaths to lubricate his dry throat and felt the blood returning to his face. It was all over, and no blood had flowed yet.

Poston looked at Lombardi, who shrugged his shoulders and said in a low tone, "This one won't fight us."

The Spanish captain sighed. "Had I known, I would have put up a fight, but it wouldn't have lasted long. At least my honor would have been preserved."

Poston replied, "You may have saved your honor, but you would have paid with your life and the lives of many others. I will send over small prize crews to all of your ships. I will find out in due course what your merchant ships are carrying. Would you tell me please?"

The Spanish captain shrugged. "As you say you will find out anyway. Gold bullion, rum, and tobacco. You will all be very rich now."

As they left the ship, Poston said to the Spanish captain, "I will send over a prize crew soon. The senior officer will be directed to trust you and the crew and to show all restraint in commanding your ships until you arrive in England. You will find that our Navy will treat you and your crew with the utmost civility and courtesy. I would guess that you and your crew will be exchanged for British sailors within a month or so."

The Spanish captain, now much calmer, said, "I would like to see Mister Lombardi again in England."

Poston said, "I will honor your request."

Poston took Lombardi and the marines to one of the merchant ships to satisfy his curiosity as to what they were carrying. The merchant captain received them with curiosity and said in Spanish, "What is this?"

Poston turned to Lombardi. "What did he say?"

Lombardi answered, "Plain as day in any language. He said 'What is this?'"

"Tell him we are at war with his country and he is our prize. We want to see the cargo."

When the merchant captain had absorbed Lombardi's kitchen Spanish, he turned purple and let out a string of oaths.

"I take it I don't need to translate all of that," Lombardi said. "Some of them are even new to me."

"Of course. Tell him to lead us below."

Lombardi pointed to the nearest hatch. "Vamonos," he said, and the procession started below. On the first deck below were hogsheads of tobacco. On the second deck were barrels of rum. "Not bad," Poston said. "Tell him to show us the really good stuff."

Lombardi said, "El oro."

The merchant captain rolled his eyes and led them below to the orlop deck. In the dim light Poston could see stacks of boxes of gold bars. He whistled. "I'd hate to have to count all of this gold."

Lombardi laughed. "You won't. We couldn't even move it until we get it to port."

"Ask the captain if the other two merchant ships have the same cargo."

Lombardi launched into a torrent of half Italian and half Spanish. When he finished the captain shrugged his shoulders and said, "El mismo."

Without waiting for Poston to ask, Lombardi said, "He says 'the same.'"

Poston said. "That's enough for me. Let's go back to our ship."

When Poston returned to the *Daring,* he found Fergus sitting anxiously in a chair. "Well?" he asked.

Poston laughed uproarishly. "Commodore, I did it, with Lombardi's help. Didn't even fire a shot. Neither did he. By the way, you will be as rich as Croesus."

"I don't think so. He had more money than the rest of the world possessed. You should read more."

"Well, you'll get a lot of prize money. Those merchantmen are full of gold, and the four ships are valuable, too. I won't be so poor either, now that I have asked Carlita to marry me."

"What? Do you want to live in Gibraltar?"

"No. Surrey. Not far from Admiral Nelson's estate. Now I can keep my farm. I will be able to retire there with Carlita in only a few years."

Fergus began to recover slowly, his constitution weakened by years at sea and overwork. By the time Poston brought the flotilla into the Royal Navy dockyard, Fergus was able to walk down the brow with help and get into Jeris's carriage. The driver moved slowly, trying to favor Fergus's wounds, but eventually they arrived at the hospital.

Pollitt met them there and conferred with the hospital medical staff. After a lengthy and thorough examination of Fergus's wounds, particularly the deep one in his left leg, they came in to talk to him.

Fergus said, "I see you fellows have your serious expressions on, but not your no-hope ones."

Pollitt laughed. "You are right. You will recover completely, but the wound in your thigh is a deep infection. It will get careful treatment here for a month or so, and you will be able to travel in due time."

"Does that mean I won't be able to go to Admiral Nelson's funeral?"

"Under no circumstances. You won't be able to walk or ride a horse. You will be here being soaked daily."

"And at the end of the month I will be able to travel?"

"Within limits."

"By coach and by sea?"

"I think so. What's on your mind?"

"I can't say. I have to talk to my wife and to Jeris Fairlie about my plans first."

Shannon came in to see him in the early afternoon. She took him in her arms and held him closely. Then she stepped back and took a look at him. "My God! What have they done to you?"

"Here they're just getting me well. I'll be out in a month, they say."

"And then what?"

"That's what I wanted to talk to you about. I have been thinking about retiring. What do you think?"

"I've always wanted you to be home with me. But you must take other things into account. Will there be much for you at sea soon? There is talk that the Royal Navy has done itself out of a job by defeating the French and Spanish navies so completely. Many people in high places think that most of our ships are no longer necessary."

"That's probably true. There will be fewer ships kept in commission, of course. Fewer officers will be needed and fewer flag officers, too. I have probably gone as far as I can. I will talk to Uncle Jeris. If he agrees, I will ask to be retired."

Jeris came by to see him the next morning. "Well, lad, how do you feel?"

Fergus moved slowly under the sheets. "All right, I guess. I'm getting well slowly. The doctors are very hopeful. Uncle, I want to ask you a question. I have talked to Shannon about this, and she agrees with me."

"This sounds serious."

"I think I should retire."

Jeris paused, got up, and paced up and down. Then he stopped suddenly and said, "I agree. The Navy is already starting to shrink. The ships that were damaged at Trafalgar will not be repaired. But should you return to duty now, you will be allowed to retain your rank. You may never go higher. Also you will remain a commodore on the retired list should you retire."

"And if war starts again some day soon, and I am recalled, what will happen?"

"Your record is superb, and you were on the verge of being made a rear admiral. If you are really needed, you will be recalled at least in the rank of commodore, and I would bet even that you would be made a rear admiral. I am sure the king will remember the one who brought millions of pounds to his treasury. As a matter of fact, his treasurer is still trying to find places in London to store the bullion. By the way, the size of your part of the prize will be unbelievable."

Fergus said, "You've made up my mind. I am tired, wounded, and in need of time with my family. Go ahead and process my papers."

Jeris sighed. "I know you are doing the right thing, but the Navy will miss you."

CHAPTER 25

Retirement

THREE DAYS LATER Jeris came back to Fergus's hospital room. Under his arm were two large manila envelopes. He tossed both on Fergus's bed. Then he pulled several documents out of one of them. "Here are your retirement papers," he said. "You may want to frame them."

"What good will they do me?"

"You might want them some day if the French get better and we need to build our Navy back up."

"And then?"

"You can take it off the wall and send it back to the Admiralty with a request that they recall you to active duty."

"I don't think they'll bother with a bunch of old paper. If they need me, they'll just send for me."

"Well, if they do, your sons will want this to keep." Jeris then extracted a silk pennant from the second envelope. "This is your commodore's pennant, now hauled down. It is yours to keep and no one else will ever fly it. Your flotilla no longer exists."

"But the ships?"

"Now they are just individual ships in His Majesty's Navy working for various commanders."

"And what will happen to their captains?"

"Poston will stay as a post captain of the *Daring* for at least a year after a long overhaul. It seems the king took quite a fancy to him for the way he captured all that gold without losing a man. Poston and all the other captains have been decorated by the king in person."

"And mine, if any?"

"Your decoration, somewhat more important, and your baronetcy, will be along in due time. They require a little more paperwork."

"And Puller, Sherrill, and the sloop captains?"

"The sloop captains are already en route to frigate captaincies. Sherrill has asked for retirement, and he is due for it. A sycophant from the Admiralty will relieve him. Puller is another favorite of the king, it seems, and will, after a lengthy overhaul, take his ship to the Caribbean. I expect to hear great things from him in the future."

Fergus nodded. "So do I. He will be very successful. Now tell me about the arrival of the ships at the dockyards and what happened after that."

Jeris laughed. "I do owe you an explanation. Shortly after you arrived, you had to be hauled away to the hospital. Captain Poston, of course, took charge. He was very clever about not letting anyone know about the gold in the merchant ships until he could enlist the dockyard commander's services. As soon as the commander and the captain of the port knew about the gold, they rounded up every marine and soldier they could gather and put a cordon around the ships—over three hundred men."

"Must have looked like a war."

"Might have been if the yard workers had heard about it before it was properly guarded. In any event the security gave the captain of the yard time to organize the unloading of the ships. It took at least a hundred heavy wagons to take all of the tobacco away, and then they had to come back for a second trip for the rum barrels."

"And then they got to the gold?"

"Yes. Poston and the yard captain worked closely together. It was now the third day after they arrived, and the workers began to bring the gold bars up from the orlop decks to the main decks by hand. From there the bars were swung over by cranes to wagons."

"Did the king know about all this?"

Jeris laughed. "Of course. On the first day he found out about the gold. On the third day he and all his court came down to the piers. He went down below before it was moved and looked at it. Then he watched carefully as the first load was brought up. As it passed by him, he said to the representative of the treasury who was counting it, 'What! What! What!' in his high-pitched giggle. 'Count it carefully and don't let any rub off. Don't even lose a jot or a tittle of it. Each rub could lose a pound for me.' Then he did a little jig and giggled again. 'What! What! Dammit, it's beautiful!' he said."

"What is this 'What what what' business? Is he out of his mind?"

Jeris laughed. "There are those who say he is a little crazy. After all, if you had been king of this complicated government for as long as he has you'd be a little off, too. Apparently he ends most of his conversational sentences with 'What! What! What!' and most of the courtiers are used to it."

Fergus sighed. "That's beyond me, but it must have entertained the crowd."

"Yes, they applauded when the king did his jig. It also must have entertained the king, for he invited Poston and Lombardi to the palace for dinner."

Fergus laughed. "Did Lombardi sing?"

"Oh, yes, and he was a hit. The king and the whole court stood up and asked for several encores."

"Operatic arias, I suppose?"

Jeris shrugged. "Poston doesn't know one selection from another, but he thought they were operatic arias. After the affair Lombardi told him the court smelled much better than most Italian opera houses."

"Was there more?"

"Oh, yes. The unloading ended the next day, and the prize court took over. The valuation of the tobacco, rum, and gold will be easy, but there will be some dickering over the value of the merchant ships and the frigate. In any event, the king let them know that he expects prompt action, or he'll confine them in the courtroom until they're finished, and I'm sure he'll get it done. This means that you will get your share."

"And what about Admiral Nelson's remains?"

"His body was brought back on the *Victory* and landed at Portland. From there it will be transported to Greenwich. I understand the body will then be shifted from the large keg of rum in which it was carried here to a casket and taken to Whitehall to lie in state. Someone is building an inner casket of wood and then another one of lead. An outer one will be made of the wood of the foremast of the *L'Orient,* the flagship of the French admiral at the Battle of the Nile, as you know. I hear someone else is building a carved one of large wooden plates, but we'll hear about that later."

"And the final arrangements?"

"After a period at Whitehall there will be a large procession. Surgeon Pollitt will be right here with you and will give you the final arrangements. I think you can see most of the ceremony except for that inside the cathedral from your fourth-floor window. I'll make arrangements for Shannon to be brought up here to join you and to be returned home after the service."

"Thank you, Uncle. Now if you'll excuse me, I think I'll get a little sleep. This has been a long day."

"I think Surgeon Pollitt is due here soon. When you wake up he'll tell you some arrangements he has made to get young Radcliffe into the very bosom of the cathedral to see the ceremony."

When Fergus woke up an hour later, Surgeon Pollitt was standing at his bedside with Radcliffe.

Fergus said, "Radcliffe, I'm glad to see you. I understand you are going to the University of Edinburgh to study medicine."

Radcliffe shifted slowly from one foot to the other. "Well, sir, I think I've changed my mind."

"And how is that? I thought you wanted to be a doctor."

"Well, sir, I've been talking to your wife."

"She talked you out of it?"

"Well, not really. She suggested I might like to study veterinary medicine."

"Oh, oh, I'll wager she offered you a job to take care of all the horses she's buying these days."

"Well, sir, I could travel to Ireland, England, and Scotland looking after her horses. This seems like a very inviting career."

"I'm sure she pointed out that it will be more interesting than sitting in an office all day tending to runny-nosed children."

Radcliffe grinned. "You sound just like her."

Pollitt broke in. "I tried to talk him out of it, but he's convinced. Now let me tell you what I have in mind for him tomorrow. I've given him some money to go to a costumer when he leaves here to get a velvet suit and all the trimmings to make him look like a young son of a wealthy aristocratic family."

"It wouldn't take much to do that. He almost looks like one now. Now what is he to do?"

"I have asked him to walk down the path of the procession just far enough back to be able to make his way through the crowd and still close enough to see the moving procession. He should get to the cathedral before the coffin is carried in. Then he is to go to the front of the cathedral near the entrance and attach himself to the family of some aristocrat that is about to enter. He is to follow them in and, after entrance, leave them and enter a side door I've already found out about. It will allow him to go up a winding staircase to a room overlooking the main floor from where he can see the whole ceremony. Then later he will come back and tell us about what he has seen."

Fergus looked at his former steward. "That will be a big day for you if you can pull it off. Can you do it?"

Radcliffe shrugged. "Not hard. I've been through worse native markets while shopping with the purser."

CHAPTER 26

The Funeral

ON THE MORNING of 9 January, Shannon arrived at the hospital at 8 A.M. She came in, took off her coat, and asked Fergus to send for breakfast for her. "I've been on the road for some time," she said.

Fergus sent for a tray for her and a cup of coffee for himself. As Shannon ate, she said, "Maybe you don't get much news in here unless I bring it to you. Today is the final day in the funeral ceremonies for Admiral Nelson."

Fergus said, "I have talked to Radcliffe and he is busy on his assignment. I haven't told you yet what he is doing. Surgeon Pollitt made arrangements for him to dress himself as a member of the aristocracy and travel the route of the funeral procession. Then he will try to follow a family inside and secrete himself in the upper part of the cathedral so he can see the ceremony. Then he'll come back and tell us all about it."

Shannon frowned. "He will unless the police pick him up. You are risking my new veterinarian."

Fergus nodded. "He told me all about it. You were very sly."

"Why so? He really wants to do it."

Fergus changed the subject. He said, "I've heard that his casket was moved from Greenwich up to London and is now lying in state in the Admiralty building at Whitehall."

"Right you are. The final movement of the casket will be in about an hour. It will be taken to St. Paul's Cathedral for final ceremonies and interment."

Fergus looked at a large wall clock. "That should be soon now."

"Yes, silly, that's why I've been busting my bustle to get here. Come on over to the window and look at the scene below and across the river. You have a wonderful view."

Fergus got up with some difficulty and moved over beside Shannon. For a full minute his eyes swept the scene below. Then he said, "My God! There are millions of people down there. I can't see bare pavement or grass anywhere. Poor Radcliffe will be trampled."

"They've been coming into town for two days. An Englishman will go anywhere or endure any hardship if he wants to see something badly enough."

Surgeon Pollitt came in. "Ah, there you both are. I'm here to keep you posted on the ceremony. Fergus, you've now seen the stage. Now I suggest you get back in bed and resume your treatments and we'll take turns describing the events to you. We can see well enough to describe the general scene to you. Radcliffe will fill it in later."

Fergus sighed. "I am very tired. Tell me later if I go to sleep."

Shannon said, "I can see a lot of action around the Admiralty at Whitehall. The large vehicle designed to carry the casket is being pushed about. It won't seem to come out through the gates."

Pollitt said, "I made a trip through St. Paul's two days ago to see the arrangements there. A large section of the floor has been removed in order to lower the casket to its final resting place. They installed a large chandelier that carries over a hundred lanterns over it. Someone said the engineering arrangements to handle the casket and the chandelier were made by a Scottish engineer."

Fergus smiled wanly. "Admiral Nelson would have liked that. He liked Scots."

Shannon asked, "Did you see the funeral carriage at Whitehall?"

"Yes. That's the huge gray thing they're having trouble with. It's built on four large wagon wheels. A twenty-foot-high canopy towers over it. That's what's troubling the men trying to get it through the gate. They will have to disassemble the top and sides and put it back together after they wheel it out. They will have to carry the casket out to the street, and it will take fifty men to carry it."

Shannon nodded. "Oh, yes, I can see it plainly now. It looks like a ship on a sea of gray."

"It should. Someone designed it so it would look like the *Victory.* They've even painted the name on the stern. Frankly, I think it looks tacky."

Fifteen minutes later Shannon said, "They've made it through the gate at Whitehall and the procession is moving forward toward St. Paul's Cathedral."

Fergus asked, "What is that strange noise?"

"As the casket moves along through the gray sea of humanity, they take off their hats and say short prayers. What you hear is a combination of the noise of the removal of hundreds of hats and the murmur of many prayers."

Pollitt shook his head in wonder. "I never saw so much gray. Everyone is wearing some sort of gray winter coat and hat."

In an hour the casket had arrived at St. Paul's. Pollitt said, "They're carrying in the casket for the final ceremony."

This was too much for Fergus, and he turned his face to the wall, put a pillow over his head, and wept silently.

The sounds of the uncoordinated playing of marches by some twenty military bands and the swelling of the hymns coming from St. Paul's mixed together in a not-unpleasant cacophony.

At 5 P.M. the noise died down. Pollitt looked at the clock. "It's over," he said. "But I think the ceremony inside the cathedral is still going on."

Shannon looked down at the sea of people. She said, "The people think it is over, too. They're beginning to move along the streets and out of town."

Fergus sighed deeply, took the pillow off his face, and said, "Yes, it is over, for Nelson and for me. I will think about him as long as I live."

Shannon came over and sat next to him on his bed. With a wet towel she wiped away the remaining traces of tears on his face.

Pollitt came over from the window. "Now it is time to look at the future. By dark, Shannon, your carriage driver should be able to get you home. I will have Fergus ready to travel two days from now. Have your carriage here at noon, and I'll have him home by dark."

Shannon nodded. "And you'll be with him?"

"If you have room for me I'll come home with him and stay until you get settled in Scotland. I'll bring Radcliffe with me, too."

"You mean Evan?"

"Yes. He has been discharged from the Navy. He will stay with Fergus as long as you need him and then go off to Edinburgh to enter veterinary medical school, as you persuaded him."

"Can he afford that?"

Pollitt laughed. "Many times over when he has all of his prize money. He can afford to go to any school, set up a practice, and build a house."

"And you?"

"I'm joining the medical staff of this hospital. As soon as Fergus has no further need of me I'm coming back here."

Pollitt looked at the clock. "Radcliffe should be back any minute now."

In an hour he came into the hospital room, bright-eyed and breathless.

Pollitt asked, "Are you all right?"

"Oh, yes, but a little hungry and out of breath."

Pollitt smiled. "I'll send for a large tray for you. Now tell us about your day."

Radcliffe sat down and took several deep breaths. "A policeman chased me all around the cathedral to start with. I guess he was too old and too fat to catch me."

"Then how did you get in?"

"I got a fifty-yard start on the lap around the cathedral. I attached myself to a rich-looking family and went inside with them. I left them inside and went to the small door you told me about. The policeman didn't want to follow me in and make a scene so I went in the side door and climbed the winding stairs to an area where I could see the cathedral floor below."

Pollitt said, "Now go back to the beginning and tell us about what happened earlier."

A huge plate full of food arrived. Radcliffe picked at it as he talked. "I went out early dressed in the clothes I had bought the day before. Velvet suit, fancy shirt, velvet hat with feather, and buckled shoes. All black."

Pollitt nodded. "Very appropriate. Go ahead."

"It was still dark when I left here, but I made it through the crowd to Whitehall. It was a terrible mess. Mostly spectators, but also ten thousand soldiers and a dozen artillery pieces and their ammunition carts and their horses."

Pollitt shook his head. "I don't see where they could have assembled them all."

Radcliffe said, "On the side streets, on the park grass, and on the private house fronts. The house owners and park keepers came around and raised Cain, but it didn't do any good. At 8:30 A.M. the drummers started to play and some twenty bands began all at once, with no apparent effort to coordinate them. I remembered a word from my school times. It was 'cacophony' and it was the appropriate word for it."

Pollitt said, "That was the word I thought of, too."

"In the courtyard at Whitehall, someone had decided that the monstrous funeral carriage would not fit through the gates. It had been assembled by a horde of carpenters the day before, and nobody had thought to measure the gate size. Now they had to disassemble the sides and top, push it through the gate, and reassemble the whole thing. Then a group of fifty pallbearers brought the casket out and pushed it into the interior of the vehicle. Even that wasn't easy, and several men got injured in the pushing and shoving.

"Finally, all seemed to be ready, and the procession started off at 1 P.M., an hour late. One-minute guns began to fire and the bands doubled their efforts. I tried to follow its progress, but it was useless. Thousands of people lined the streets, and I couldn't see much, so I went forward to Saint Paul's Cathedral.

As I said, I tried to get in and had to evade the policeman. Just as I got into my viewing place the casket started to come in. It was moved to a base just in the middle of the floor that had been dug up to permit it to be lowered at the end of the ceremony. I counted 130 lanterns on the huge chandelier overhead, and it really lit up the interior like a bonfire.

"The inside of the cathedral was packed—people sitting and standing wherever they could crowd in. At every corner was a very tall Scottish Highlander dressed in a scarlet jacket, kilt, and tall hat, and holding a four-foot claymore in front of him upside down with the point on the floor. Commodore, you would have been very proud of their appearance."

"Thank you," Fergus said. "Did they keep order?"

Radcliffe shook his head. "They never moved, even when the forty-eight sailors from the *Victory* brought in the largest of the flags that had been flown from the ship during the battle. They had carried it along the procession. They were to put it on top of the casket, but just as they started to spread it out, someone started to tear off a small piece. Then the whole bunch joined in and tore it into small pieces and stuffed them under their jackets. Then they went to their assigned places in the cathedral."

"And the Highlanders didn't do anything?"

"No. All the people applauded, so they thought it must be a part of the ceremony."

"Then what happened?"

"It went on for hours. Hymn after hymn. Prayer after prayer. Finally I got tired of it all and so did a lot of people who started out. The bell kept on tolling, though. I made my way down to the entrance and out to the front. One of the policemen spotted me and started to run up the steps. I dodged behind a couple of ladies and started through the crowd. He never stood a chance. As I said, he was too old and too fat. And here I am. It was an exciting day and I thank you all for making it possible."

Pollitt said, "And thank you for a magnificent effort." Then he looked at Fergus. Fergus had gone quietly to sleep while Radcliffe had been talking. Pollitt said, "He needs rest. He knows and approves of what we are to do and he'll be ready to go. Now I'll escort you to your carriage, and, Radcliffe, your bed is ready for you."

Shannon took a last look at Fergus and then said to Pollitt, "Thank you for everything for both of us."

Pollitt shrugged. "It is I who should be thanking you on behalf of our country. It can never thank your husband enough for what he has done."

CHAPTER 27

Family Life

LEAVING THE well-organized atmosphere of a hospital was not easy for Fergus, but he enjoyed the carriage ride through the winter air.

The arrival at the flat was something that Fergus was not prepared for. The chaos of small children at first startled him as the older girls smothered him with hugs and kisses. The two small boys, at first curious and restrained by this stranger, soon swarmed all over him, too, mostly around his knees. This threatened to knock him off his weakened legs.

Shannon rescued him and soon set down rules for treating him. "We have to protect him until he is 'broken in,'" she said. "Just like a horse. You'll have to learn to ride him."

Fergus laughed. "I can see I'm going to like this family life, but you'll have to bring me in slowly."

Dinner was a controlled bedlam of a different variety. Fergus sat quietly at first while the little ones plied him with questions. The protection of the dinner table gave his legs a safe platform from which to operate, and he was soon deep in conversation with all of them.

By the end of the week Fergus was well "broken in." Shannon, with Evan's help, had packed all they were going to take to Scotland.

Pollitt had made all the arrangements for carriages and had procured reservations for ship passage from Southampton to Glasgow. Jeris came in frequently to lend a hand, and Shannon and Pollitt did the rest.

Jeris and Martha came to see them off, and the children became ecstatic over the prospects of a sea voyage.

The trip went well, and soon they were pier-side at Glasgow, met by Liam and Angus with two carriages and a large wagon "for Shannon's gear," Liam said.

Fergus had recovered most of his stamina with the sea voyage and insisted on sitting up with Liam on the box so he could question him.

Liam said, "Let me get this carriage safely out of the streets with these damned Scots. They drive horses like madmen. Then we can talk on the road." He brought the carriage to a halt just at the top of the road leading down to the big house. "Now you can see for yourself," he said, waving at the expanse of field below.

Fergus gasped with pleasure. "The barns are just what I wanted. I see you are already running horses on the track."

"Yes. About six good ones this year. Another six are in Ireland just about ready for England and maybe more now that Ennis has gotten some help."

"Irish revolutionaries?"

Liam laughed. "There isn't much revolution left in them, but they are still good with a pitchfork. They even help my exercise boys who are working the current crop now. We'll breed more when Ennis says he can handle them."

"All right, Liam," Fergus said. "Let's go down to the house and unpack and then I'll be ready for a tour."

When they were unpacked, Fergus brought Shannon out on the terrace. She pointed to his chair still placed so he could watch the sea traffic below. "Well," she said, "point it in the direction you want to watch now."

Fergus laughed, walked over to it, and turned it to the hills and trees behind the house. "This will stay like this for some time. If I ever feel the urge to go to sea again, you'll know it. I will have turned my chair back so I can watch the sea for the daily packet bringing my orders."

"Now you want to watch the salmon runs?"

"Oh, yes, and now and then the horses. But I'll leave them to you most of the time."

About the Author

Vice Adm. William P. Mack graduated from the U.S. Naval Academy in 1937 and served in battleships, destroyers, and amphibious forces. In his thirty-seven-year career, his many assignments included chief of information, chief of legislative affairs, and deputy assistant secretary of defense. He also commanded the Seventh Fleet during the mining of Haiphong Harbor and ended his career as superintendent of the Naval Academy.

Among Admiral Mack's many books are three Naval Institute professional guides. His first attempt at fiction was a award-winning selection of the Book-of-the-Month Club titled *South of Java,* which he wrote with his son. Five other novels about destroyers in World War II followed and, most recently, *Captain Kilburnie,* the prequel to this novel.

The recipient of the Navy League's Alfred Thayer Mahan Award, Mack lives and writes in Annapolis, Maryland.

The Naval Institute Press is the book-publishing arm of the U.S. Naval Institute, a private, nonprofit, membership society for sea service professionals and others who share an interest in naval and maritime affairs. Established in 1873 at the U.S. Naval Academy in Annapolis, Maryland, where its offices remain today, the Naval Institute has members worldwide.

Members of the Naval Institute support the education programs of the society and receive the influential monthly magazine *Proceedings* and discounts on fine nautical prints and on ship and aircraft photos. They also have access to the transcripts of the Institute's Oral History Program and get discounted admission to any of the Institute-sponsored seminars offered around the country.

The Naval Institute also publishes *Naval History* magazine. This colorful bimonthly is filled with entertaining and thought-provoking articles, first-person reminiscences, and dramatic art and photography. Members receive a discount on *Naval History* subscriptions.

The Naval Institute's book-publishing program, begun in 1898 with basic guides to naval practices, has broadened its scope to include books of more general interest. Now the Naval Institute Press publishes about one hundred titles each year, ranging from how-to books on boating and navigation to battle histories, biographies, ship and aircraft guides, and novels. Institute members receive significant discounts on the Press's more than eight hundred books in print.

Full-time students are eligible for special half-price membership rates. Life memberships are also available.

For a free catalog describing Naval Institute Press books currently available, and for further information about subscribing to *Naval History* magazine or about joining the U.S. Naval Institute, please write to:

Membership Department
U.S. Naval Institute
291 Wood Road
Annapolis, MD 21402-5034
Telephone: (800) 233-8764
Fax: (410) 269-7940
Web address: www.navalinstitute.org